The Adventures of
Megan Martin
The Medallion Mystery

by

Bryon Smith

Publishing Services Provided by
Write to Print
http://www.writetoprint.com

Library of Congress Control Number: 2002103299

1951 -

The Adventures of Megan Martin
The Medallion Mystery / Smith

ISBN **0-9714272-9-1**

Publishing Services Provided by:

Write to **Print**
P.O. Box 1862
Merrimack, NH 03054
http://www.writetoprint.com

Cover art by: Todd Jumper

Printed in the United States of America

Address all inquiries:
Write to **Print**

P.O. Box 1862
Merrimack, NH 03054-1862
Attn: Authors : Bryon Smith

Acknowledgements

Laura Smith as Megan Martin
Cover Graphics by Todd Jumper

With special thanks to:

*Dawn Smith for editing and support
Laura Smith for inspiring me to write the
story, character development and plot
consultation.*

Chapter 1
To Grandmother's House We Go

It was a warm sunny Friday morning when Megan, her mother, and her best friend May were on their way to the country to spend a week with her grandmother. This was a special occasion for Megan. She loved to visit the farm to run through the fields and play with the animals. Not the least of her favorite things, however, was her grandmother's homemade apple pie.

Megan was an attractive teenager with shoulder length blond hair. She was somewhat impulsive, loved to play pranks on her friends sometimes and especially on her brother, with whom she normally didn't get along very well. She loved physical activities like hiking, biking, climbing, swimming - things like that. Sports were ok to watch when there wasn't anything else to do. She liked science and loved her new laptop computer that her dad bought her for her last birthday. She frequently surfed the Internet searching for interesting websites about UFO's, ghosts, hauntings, and important things like that. She liked to e-mail her friends and relatives, mostly because she enjoyed getting e-mail and believed she got back out of it what she put into it. She even built her own website to tell about some of her adventures. She liked to write and even direct little productions with her friends using her mom and dad's home video camera. Halloween was a huge blast. She always threw a big party and called it her "Happy Pumpkin Day Fest." She would put on a stage play in her studio room that her dad had built for her and everyone would play games and have a good time. Megan was curious about what made things work. If it broke she wasn't long finding a screwdriver or wrench to take it apart and find out if she could fix it. Sometimes she even amazed her dad when she would find something in the trash take it apart and fix it. Usually it was something as simple as a broken wire or blown fuse but still she had accomplished something that no one else had given a thought. If they had, it wouldn't have been in the trashcan in the first place. She really enjoyed the sense of accomplishment that a successful venture, or adventure, gave her.

The only person she knew who was more impetuous than Megan was her best friend May. May was the same age as Megan and about the same size but she had brown hair. May and Megan were very much alike in many ways. They had many of the same interests and could frequently be found together. May had some religious background and some knowledge of the Bible. She was also somewhat superstitious. She hated snakes and spiders, and bugs in general gave her the willies.

Martha Martin's farm was in a small farming community known as Peaceful Pond about an hour's drive from the city where Megan lived. The local country church was built right beside the pond and completely surrounded by a large cemetery. Just a mile or so south of the pond was the old Martin family farm.

Megan's grandmother had lived alone for the past 5 years since the death of her husband, Fred. She kept herself busy with the farm despite the coaxing of her friends and certain relatives to sell out and move to the city. She insisted that her work on the farm was the only thing that kept her going. "Why if I were to sell this farm, I would surely die from boredom," she would say.

As they neared the farmhouse, Megan could see her grandmother standing on the front porch awaiting their arrival. She waved and smiled as they pulled into the driveway. Megan's mother, Donna, brought the van to a stop in the driveway. Everyone got out and started to unload the van. Megan had her suitcases and backpack in hand as they walked toward the porch. Scratches, her cat, ran along ahead of them to meet grandmother on the porch.

Megan and her grandmother exchanged greetings and hugs while Scratches rubbed up against grandma's leg affectionately.

"I see Scratches is doing well," grandma said as she reached down to pat the black and tan cat on the head.

The girls started into the house with their bags. Megan knew exactly where she was going but her grandmother called out instructions just the same, "Don't run up the stairs, girls!"

Megan and May slowed down, took several regular steps up the stairs before running the rest of the way to their upstairs room. Megan and May had the first room to the right and Megan's mother had the first room to the left. Megan and May went into their room. It was a pretty little room with two small beds. One bed was against the south wall with the headboard against the southeast corner of the room. The other bed was against the east wall with the headboard at the northeast corner of the room. There was an old wooden desk between the beds. There was a window above the desk in the east wall. There was a window above the bed on the south wall and another window in the south wall just beyond the foot of the bed. In the northwest corner there was an antique wooden toy box. Near the toy box was a small wooden table with a tea set that had been made by her grandfather long ago. Without a doubt this was Megan's favorite area of the room, and this room was her favorite part of the entire house. She had many fond memories in this room as a young child.

In the southwest corner of the room, a few feet from a window, was an antique dresser with a mirror. Near the foot of the south bed and a few feet from the southwest window there was a larger round antique wooden table at the opposite end of the room from the beds. On the table were a hand made tablecloth and a big old white candle. Lying beside the candle was a small box of matches. In the country, power failures were common during bad weather and each room had either a lamp or candle ready to be used in just such an emergency.

The girls put their suitcases on the floor beside their beds. Megan jumped onto her bed and bounced as she grabbed her pillow in a hug and rolled over facing the window beside her bed. A thoughtful expression came over her face as she recalled fond memories of this place. - memories of her Grandfather when she was only 8 and the kitten he gave her as a birthday present that she lovingly named Scratches. Scratches had been with her now for 6 years. She had been the last thing her grandfather had given her before he became sick and died.

Scratches, as cats go, was somewhat above normal and at times appeared to have an uncanny understanding of things in general. She was occasionally aware of things that people either are not aware of or take for granted. This was not to mention her strange understanding of the human language. Sometimes it was almost as if she could understand what people were talking about and sometimes it even appeared she knew what they were thinking. Still she was a cat and therefore independent in an eccentric sort of way.

Megan was too young then to understand, but now she had questions and wanted answers. Why did grandpa have to die? What was it that caused him to become sick? Why couldn't they help him at the hospital?

Megan was shaken from her trance as a pillow pelted her over the head. It was May wanting a quick pillow fight. Megan threw the pillow back at May along with the pillow she had been clutching. The girls laughed and smiled at each other. May opened the window beside her bed and looked out across the south field. "What is that over there?" she pointed.

Megan got up and joined her friend kneeling in the bed at the window to see what she was pointing at. "Oh, that's the old family cemetery," she answered.

"A cemetery? How cool!" May answered as a sly look came over her face.

Megan saw the expression on her friend's face and couldn't repress a smile. "I know what you are thinking May and..."

"And what?" May said as she pelted Megan one more time with her pillow and ran from the room into the upstairs hallway giggling and calling out, "Cemetery! Cemetery!" over and over.

May stopped, then, looking over the handrail to the floor below, she remarked, "Man this is a big house. Your grandpa must have been rich."

Slowly she walked the length of the upstairs hallway checking in each room to see what might be concealed behind closed doors. At the end of the hall she found a door that was locked. "What's behind this door?" she asked Megan.

"That's the old study. The library is in there," Megan answered.

"Library? Neat! But why is the door locked if there's nothing in there but books?" May asked as she bent down to peek through the keyhole.

"I don't know. I just remember that grandpa spent a lot of time in that room when I was small. He was always reading or working on something in that room," Megan answered.

Just then the sound of Grandmother's voice echoed up the stairs. "Girls, come down here and help me fix lunch."

The girls turned and started back down the stairs as Scratches was coming up. Megan picked her up and brought her back downstairs, placing her on the floor in the living room as the girls went into the kitchen.

May asked, "What are we going to fix?"

"We are going to fix sandwiches," answered grandma. "Now Megan you get some bread and, May, you get some lettuce."

As Megan pulled the refrigerator door open, something caught her eye. There lying on the windowsill behind the sink was an old key. "That might be the key that opens the study upstairs," she thought to herself as she turned back to her task of making sandwiches.

They made some sandwiches and took them into the dining room.

After their meal, May and Megan took the plates back to the kitchen and put them in the sink. Megan reached up and took the key from its resting-place and looked at it.

"A key?" May asked. "Uh, you don't think that's the key to open the study door upstairs, do you?"

Chapter 1

Megan turned to look at May as a sly smile came over her face. Quickly she tucked the old key in her pocket. "I think we shall find out, Watson," she answered in a very Sherlock Holmes way.

Chapter 2
A Solid Gold Mystery

     May looked out the kitchen window that faced the old barn. It was in need of paint and a few repairs but was still in fair shape. Megan also looked up to see what May was looking at and saw Scratches entering the narrow opening left because the large double barn doors had not been fully closed. For a moment Megan drifted back remembering watching her grandfather working in the barn with the animals as she played in the barn loft in the hay.

     "What are you doing, Princess? Hunting mice? Looks to me like you need to go on a diet," she said as she patted the old fat cat on the back. Princess raised her back as she always did when someone would pet her. Then she walked away and disappeared behind a bale of hay.

     Princess had been there since Megan could remember and was, in fact, Scratches' mother. She ruled the barn like she owned the place and that loft was her throne room.

     Megan came over to the ladder bent down and looked into the lower area of the barn. She remembered seeing her grandfather working with a mare as she was about to give birth to a beautiful foal. Megan was anxious, she had many questions that children think of but her grandfather had told her to keep her distance and be still so she had climbed up into the loft to play.

"A barn," May proclaimed. "I've never been in a real barn before."

Megan looked over at her friend and smiled. "I haven't been out there since my grandfather died," she said as she walked toward the kitchen door that opened into the back yard.

"Grandma, we're going outside to play," Megan called to her grandmother.

"Ok, but don't go too far," Grandma Martha answered.

Megan and May ran out the door into the yard and ran to the barn door.

Outside they heard a noise in the barn, then the sound of music faintly playing. The barn door had been tied closed with an old piece of rope that hung loosely around the door handles. Quickly Megan untied the rope and the girls ran into the barn as fast as they could. They stopped at the foot of the ladder that led up into the loft and listened but the music had stopped. The two looked at each other with puzzled expressions.

"Where is Scratches?" Megan asked as she quickly looked around the barn.

"I thought I heard music, like one of those little music boxes," May said as she also started to look for the cat.

"Scratches! Scratches!" Megan called for her cat. Then a sound beckoned to the girls from the loft. "The loft! Scratches used to hunt mice and rats up in the loft with her mother when she was little."

Megan lead the way up the ladder into the dimly lit barn loft with May following close behind. There was still a good deal of old hay laying here and there around the loft and a big pile of hay and a few bales at the back wall of the barn. The girls looked around but there was no sign of Scratches. The smell of the hay in the loft was strong.

"It's kinda' spooky up here," May whispered as she turned and looked all around. "And it stinks, too." May noticed something out of the corner of her eye. "What if..." May paused for a moment as a shushing sound of something moving through the large pile of hay caught her attention. "...It isn't the cat making that sound. What if something else is back there?"

Megan walked slowly toward the pile of hay. Suddenly the music started to play, just a few haunting notes but it was all it took to cause Megan to freeze right in her tracks. Her eyes grew wide and her blood ran cold. There was nothing in that barn that she could remember that could even make a sound like that.

"I don't know about you, but I'm for getting out of here!" May said as she mounted the ladder and started down.

"Scratches stop that!" Megan shouted. "It has to be Scratches."

May stopped with her head still peeking through the hole in the floor. "What? Scratches playing music? Right! Let's get out of here!"

"No, Scratches is up here," Megan answered. "I want to know what's going on here."

At that moment Scratches jumped up on a bale of hay high up on the stack and meowed. "Scratches, you silly cat, what are you doing up there?" Megan said as she started to climb up on the hay to get her cat.

"Are you sure you should be climbing up there?" May cautioned.

"I used to climb all over these bales when I was little," Megan told her friend. "In fact, I had more fun in this old barn loft than just about any place I have ever been. I have always felt safe here."

May looked around as she clung to the top of the ladder. "Spiders, bugs," she spoke softly. "And spider webs!" she yelled. "And, who knows, there might even be snakes up here." She spoke as she brushed a spider web away from the ladder.

Megan reached the bale of hay where Scratches sat majestically and took a seat beside her cat. She looked all around the barn loft remembering fond memories of how she would hide behind that bale of hay and how her grandfather would always find her.

"Ah, found you my little honey bee,"
grandfather said as he peeked over the bale of
hay and saw Megan hiding in her secret hiding
place. Megan jumped up and hugged her
grandfather lovingly.

Megan smiled as she turned to look down into her secret hiding place. There was an attractive small wooden box setting there now. A box that she remembered from another place and time. But where? Slowly she reached down and picked up the little wooden box and music started to play. It was a music box. She recalled that tune from somewhere but at the moment she could not remember where.

"It's a music box," Megan said so that her friend could hear.

May climbed up to join Megan on the hay to see the box she had found.

Megan tried to open the box. "It's locked," she said as she studied the little keyhole for a moment and then looked up with a puzzled look on her face.

"What is it Megan?" May asked.

May held the box up, "I know this music box from somewhere. There is something about it. If I could only remember."

"It looks really old," May assessed. "It must have belonged to someone a long time ago.

"Yes, that's it. It belonged to..." Megan hesitated. "My great grandmother." Megan ran her fingers over the box remembering how her grandfather had told her that one day that music box would belong to her.

"This music box is very old. It belonged to my mother and one day it will belong to you, Megan," Grandpa told her.

"To me grandpa?" she asked.

"Yes, Megan, one day when you are old enough this music box will belong to you," he answered.

"How do we open it?" May asked. "Where is the key?"

"Until then I have something for you that also belonged to my mother." Grandpa reached into his desk drawer and pulled out a beautiful gold heart-shaped locket and opened it to show Megan a picture of her great grandmother. Inside the back of the locket was also a small key.

"I know," Megan said as she reached for the locket that hung around her neck. Slowly she opened the backside of the locket to reveal the small key hidden inside. She took the key and placed it into the lock and turned it slowly until the lock made a clicking sound. The two girls looked at each other anticipating what they might find in the box, wondering why someone would have placed that box there in Megan's old secret hiding place.

"Open it," May insisted eagerly.

Megan slowly opened the box and looked inside.

"What is it?" May asked.

Megan removed a folded piece of paper. Under the paper, wrapped in felt, was a round piece of gold metal with pictures on it. She picked up the metal thing. "It's really heavy," she remarked as she inspected the object. On one side it had a picture of a triangular thing and at the top was a thing shaped something like an eye. There were other pictures and symbols on the object that she did not understand. On the back of the object was a map, but it made no sense to her as it didn't look like anything she had seen before. She handed the object to May.

"It looks like gold," May remarked when she held the object in her hands.

Megan opened the paper to find a letter there with her name at the top. She started to read.

"What is it Megan?" May asked.

Megan started to read out loud.

My Dearest granddaughter Megan,

I fear that I may not be with you much longer. My grandfather, your great great grandfather Arthur was an archeologist. He studied old things. He believed he was on the verge of solving an age-old mystery, the mystery of Atlantis. He believed the ancient Atlantians actually built the great pyramids of Giza in Egypt long before the ancient Egyptians came to live in that land. He found evidence of Atlantis and Atlantian culture in several of his travels around the world. Almost everything that he discovered was either sold or donated to museums but for some reason he would not turn loose of this solid gold medallion that he unearthed on an expedition to the Bahama Islands. The gold medallion alone is worth a king's ransom and people would kill to get their hands on it. There are those who would steal it simply for the value of the gold. There are some who would steal it for its value as an archeological treasure and there are those who would steal it to prevent the knowledge it holds from being made public. I trust you will keep it safe and secret.

I knew of the medallion long ago and how my father worked to solve the mystery. He kept many papers concerning his research hidden in the old house. These papers and other evidence were never given over to the knowledge of the general archeological world. He believed his life and research depended on his keeping the knowledge of these things a secret until the time would come when he could tell the world what he had discovered.

One day on a trip to South America to investigate the opening of an ancient tomb, he contracted an illness and was forced to return home. He made several notes of his findings before he died. The doctors then had no idea of the nature of the illness he had contracted and so could do nothing to help him. He soon died of that illness and his secrets, including this medallion, were buried with him. His papers however were not buried with him and are still hidden in the old house where I was born.

Chapter 2

Dearest Megan, my precious little honeybee, I fear that when I unearthed my father's grave to recover this medallion that I have also contracted the same illness that killed my own father. It was said the tomb was protected by a curse and that who ever violated the tomb would be cursed and their life forfeited. Even now I find it hard to breathe and my fever runs hot. I believe the illness is a type of fungus that has taken root in my lungs and my time is short.

I have placed these things in my mother's music box for you and put it where I believe you will be the first to find it. You will find more information in the old study in the house. If I do not live through this, I pray you will take up my, no, your great grandfather's quest for the answers to these questions. Be very careful and always remember that I love you.

Your grandpa,
Fred.

Megan looked down as tears rolled down her cheeks and dripped onto the letter.

"You must have loved your grandpa a lot," May said.

Megan, unable to speak, only nodded her head. Scratches meowed almost as if she understood and then jumped from the hay, making her way to the ladder. The girls looked up watching the cat and the cat looked back at them as if saying, "Follow me."

Megan placed the medallion and the letter back into the little music box, locked the box, placed the key back in the back side of her locket and both girls followed after the cat.

Scratches ran out into the barnyard, across the barn lot past the fence and out across the field. The girls ran after her opening the first gate and climbing over the fence at the back of the yard. They ran though the alfalfa field to the cemetery fence. Scratches slowed her pace as she squeezed under the old cemetery gate. Certainly the cemetery was old but the chain link fence could not have been more than 10 or 15 years old. The girls paused at the gate watching as Scratches walked up in front of a tombstone and sat down. She looked at the tombstone then turned, looked over her shoulder and meowed toward the girls.

The two friends looked at each other and then back at the cat. Megan reached for the gate latch and opened the gate. She took another glance down at the music box she held in her left hand and in a sign of trust handed the box to her friend May. Then she turned and took several steps into the cemetery.

"Megan, that's a cemetery," May spoke with a tone of uncertainty.

"Yes, I know," Megan answered as she took another step toward the place where Scratches was seated.

"I mean, you are walking on the graves of dead people in there," May spoke, almost pleading.

Megan looked down at the ground and then over at the tombstones. She paused momentarily then turned to her friend at the gate, "But they are my relatives." With that she continued on to take a position behind her cat Scratches.

May reluctantly proceeded into the graveyard and stood beside her friend Megan. There before them was the newest of all the stones, Megan's grandfather's tombstone.

Each of them read the words on the tombstone. "You know, this is real spooky," May remarked.

"What do you mean?" Megan asked.

"Well, it's almost as if Scratches knows what she is doing. Like she led us to the box and to the grave," May answered.

Both girls turned to look at the cat who was still seated in front of the tombstone. Slowly they turned and looked back at each other with an expression of wonder and with a hint of fear. "I think we should get back to the..." May would have said "house" but something in the trees caught her attention. It was a very old run down house. "What is that?" she asked.

"Oh, that's my great grandpa's old house. That's where they lived when the family first moved here," Megan answered.

"Let's go check it out," May insisted.

The girls started for the gate, walked around the little cemetery and started into the woods. The old house had weeds and trees growing all around it. The old path was almost completely grown up with shrubs. They stopped a few yards away and Megan just stood there looking at the old house. It was all rough-cut lumber and logs. Originally it was a log house but some additions had been made to the old house later on and they used rough cut lumber.

"My grandpa and dad wouldn't let me get any closer to the old house than right here when I was little. One day though, when no one was looking, I walked up and looked through the old door." Megan walked up to the old rotting porch. She could see the ground through it in most places.

"What is it?" May asked, detecting a note of concern on her friend's face.

"Well, that day when I peeked through the door, when I turned to leave, I stepped off the porch and stepped on an old rusty nail. My grandpa heard me crying when I came out of the trees. He ran all the way across the field and carried me back to the house." Megan looked down at the ground in front of the door where she had stepped on the nail. The nail was still there, sticking up through a very rotten board. In fact, the board was so rotten you couldn't even hardly call it a board anymore.

"Sounds painful!" May replied as she watched Megan make her way over toward the door.

Megan reached down and picked up the old rusty nail. It was a flat nail something like a horseshoe nail and was rusted until there wasn't much left of it either. "Yeah, I had to have tetanus shots. Grandpa soaked my foot in some blue stuff he used on the animals when they got cut." She turned her gaze from the nail in her hand to push the old door open. The door groaned almost as if it were in pain and cobwebs stretched and broke. A big black and yellow spider fell to the floor and ran off into a dark corner.

Slowly Megan stepped up on the doorstep and looked inside as May made her way across what was left of the old porch. She peeked around Megan to see what was inside the old house. "What's in there?" she asked. Megan took a step inside the old house and the floorboards creaked under her weight. May followed a few steps behind.

Inside the front room was an old wooden table with cobwebs draped from the tabletop to the legs on every side. In the corner to the left of the door as you entered was an old chair and beside the old chair was a

18

box crate that had been used as an end table. To the right of that was the old stone fireplace that still contained charred black fragments of burned wood and ashes. Across the room opposite the door and slightly to the right was another door and to the right of that door was a very old roll top desk that was closed.

The girls made their way cautiously across the room to have a look in the next room. In there they found an old cobweb-covered bed. The mattress was very old and lay flat on the bed platform without box springs. The wooden frame of the bed appeared to have been quite nice in its day, but now it showed its age as well as its antiquity. It had tall wooden legs with wooden balls on top. The old mattress was made of feathers, no doubt, chicken feathers. It had been damp many times and had smelled strongly of mildew.

"Phew, that smell is going to make me sick," May said as she covered her nose and looked around the room at the cobwebs, her eye catching a small black spider working on a web in the corner above the bed. Then she noticed the rafters on the ceiling were literally covered with tiny spiders and spider webs. "Oh my," she muttered in a tone of disgust, shaking her head. "Spiders! I hate spiders!"

"Maybe if we open the doors and get some fresh air in here," Megan said as she tried to open the door beside the bed. The door had not been opened in many years, perhaps even long before Megan was born. Megan leaned into the door pushing hard and finally the door gave way and opened with a loud screeching sound.

Scratches had been hunting in the tall grass in the back yard of the old house when she heard the door open, but when she saw Megan standing in the doorway she ran hopping over the tall grass to rub up against Megan's leg. A gust of fresh air blew through the building at that moment and suddenly in the heat of the day a cold feeling blew over Megan like the wind, leaving her with goose bumps.

"That's strange," she said as she rubbed her arms and looked out into the weed-covered back yard of the old house. There was an old shed that was still standing, if you could call it that. She could see through the boards in many places. There was an old outhouse a few yards to the left of the shed. There was what was left of an old horse drawn plow, an old tractor with iron wheels and a few other farm implements that she could not identify. What was that strange cold feeling she had felt? It was so strange. It was something she found hard to describe.

"Aaaah-Choo!" May sneezed, waking Megan from her trance. "Oh, this place is, uh, really old and smelly and dusty and, look I found another room back here."

Megan turned to see what May was looking at when a board May was standing on cracked and broke catching May's leg between the broken boards. Frantically, she tried to pull her foot free of the boards but the harder she pulled the tighter the boards cut into her ankle.

"Megan, help me!" she pleaded as Megan ran to her assistance. May was pulling and struggling as hard as she could to pull her leg free from between the broken boards.

"I don't like this place! I want to leave now!" May cried as Megan worked with her leg, trying to free her friend.

"Don't pull! I can't get your foot out if you pull like that," Megan told her.

"Oh, I just know there are snakes and wild animals and SPIDERS and God knows what under this house!" May cried and shook with fear. "I just know they are going to bite me! I just know it!"

"Be still. There's nothing under this house that could stand the taste of you," Megan said jokingly, trying to repress a giggle. "Lions and Tigers and Bears OH MY!"

"Stop it! This isn't funny," May responded, wishing she could find the humor that her friend could see in all this.

Megan pushed May's leg down again and one side of the old board broke off and fell beneath the house allowing May's leg to pull free.

"There, see that wasn't such a big deal, was it?" Megan told May.

"Big deal, big deal, right," May said as she examined the scratches on her ankle, then cautiously leaned over to peer into the hole under the house where the broken board had fallen.

"See any monsters under there?" Megan asked, smiling as she walked into the third room of the house.

The walls were lined with old wooden shelves, some of them still holding old jars, a few boxes and antique utensils. There was a very old oil and wood burner stove against one wall. It had oil jars at each end of the stove and wood compartments in two places at each end. At the end of the stove was a small shelf that was evidently used as a table to prepare food. Several old utensils, jar lids, and some large wooden spoons lay on that table.

"It's too dark," May called loud enough that Megan could hear.

"Dark?" Megan questioned.

"Yeah, it's too dark to see anything under there. Just some dirt," May answered, still looking through the hole in the floor.

"Just watch your step and come check this out," Megan instructed.

May got up and joined Megan. "It's the kitchen, I guess," Megan told her.

May walked over to the old shelf-like table, totally forgetting her near brush with certain death at the hands of a dark ominous hole in the floor. She picked up a large wooden spoon and made gestures as if she were stirring something in an imaginary pot on the stove while Megan pulled the doors open on the old wood-fired oven on the stove. She smiled and pulled out an old large heavy black frying pan and placed it on top of the stove.

"Here, you might need this," Megan told her friend. "And you might need this too," she added as she pulled a huge heavy black pot out of the oven and, not anticipating the weight, dropped it on the floor.

"Ha," May spoke in a somewhat sarcastic tone, perhaps to get even with Megan for the incident in the bedroom. "Yes, my dear, but not on the floor." She moved her head back and forth in a haughty way, implying she was in charge of the cooking.

Megan took hold of the pot handle with both hands and strained to place the pot on the stovetop. "Wow, I can't imagine cooking with pots and pans this heavy."

"I can't imagine living back then, let alone cooking," May replied as she tossed the old wooden spoon into the big black heavy cast iron pot. She had lost her fascination with the game of house she was playing. "So why in the world would they build a kitchen and storage room off the side of the bedroom?"

"I don't know, May. They did things different back then than they do now," Megan answered. Megan stood looking at the jars on the shelves. "I wonder what's in them."

"Who cares? Let's get out of here and go back to the house," May insisted.

Megan turned and started through the door back into the bedroom when suddenly she was struck by that cold feeling of something literally passing through her. "Oh, there it is again." Once again goose bumps rose up on her arms.

"There is what again?" May asked, but then at that moment the cold presence passed through her as well. "What was that?" she asked in surprise as goose bumps rose up on her arms as well.

Both girls stopped, frozen in the old bedroom, as a ghostly mist moved through the room to a baby bed at the foot of the big bed and then vanished from sight. At the foot of the old big bed was now a baby bed that had not been there before. The girls looked at each other, both having their arms crossed and rubbing their arms for warmth, and then looked back at the baby bed.

"That wasn't there before," Megan stated. "I know that wasn't there when we came into the house."

The two girls looked at each other again with surprise because both of them knew there was nothing in that bedroom except the main bed. And when they looked back the baby bed was gone again.

"I-I-I'm out of here!" May spoke in a loud and frightened voice as she hurried through the living room and out the door. Megan stood frozen in her tracks unable to move but was shaken by the sharp growling sound that came from beside her at the floor. It was Scratches, her cat.

"Holy cow!" Megan yelled as she looked down to see Scratches there beside her with her back arched, all her back hair standing up, and a strange frightened look on her face. It was the same look that Scratches got when she was having a tiff with the neighbor's dog back in the city.

"Megan, come out of there!" May called to her from outside the old house.

Megan reached down, grabbed her cat, and ran out the front door of the old house to join May. They both turned and took one last look at the old house and then set out in a dead run toward grandma's house. They had only gone a few yards when Megan came to a dead stop, dropping Scratches to the ground. May ran a few more yards and also stopped.

Megan looked up at May, held out her hands and shook her head. "I can't believe I did that! I just can't believe it!" she said as she turned around and looked back at the old house.

"Can't believe what?" May asked.

"I left the music box with the medallion in it, in there on the old stove," Megan answered almost in tears.

"Leave it," May said.

"I can't leave it. My grandpa gave me that and I can't let anything happen to it," Megan answered.

May walked back to join Megan. "Well," May spoke, paused, and then continued, "we can come back and get it in the morning then."

Megan stood there pondering on the plan for a moment but then responded, "I can't allow anything to happen to it. If I leave it there, something might happen to it. I must go back and get it right now." With that Megan took off running back toward the house. May hesitated before following, but Scratches just sat there unwilling to join the girls on this return trip.

When they got back to the house, Megan walked right up and cautiously entered the front door but May stopped short of the house standing by a big tree in what was once the front yard. "Be careful!" she called to her friend.

Megan did not answer, but moved slowly and deliberately through the front room of the old house looking this way and that to see if anything was about to jump out and get her. Then she passed into the old bedroom, but as she did she looked to see if the baby cradle was in the room. When she saw that it was not there, she moved quickly into the kitchen, grabbed up the music box, and hurriedly departed the old house as quickly as she could.

"Did you see anything?" May asked as the girls started quickly back toward the big house.

"No, there was nothing in there this time," Megan answered faintly.

About half way back to the house Megan slowed down to a walk for a few steps and then stopped. "What is it, Megan?" May asked.

"I don't feel well," Megan answered as she teetered back and forth.

May reached out and steadied her friend to keep her from falling. "Take a few deep breaths. You will be all right," May insisted. "You will be just fine. We will go back to the house and you can lay down there and rest."

"Yes, rest. That's what I need to do. Rest," Megan agreed as they proceeded on to the big house.

As the girls entered the house through the back door they found Megan's mother and grandmother seated at the kitchen table having a cup of tea and talking about what they were going to do for dinner.

"You girls having a good time?" grandma asked.

"Sure, having a real fun time," May answered with a touch of sarcasm.

As they passed the chair where Megan's mother was seated she reached out and took hold of Megan, stopping her. "Megan, are you all right?" her mother asked. "You look a bit pale, dear." Megan's mother reached up to feel Megan's forehead. "You feel cold and clammy. I hope you aren't coming down with something."

"No, Ma, I'll be OK. I just need to go lay down for a little while and rest," Megan answered.

Megan's mother looked up at May as if searching for some clue in May's expression as to what the girls had been up to. May sensed what was happening and answered, "We were just running in the field. I guess the heat got to her."

"All right, Megan. You go upstairs and lay down for awhile and I will come check on you in a few minutes," her mother instructed.

Grandma noticed the box in Megan's hand but did not say anything. She had wondered what had become of that old music box as it was handed down from generation to generation and had been hers at one time. The fact that it had come up missing about the time of her husband's death was curious to her but she knew that her husband had already given the gold heart with the key and the picture to Megan. He intended for Megan to have the music box when she was old enough.

Still grandma sensed that something other than the heat might have been what was affecting Megan's health.

"What do you think?" Megan's mother asked

"Oh, girls will be girls. I expect they were just playing and over did it a little bit," grandma answered as she opened the refrigerator door to assess the quantity and types of food required for the dinner that night. "Looks like we are going to have to go to town and get a few things," she added as she closed the refrigerator door.

"I'll drive you to town," Megan's mother said as she got up and headed toward the front door. "Do you think the girls will be all right?" she added as she passed the stairs that lead up to the girls' room.

"I'm sure they will be all right," Martha told her as she picked up her purse and headed for the door.

"Megan, we are going to town to get some things. We'll be back soon," Megan's mother called up the stairs.

"All right, Mrs. Martin," May called back.

The girls heard the door close behind the women as they left. "Well, how are you doing?" May asked.

"I feel better now. It's just that..." Megan stopped as if she wanted to say something but didn't know what it was that she wanted to say.

The key to the upstairs study slid out of her pocket as she lay on the bed and May saw it fall to the bedspread. "The key to the study, and we are all alone, no one to bother us." May reached out and picked up the key.

Megan sat up on her bed, looked over at May, and said, "It's just that, well, it's like I have a real strange feeling we are not really alone at all." She turned, put her feet down on the floor, looked at her wristwatch for a moment, then stood up. "I guess if we are going to do this we had better do it right now."

The girls made their way to the end of the upstairs hall and stood in front of the study door. May placed the key in the lock and turned it first one way and then the other. The door lock clicked, she turned the knob, and the door swung open. There before them was the big old wooden desk that Megan's grandfather used to spend so many hours at. There were bookshelves that went all the way to the ceiling, full of books. The old office chair that Fred had spent countless hours in was by the desk. The carpet on the floor was old and tattered. Paths were worn back and forth in the carpet as if someone had made many trips back and forth over it. Scattered around the room in different places were old pots, statues, bones and other items Fred had brought back from his archeological trips.

The girls walked over and stood looking at the old desk. "It's just the way I remember it," Megan told May. Megan reached out and looked at an open book that had been left on the desk. There was a one-dollar bill inserted between the pages, evidently being used to mark the page.

"Do you think he was reading that book when he died?" May asked.

"It's filled with little picture writing symbols, like on the Medallion," Megan said. Megan placed her fingers in the open page, marking the location where her grandfather had been reading then she closed the book and looked at the front. "Egyptian Book of the Dead," Megan read.

"What's that?" May asked.

"I don't know, but if we are going to solve this mystery I guess we are going to have to find out," Megan answered.

Megan noticed a small piece of paper that had been lying in the book like a bookmark. The paper had some markings on it, a hand-drawn triangular thing with a line marking the top as a segment separate from the lower part and the words 'REV. 14' "REV 14?" Megan questioned.

"That's short for Revelations 14 in the Bible, I think," May remarked. "Look, there's a Bible right there."

Megan looked and there on the far right of the desk was a big black Bible.

"I learned some of that in Sunday school," May said as she made her way over to the old book. "It's the last book in the Bible." She opened it to Revelations 14 and read silently to herself.

Megan, still looking at the piece of paper, noticed something on the back of the dollar bill. Suddenly she laid the paper down and ran from the room. "I'll be right back," she said.

In moments she returned with her music box with Scratches following close behind. She took out her little key, opened the music box, and removed the medallion. She laid it down beside the symbol on the back of the dollar bill. "Look, it's almost the same."

May looked, "Why, that's the eye of Ra, the ancient Egyptian sun god."

"Yeah," Megan said as she picked up her medallion and the dollar bill and took a seat in her grandfather's chair. "If that is all there is to it, why did my grandfather have to die? Why did he keep searching for the answers until it killed him?"

Megan looked up at May and then back at the items in her hand. "And why did my great grandfather do the very same thing?" she added.

May reached out and took the dollar from Megan and looked closely at the symbol of the pyramid and the eye. "And why did our forefathers use a similar symbol on their money?" she questioned.

"I've seen that symbol in other places, but if it was the eye of Ra originally then it must be very old. Perhaps it was adopted by other people for different reasons," Megan spoke, thinking aloud.

"Yeah, I saw it last night on one of those psychic phone service advertisements," May said sarcastically.

Megan looked up with a smile, "You don't believe in that stuff do you?"

"Who me?" she chuckled. "What difference would it make? I'm not even old enough to call them."

"The answers must be somewhere in this room," Megan spoke as she sat up straight in her chair. "This paper says this one design, the triangle and the strange writing, was found on the front of a church in the South of France believed to have been originated by the Apostle Paul."

"Maybe there's something in the desk," May spoke as she pulled out one of the top drawers. "Look here's an old book of some kind." She removed the old book, opened it and her mouth fell open.

"What is it?" Megan asked.

"It looks like your grandfather's journal," she answered as she started to read.

"If it is, there may be some clues in it," Megan told her.

"And if it isn't, we get to read all these books," May answered, waving her right hand about the room in a matter of fact 'how do you like that' kind of way.

Megan flipped through several hundred pages of the journal then looked back up at her friend. "I can see it's going to be a long night."

May walked over, gazed out one of the windows and saw the South field, cemetery, and the top of the old house in the woods and realized the room was facing the South. "Is this room right over the kitchen?" she asked.

"Yes," Megan answered as she continued to read through different pages of the old journal, hoping to find some clues to the mystery.

Scratches had prowled all the way around the room and was sniffing around one of the book cases directly behind where Megan was sitting. "Meow!" she called almost as if she was trying to say something. Megan turned around to see her cat sniffing at the books on the bottom shelf. "What is it Scratches?" Megan looked down at the cat and then at the bookshelf. "Did you smell a mouse back there?" Megan questioned as she spoke to her cat. Slowly her eyes scanned up the bookcase and back to the floor. "There's something really strange about this," she thought to herself, but she just couldn't put a finger on it.

Suddenly she was distracted by the sound of May trying to open one of the old windows. Grunting she finally managed to open it. Then she proceeded to the second window and did the same thing. "I just thought we should get some fresh air in here." Seconds later the door slammed shut causing both girls to jump.

The breeze from the windows blowing through the room had caused the old door to slam shut. May walked over, opened the door and used an old doorstop that lay on the floor beside the door to prop it open.

Megan went back to her reading as May walked around the room looking at all the books and archeological do-dads scattered around the room. She noticed several strange looking ceremonial masks hanging from the wall and an old black steel floor safe in the corner. She bent down and was looking at the front of the safe. "Hey, check this out," she said as she tried to open the safe, but it would not open. Then she looked at the combination lock on the front of the safe. "I always wanted to do this," she said as she placed her ear against the door of the safe and started turning the dial back and forth.

Megan looked up for a moment to see what May was up to and then continued reading the old journal. Time seemed to fly by and before they knew it they heard the sound of Megan's mother's car pulling back into the driveway on the west side of the house.

"Oh, uh, quick close the doors! I mean close the windows. We have to get out of here quick before grandma catches us," Megan instructed as she jumped from her seat and closed one of the windows while May closed the other one. Passing by the desk she picked up the old journal then they quickly ran out into the hallway and closed the door. They could hear the women closing the car doors and knew it would only be moments before they entered the house. "Oh, no! We forgot Scratches in there," Megan whispered as she quickly reopened the door and called for her cat. Scratches ran into the hallway. Megan then quickly closed the door just as the women entered the house. May peeked out around the corner of the hall where she could see down into the front room of the house. Seeing the women pass through the room, she motioned to Megan to follow. As quickly and silently as they could they made their way back to the other end of the hall to their room.

"Whew, that was a close one," May said as she threw herself on her bed.

"Close enough, I would say," Megan agreed as she sat down at the old wooden table in her room and reopened the journal.

May got up and walked over to see what Megan was reading. "Say, look! There are dates on each entry. I'll bet if you go to the last entry you can start sorting this out quicker."

Megan flipped to the end of the journal and started to read.

The Journal...

Chapter 2

I did something last night I never thought that I would do. I dug up my own father's grave in order to find the missing medallion. I had searched everywhere, the old house, the barn. Everywhere but could not find the medallion. I knew he would never sell it, and I remembered that he kept it either under the mattress of the old crib or with him in the old secret compartment book he kept near him most of the time. When I did not find it in any of the usual places, I considered that he might still have it with him. The only way I could find out was to dig up his grave to look and see. Evidently he had given instructions for a sealed package containing the medallion to be buried with him. It was evident that no one knew what the package contained, no one perhaps unless my own mother knew, but she never said.

I am aware this medallion is worth a great deal and people might even kill to take possession of it. I guess the reason he wanted to be buried with it was to protect his family from the curse that goes along with it. I didn't believe in the curse myself and never understood what the curse was about until after I held the medallion in my hands. I would guess that the curse of the medallion is that of the greed of those who would possess it for their own. This is why I must also keep the medallion a secret. If Martha knew what I had done, I would never hear the end of it.

The next entry…

Evidently there was more to the curse than what I had first thought. I have taken ill and must prepare for the worst. I thought that whatever had caused my own father to take ill would have been gone. But as I remember he died of a lung disease caused by some unknown illness. In my research I have learned he died from a strange, perhaps even alien, fungus that took root in his lungs and suffocated him. Should something happen to me someone else must carry on the search for the truth, but whom?

Last entry...

My dearest Megan, if you should find this journal I can only assume you found the music box with the medallion in it, and that I am no longer among the living. The illness I have contracted came from the grave of your great grandfather. It is no danger to you as long as you don't dig up his grave or mine. If you decided to continue the quest for the truth you should find helpful information here in my study and in my journal. There are so many things I need to tell you, but time will not allow it. I am very ill and headed for the hospital now.

God bless you, my little Honey Bee.
Your grandpa Fred

A tear rolled off one of Megan's cheeks as May reached out to take the journal from her. "Let me read for awhile. If I find anything, I'll read it to you," she offered.

Megan got up and went to lie down on her bed. Life just wasn't fair to take her grandfather from her like this. Scratches jumped up on the bed and lay down beside Megan while May continued to flip back through the pages of the journal looking for any information that might be helpful to solve the mystery.

Megan fell asleep while May was reading and before she knew it she was being awakened by her mother. "Wake up dear. It's time to have supper."

Megan sat up in her bed, rubbed her eyes, and looked at her wristwatch. It was 7 PM. Where had the afternoon gone? Then, realizing May had been reading her grandfather's journal, she looked over and saw May laying on her bed with her hands under her pillow. May was not asleep, but winked at Megan. Megan smiled and looked up at her mother.

"Have you girls been having a good time so far?" Donna Martin asked.

"Sure mom, I'm just a little bit tired," Megan answered.

"You will have to tell me what all you have been up to at supper," Donna told her as she walked back out the door and started down the stairs.

"Yeah, right," May spoke softly after Donna had left the room.

May sat up on her bed and lifted her pillow showing she had hidden the journal under her pillow so that Megan's mother would not see it.

Megan just nodded her head indicating her approval of May's solution to the problem. The girls got up and headed for the door. "Did you find anything interesting?" Megan asked.

"Yeah, the book is filled with all kinds of little clues that date way back to memories and things that your great grandfather told your grandpa about," May answered as they walked out into the upstairs hall and started down the steps.

Megan looked down at the steps to see where she was walking. "Little clues you say?"

"Well, I look at it like this, if it had been easy, your great grandfather would have solved it long ago," May added.

"I guess your right," Megan replied.

When they entered the kitchen, the table was all ready set so the girls took their seats and, after saying a short blessing, everyone began to chow down.

"Fried chicken, mashed potatoes and gravy, corn on the cob, my favorite!" May expressed her pleasure with the sight of the culinary delight before her. "Say, Grandma Martha, you wouldn't be of a mind to adopt a teenage girl, would you?"

Martha just smiled as she continued to load her plate. There was no finer compliment than to have someone raving about how her food was so good. If there was one thing she could still give to her family and friends it was these special taste treats she was an expert at making. These kinds of compliments gave grandma a warm feeling inside.

"Are you feeling better, dear?" Donna asked as she placed her hand on Megan's forehead feeling to see if she was running a temperature.

"Yes, mother. I guess it was just the heat," Megan replied.

Donna picked up her fork and started to dish up some of the food on the table over onto her plate. "You know you have always been sensitive to the heat Megan. You be careful this week and don't over do it."

"I will, mom," Megan answered.

"And I will leave your medical kit with instructions with Grandma should you need anything from it," Donna added.

"Oh yes. Let's not forget the medical kit," Megan thought sarcastically. She had certain allergies as a child - asthma, being sensitive to heat and sunlight, dust and bug bites, but for the most part she had grown out of nearly all of these except perhaps her sensitivity to heat & sunlight. She had fair, sensitive skin like her mother and perhaps her mother, remembering her own frailties, was over protective of her daughter. Megan remembered the time her grandfather found her in the barn loft overcome with dust and gasping for breath. She had been throwing the hay up into the air. The air filled with dust, and she nearly passed out before she could get to the ladder to call for her grandfather. The next thing she knew she was waking up in the doctor's office with a tiny pill under her tongue. She had literally stopped breathing and had it not been for her grandfather she might have expired that day. That was the day her mother put her foot down and said, "No more playing in the barn loft, young lady!" Of course that didn't stop her from sneaking up into the loft when her mother wasn't looking. But that was the last time she threw the loose hay up into the air and let it fall down over her head.

"So did you girls have a big day today?" Martha asked.

"Sure. We checked out the barn and the field and..." May hesitated fearing she might say the wrong thing, "...and then we ran around in the field until we got tired and came back to the house."

Donna looked over at Megan in one of those 'you just remember' looks that warned Megan to be very careful. It was evident to Donna that her daughter had also forgotten the ordeal with the dust in the barn.

"You girls haven't been playing around the old house have you?" Martha asked.

Megan looked down at the food on her plate and scraped up some mashed potatoes, "Well, Scratches ran off and we went after her. She went back to the old graveyard and then ran over to the old house. We had to go get her, grandma," Megan answered.

"You know that old house is dangerous and I don't want you two girls getting hurt back there. You remember what happened last time you went back there, don't you?" Martha warned as she made reference to the time Megan had stepped on the old nail.

"Yes, grandma, I remember," Megan answered. There wasn't any point in telling grandma that she was older now and more careful than she had been when she was younger. Grandma was set in her ways about many things. To grandma everyone at the table was still a child including Megan's mother. Grandma Martha was many things - she was set in her ways, she was a strict governess and kept a neat house, but she was still loving, kind and thoughtful of others. Making sure that no one got hurt was one of her priorities and Megan of all people was well aware that while grandma was in charge and within sight, the girls were not likely to get away with very much. She dreaded what grandma might say or do should she become aware that the girls had been inside the old house not to mention the fact they had been inside Grandpa Fred's old study reading the books and going through things.

When they finished their meal, May and Megan got up and started clearing the table. It was commonly understood that the children cleaned up the table and did the dishes after meals. Megan made the first move and May followed her lead.

After supper they all settled down in the living room which was off to the right of the front room to watch TV. Grandma wasn't into the soaps of any kind, but she enjoyed documentaries, news and other educational programs. While listening to the radio, if music came on the station she would frequently change the station to a news broadcast or something else where someone was talking. She said she just didn't care much for today's music and would rather hear someone talking any time than someone trying to sing.

Another kind of program that fascinated Grandma Martha was those that dealt with UFO's, ghosts, and paranormal subjects. In some cases she had been known to literally forget to fix dinner in order to watch a program dealing with these subjects. It just so happened that on this night there was a special program about the pyramids of Giza.

As the program started, the girls pulled cushions from the couch, tossed them on the floor and laid down upon them. Megan looked over at May and whispered, "Just a coincidence, right?" May smiled in a way indicating her suspicion that something more than a coincidence might be the case.

The program challenged the common beliefs that the ancient Egyptians had constructed the pyramids. In fact, it gave evidence that someone had built them long before the ancient Egyptians had come along. The evidence included the signs that the pyramids and sphinx had all been submersed in water perhaps for over 100 years before anyone else came to that land. The program indicated the location of the water line on the second largest pyramid of Giza showing the level of the water and how only the top of the larger pyramids had been above the water line. It told how the Great Pyramid of Giza had been protected by the outer casing stones that had later been removed by stone robbers, and as such did not show the same water damage signs as the second largest pyramid of Giza. The girls looked at each other again, both thinking these were the very same things that Megan's great grandfather had discovered many years ago, but no one would listen to him. While all this was very interesting, if the ancient Egyptians had not been the ones to construct the ancient Pyramids of Giza, then who had?

Chapter 3
More Clues to a Greater Mystery

Later that night in their room, the girls locked their door, lit the big candle in the middle of the table, took out the old journal, and started to read. They discussed the contents of the journal in detail going over some sections several times before moving on to the next entry.

"Ok, right here, there is another reference to the idea that your grandfather believed the pyramids and Sphinx of Giza had been built by a race of people who lived on earth long before the great flood. He says he believes it was near the end of the last ice age." May read from the journal with Megan looking over her shoulder. "And over here is a reference to a legend of an object like a crown that was worn by the ruler of that land and this crown gave him special power."

"Crown?" Megan thought aloud.

"Yes, and over here there is a reference to the people of Atlantis and a notation that says your grandpa had a theory that these people who lived long before Adam and Eve actually came from outer space," May continued.

"Aliens?" Megan questioned.

"Yep, that's what it says here," May answered.

"Boy, this just gets better and better, doesn't it?" Megan said.

"He didn't use the word alien in this text, he just says," May pointed and ran her finger along the text as she read, "'the people of Atlantis evidently had a great understanding of the stars and of the planets. They were able to construct a great city on Earth and they had the ability to travel back and forth to other worlds.'"

"If they had all that knowledge and the ability to travel back and forth to other worlds they had to have been smarter than we are today," Megan spoke as she reached out with the burnt matchstick and re-lit it in the candle flame. "So if they were so smart and had space ships, where are they today?" She spoke as she watched the flame on the end of the matchstick for a moment and then blew it out.

"Spaceships," May said, almost questioning what she was thinking. "And then here," she pointed, "it says that he found references to these things in several texts written by different people at different times. Like here he refers to a text in the Egyptian Book of the Dead where it says these beings or gods went back and forth to the god Ra who dwelled in the great abyss, the land of the fishes, upon which float the bark of the ages."

Megan laughed, "Ra in the land of the fishes." She shook her head. "Does it say what kind of stuff he was smoking when he wrote that?" She continued with a smile, "Funny, I never really took him to be, uh, well mentally off tilt."

"Hey, these were just theories, right?" May responded. "And here it says there was a god known as Horras of the double horizon and it says," May pointed and read again, "'Evidently at that point in the history of this earth, the earth and sky were very different. If, therefore, there was a different canopy over the earth and the sky appeared thick like water and volcanic ash floated in the air high above the earth, it may be possible that when the Sun came up in the morning a refraction of the light may have taken place giving the sun the appearance of a huge eye in the sky.'" May gasp for breath after reading the long sentence.

May turned the page. "And here we find a reference to another entry." She turned several pages and started to read again. "'I was able to simulate the refraction effect using a simple glass of water and a flashlight,'" she read. "And then it goes on to say, 'certainly this demonstration would not have the same magnitude or effect but I feel it is a lead, perhaps a clue into a greater mystery.' "

Megan leaned over and put an arm up on May's shoulder, "I can see this is going to take awhile."

"Yeah, we are going to have to learn everything we can from these notes, those books and what ever else we can find." May stopped and looked up at the candle flame. "We have to learn things that took your great grandpa and your grandpa Fred nearly two life times to learn."

"I don't have a life time to learn it," Megan said as she lifted herself from her seat. "I just have one week to figure all this out, and then it's back to the city with us."

"What are we going to do?" May asked.

"Well, one thing I know for sure. If we have grandma looking over our shoulder at every turn, we aren't going to get very much done at all," Megan answered as she sat down upon her bed and stroked Scratches. "What do you think, Scratches? Do you think we could convince grandma to let us use grandpa's study? You know, read a few books and such?" Scratches looked up at Megan, mewed and then started licking Megan's hand as if to groom it.

"Why don't we ask her," mentioned May.

"Because if we do ask her, and she says no then we will have to disobey a direct order to stay out of that room if we intend to continue this quest of ours," Megan answered.

"Then if we get caught in the act we are..." May spoke but was cut off in mid-sentence.

"Then we may have a free ride back to the city, and if my Mom and Dad find out I got in trouble here, they will make life heck on me when I get home," Megan added as she got up and walked over to one of the windows. She gazed out across the field toward the old cemetery. "I just don't know what grandma might say if she caught us reading grandpa's journal, or knew that we had opened the old study. You saw how concerned she was when she knew we had been out to the old house."

"That house gives me the creeps," May spoke as she joined Megan at the window. Megan's mouth fell open and a surprised curious look came over her face. "What is it Megan? Did you see something out there?"

"I thought I saw a light out there by the old cemetery," Megan told her, "but it's gone now."

"Do you think someone is prowling around out there?" May asked.

"I don't know what it was. It didn't look much like a flashlight," Megan informed her friend.

"With our luck, it's probably a ghost walking around out there," May spoke softly almost as if she feared someone would take her serious.

Megan reached up and placed her hand on the bottom of the open window. It was evident the wheels in her head were hard at work on trying to find some fast solution to the problem.

"We have to find out what's inside that safe in the old study," Megan said with determination. "That old safe has to have something in it that would help us."

44

May looked at her wristwatch. "It's 11:30, Megan. Do you think we should do that tonight?"

Megan turned and started for the door, "We have to find the combination to that safe. Did you see anything in the journal, oh, like a combination to a safe or anything like that?"

"No, I saw some numbers but nothing that looked like it could have been the combination to a safe," she answered.

"Then the combination has to be somewhere in the study, and that's where we will start," Megan said as she slowly opened her door. In the still of the night the door squeaked loud enough it echoed all over the upstairs, down the staircase and into the front room. Megan turned and looked at May cringing. She said, "I hope grandma is a sound sleeper tonight." Slowly, she slipped from her doorway into the hall and started making her way toward the west end of the hall. Every so often the floorboards would creak, but the girls continued hoping they could make the trip without being caught. Slowly they slipped past the door to the room where Megan's mother was fast asleep and on down the hall until they stood in front of the study door.

Cautiously, they opened the door of the old study and tiptoed inside. May closed the door but didn't latch it. Megan picked up a match and lit the old oil lamp on the desk and then stepped back to look the room over. "If I were grandpa, where would I hide the combination to the old safe?" she spoke, thinking aloud.

May walked over and lay down on the floor in front of the old safe and started reaching under it feeling around on the bottom of the old safe.

"Good lord, May," Megan whispered. "What are you doing?"

45

"Looking for a piece of paper, maybe an envelope that may be taped to the bottom of the safe," May whispered back.

"There might bc spiders under there, big black spiders," Megan cautioned.

May quickly pulled her hand out from under the old safe. Seeing cobwebs all over her arm, she made a face and quickly brushed the cobwebs off her arm. "It wasn't under there," she added.

"Doesn't take you long to look under a safe, does it?" Megan chuckled under her breath.

May stood, brushing both hands against the hip pockets of her jeans. "Yuck, that's disgusting," she whispered, shaking her head and making a face. "Grandma hasn't cleaned under there in awhile, that's for sure."

Megan walked around the old desk. "Maybe he taped it up under a drawer or something," she said as she crawled under the desk and started her search. "I can't see anything," she said. "It's too dark under here."

May took the old oil lamp down from the desk and sat it on the floor near Megan. Megan swallowed hard. May could see the expression on Megan's face as it changed from one of curiosity to one of disgust. "What is it?"

"Grandma hasn't cleaned down here in awhile either," Megan answered.

May started pulling each drawer out one at a time while Megan looked up to see if there was any sign of anything taped to the bottom of them. Something caught Megan's attention and she told May to hold everything right there. She had discovered an envelope taped to the bottom of one of the drawers. "Ha," she whispered, "got you now." She removed the package and took a seat in the old chair behind the desk. Both girls were certain they had found what they were looking for. Megan opened the old envelope and pulled out a stack of papers.

"What's this?" Megan said as she examined the old papers.

May reached over and took one of the papers in her hands. "It looks like some kind of money," she whispered. "Look they have dates on them."

"Silver Certificates," Megan read softly.

"100 dollars," May whispered, "and they all look almost like brand new." May held her bill up to the light and looked it over. "Not even a single fold in them."

"These things are old as the hills, probably not worth anything today," Megan said as she flipped through them. "Must be over a hundred of them," she said as she stuffed them back into their envelope.

"Look here, this one is dated 1878," May said, "with a picture of some guy named Monroe on it."

"Like I said, worthless," Megan whispered as she sifted through several of the bills. "Must be about 20 or 30 of them like that one in here, but no combination and that's what we are looking for."

"Better put it back where you got it," May warned Megan.

"Can't, the tape is old and it broke into dust when I removed the thing," Megan told her.

"Shush," May whispered. "I thought I heard something downstairs."

Quickly Megan looked for some place to throw the envelope. She started to throw them into the trashcan but realized there wasn't anything in the trash can. If grandma came in and found it in the trashcan, she would know the girls had been in that room. Then she thought the drawer that was open would be a good hiding place so she threw the envelope in the drawer and closed the drawer as quickly and quietly as she could.

"We've got to get out of here," May pleaded as she stood at the door begging Megan to follow her. Megan wasn't far behind, though, and both girls slipped out the door and closed it behind them. Quickly they made their way down the hallway in their stocking feet, back into their room, and closed the door behind them. Both girls were breathing hard in their excitement, listening at the door, but when sounds of foot steps started up the stairs they both ran and jumped under their covers, none too soon because their door slowly swung open and there stood grandma Martha. She peeked in and shined a light around the room. Seeing the girls in bed, she closed the door and went back down the stairs.

"Goodnight, May," Megan whispered.

"See you in the morning," May answered.

Chapter 4
The Revelation of Impending Doom!

Morning came too soon as the girls were awakened at daylight by the sound of the old rooster crowing from the fence post near the chicken pen.

Megan rolled around in her bed trying to ward off the invasion of crowing that had forced its way into her room. May had all ready given up on the idea of sleeping and was just laying there looking at the ceiling still half asleep.

"I'm going to kill that rooster," Megan muttered as she grabbed her pillow and pulled it over her head.

May laid there for a few moments, listening to the rooster crowing, then pried her tired body up from the bed to have a look out the window. "Chickens," she muttered. "You didn't tell me you had chickens out here."

Megan tightened the pillow down around her head wishing it would all just go away. But it was not to be. The sound of Martha's voice calling for everyone to get up and make hay while the sun was shining echoed up the stairs. Megan rolled over and stared up at the ceiling for a moment. "Oh, boy," she mumbled.

"Oh, boy, what?" May mumbled back.

Megan held a finger in the air, "Just wait."

The girls lay there for a few moments without saying a word. "Come on, girls. I need you to go out and gather the eggs so we can have breakfast," Martha called.

May turned around with a scowling expression on her face, "Gather the eggs. You have got to be kidding!"

"Nope, she isn't kidding. This is the farm and that's just how things are out here," Megan spoke, half talking and half clearing her throat. Megan sat up on her bed, stretched and yawned.

"Least we could get a shower before we go out," May protested.

"You think you've got problems! I can't even see yet," Megan answered as she tried to shake herself awake.

Megan got up and staggered down the stairs to the bathroom. May followed along a few steps behind. Megan ran some cold water and splashed it on her face. May followed suit. The girls wiped their faces and stepped out of the bathroom. "One bathroom for a house this big?" May asked. "Why, our house isn't half this big and we have two bathrooms."

"Things are different in the country, and back when this house was built it was considered a mansion," Megan said as she picked up a small basket from the corner of the kitchen table and opened the back door.

"Mansion," May spoke as they went out the kitchen door and headed across the back yard. "I guess so," she added as she glanced back at the big old house.

"So where did your grandfather get all the money to build a place like this?"

"Well, great grandpa started it all, but he sold a lot of old archeological type things he found. That and he got grants to go on a lot of the expeditions that he went on. I guess he was kinda' wealthy, now that I think about it," Megan spoke as she opened the chicken yard gate.

"I guess he must have been all over the world," May replied.

"Yeah, I guess so. Of course, they farmed this land but that didn't really do much more than help pay its own way. Farmers usually don't get rich from farm work alone," Megan said as she closed the gate behind them.

The old rooster jumped from the fence back to the chicken yard and started strutting around checking the girls out but not wanting them to know he had a close eye on them. He would peck at the ground for food, acting as if he could care less, but this was his territory and nothing went on inside this fence that he didn't know about.

Megan put on the gloves that were in the basket.

"You know we had a mean rooster when I was a kid. It was a banty rooster. It flopped me several times. For awhile, I was frightened of it. Then I got mad at it and when it would flip up to spur me I would catch it by the feet, spin it around and throw it as far as I could. I got pretty good at it, too."

"What's a banty rooster?" May asked.

"It's a small rooster they sometimes call fighting roosters because they will fight with almost anything," Megan answered.

"Doesn't sound like it would be good to have around on a farm in the first place," May answered.

"It wasn't, if you ask me. Then one day it jumped on my sister's horse and the horse killed it." Megan answered, then added, "Stupid rooster."

The girls entered the old hen house. Some of the hens were still setting on nests in boxes built like shelves against one wall of the hen house. Some of them started to cackle when the girls entered the shed, some of them just cocked their heads and watched.

"Phew, it stinks in here," May protested upon entering the shed. "I guess your grandma hasn't cleaned out here in a long time either.

"Nah, I guess the last time this hen house was cleaned out, grandpa did it and that was several years ago," May answered. "Even then he only cleaned it about once a year."

Megan started at one end and started working her way toward the other end. May found some eggs in nests that the hens had all ready left and gathered them into Megan's basket, but she wouldn't go near a nest that still had a hen on it. She turned to watch Megan get the eggs from a nest with a hen on it. As Megan reached toward the nest the old hen started to cackle but Megan just talked to the hen, "Do you have any eggs for me today?" and reached right under her. The hen stood up, still protesting and Megan gathered the eggs. Then May tried it with another hen only to receive a swift peck on the hand.

"Ouch!" she yelled as she jumped back. "That chicken bit me!"

"Some of them will peck you when they are protecting their nest," Megan told her, "and I have to admit some of them can be down right mean, but you just have to show them who's boss." With that Megan turned around, picked up a short broom from the corner of the barn and waved it at the chicken that had pecked May. The hen jumped from her nest and hastily exited the building. "Elvis has left the building," Megan said with a laugh as she tossed the broom back in the general direction of the corner.

Megan moved to another hen on a nest and as she reached for the nest she saw something moving just a little bit at the back of the nest. "Get the broom, May."

May reached for the broom and handed it to Megan. "Another mean chicken," May said but when Megan waved the broom at the hen, it jumped off the nest to reveal a very large black rat snake coiled up in the nest swallowing a hen's egg.

Megan let go a big sigh when she saw the huge snake. "Well, here we go again," she added shaking her head.

May stood frozen in her tracks with her mouth open trying to speak but the word didn't come out easy. "Ssssssssnake! It's a snake! A great big snake!" She started moving toward the door.

"Don't worry, May. It's just a rat snake," Megan reassured her indicating it was no threat to them. Convincing May of that was another thing, though, because May had a fear of snakes. You don't see many in the city, except in the zoo, and most of what she had seen about snakes was bad. To her the only good snake was a dead snake.

Megan watched the snake for a few moments as it swallowed the egg while May watched Megan from the door of the shed. "I remember when my grandpa would find old Bud out here eating the eggs. I wondered why he didn't just kill the old snake and be done with it.

But he would just catch the old snake, carry him to the woods back by the old house and turn him loose."

"He caught the snake and, and he named it Bud?" May asked. "You mean like a pet?"

"Yeah, him and that old snake go way back, I guess," Megan moved on and chased the rest of the hens off their nests to make sure there were no more snakes in the shed. Then she gathered the rest of the eggs. "You would never know where old Bud would turn up next. Sometimes we would find him in the corn bin. He went there sometimes because the corn bin was always full of rats and mice."

"How do you know it's the same snake?" May asked.

"Because of his scars," Megan told her.

"Scars?" May questioned.

"Yeah. He has scars all over him. Some even look like bullet scars where he may have been shot," Megan said.

May cautiously moved back into the shed where she could see the old snake as he was finishing his egg.

She could clearly see the scars on the old snake and there was no doubt this old snake had lived a very rough life. "Man, that's awful."

"Grandpa used to talk to old Bud like he was some kind of friend. He would say things like..." changing her tone of voice so that she would sound more like her grandfather, "Well, old timer, you and me have a lot in common. We can set in the afternoon shade of the old maple tree and compare our scars, HA, HA, HA!" Megan tossed her head back and forth imitating her grandfather when he was in a good mood and talking to old Bud. "But then again, Grandpa Fred used to talk to all of the animals on the farm and even had names for his favorite animals. He generally never gave names to animals he didn't like unless he really hated them, like old Lucifer."

"What was old Lucifer?" May asked.

"Lucifer was a really huge old boar hog," Megan told her.

"A pig?" May questioned.

"Yeah, but not just any pig. Lucifer was mean as the devil and no fence could hold him. Grandpa was afraid that one day he would get loose and attack someone. He lost count of how many times he got called to go fetch old Lucifer from the neighbor's corn field. Then one day when Lucifer got loose and went to the neighbor's corn, grandpa went after him. When he got there the neighbor Mr. Norton asked grandpa..." Megan changed the tone of her voice again to imitate the older men talking, "'Where's the cart?' because he expected my grandpa would load the old pig up and bring him home again. My grandpa reached into the cab of his pickup truck and pulled out his shot gun and said, 'Don't need a cart today, just need your tractor to load that old boar hog with.' That was the end of old Lucifer."

May looked back at the old snake. Megan finished picking up the eggs, all except the three eggs that old Bud was still coiled around and the girls stood there for a few moments just watching the snake finish his egg and spit up the broken shell.

"That's disgusting," May said, but she said that often. Being a city girl she was not conditioned for the things that go on at the farm. She didn't have any understanding for life like children who grew up on a farm. Megan smiled because she knew that her father and grandfather had given her a special advantage by allowing her to live and work on the farm in the summer time and during spring breaks.

Megan slowly reached for the old snake as if she were going to try to catch it. Perhaps she was testing her nerves to see just how brave she was or perhaps she was testing the snake to see if it was dangerous or not. "Grandpa said that he believed this old snake had been around people before and might have even been someone's pet at one time because it was tame when he found it."

"Of course, it's been around people before. Looks to me like they all tried to kill it," May assessed from the scars on the snake as she watched Megan reach out toward the snake.

"Megan, what are you doing?" May pleaded.

Megan stopped just a few inches from the head of the old snake. Bud raised his head up, flicked his tongue out a few times testing the wind and evidently recognized the smell of the gloves.

"Grandpa would let me pet the old snake when he held it," Megan said thinking back, remembering the past.

"Not today, Megan," May insisted.

"You know, I think snakes can recognize people," Megan spoke, thinking aloud.

"Yeah, it sure recognized the eggs in that nest, I would say," May said.

"Grandpa said that usually when a snake is frightened it will buzz its tail. He showed me that with other snakes we found on the farm, but old Bud never buzzed his tail at anyone that I know of. He said that when a snake buzzes his tail, he is frightened and likely to bite," Megan spoke as she watched Bud's attention turn from looking at her to the next egg on the menu. "I saw him catch lots of snakes out here and sometimes he would get bit but he knew what snakes were poison and what snakes were not poison because none of them ever made him sick."

"I vote you leave the snake alone, or go tell your grandma, but don't mess with it," May pleaded again.

"I guess you're right. I'm not in the mood to test all of grandpa's theories today," Megan said as she turned away from the old snake leaving it with the last 2 eggs in the nest. Megan headed out the door and the girls went back into the kitchen.

"Hi, Grandma. We got 18 eggs this morning but we would have had 21 except old Bud beat us to them," Megan told her grandmother.

"Old Bud came back?" Martha spoke as she took the basket from Megan and moved it over to the kitchen sink.

"Yeah, he's in the chicken shed," Megan added as she removed her gloves and lay them on the corner of the table.

"I have not seen Bud in months. I thought he must have died," Martha spoke as she washed the eggs off.

"Where's mother?" Megan asked.

"I guess she's still upstairs. I heard her moving around up there a few minutes ago. I expect she will be down here real soon," Martha answered as she glanced over at May taking a seat at the table.

Megan stood helping her grandmother by putting the eggs in a clean bowl. When they were in the bowl she put most of them in the refrigerator while Martha selected several to use for breakfast.

"What's wrong, May?" Martha asked. May was sitting there with her head lying on the kitchen table.

May raised her head up. "Just can't believe I'm up this early," she said as she glanced at her wristwatch and then at the clock on the kitchen wall as if challenging them for errors. "It isn't even seven o'clock yet. I didn't know life started before seven AM."

"Life starts early when you live on a farm," Martha told her. "It's not that bad. You get used to it."

Megan placed a skillet on the old gas stove and turned on the burner. "Then again some of us have never known anything different. Right, grandma?"

Martha smiled. "Yes, child, I guess you are right." Slowly, a tired troubled look came over her face.

57

"If only your grandpa could still be here to share it with us."

Megan noticed the tone of her grandmother's voice change as she spoke those words but thought it must just be because she missed grandpa so much. Megan didn't realize there was more trouble that she was not aware of. In fact there blew an ill wind directly at her grandmother and the farm and if something wasn't done about it, the entire farm was in danger.

Moments later, Megan's mother Donna showed up and everyone had a nice breakfast.

"Nothing quite like farm fresh eggs for breakfast," Megan said. She had developed a taste for certain things she found on the farm that were not found in the city. The air was fresh, the food was better, and the sun just seemed to have a happy face in the country. Of course it did get hot here just like it did in the city, and there were bugs and snakes and all kinds of things like that. But still it was a refreshing change and one that Megan wouldn't trade for anything.

When breakfast was over, Megan and May washed the dishes as Martha and Donna moved on into the living room. As May walked to the bathroom she overheard the two women talking. Something about "selling the farm" caught her attention and she moved closer to the living room door to overhear what was being said.

When Megan was finished in the kitchen, she also headed down the hall that went past the living room, to the stairs in the front room. She found May standing listening at the living room door. Wondering what was going on, she stood and watched for a moment, but only caught a few words exchanged by the two as Donna got up and moved toward the front door. Donna's bags were packed and setting at the front door because she was headed back to the city today. The girls were going to spend the rest of the week on the farm with grandma, helping her do the chores and the like.

When Donna started their way Megan walked on past May, giving her one of those looks like 'I saw you there, so what are you up to' and continued on to give her mother a good-bye hug before she left.

May didn't know what to do. She was thinking about what she had heard and she slipped off into the bathroom to think about it.

"You girls be good for grandma," Donna told Megan as she gave her a hug and a kiss, then turned and departed the house through the front door.

Megan turned around wondering what was going on, but then ran up the stairs, got a change of clothes from her bag and ran back downstairs to find May standing in the bathroom just staring into the mirror.

"What's going on, May?" Megan asked.

May turned and looked at Megan as she closed the door behind her. "We have a problem."

"What's that?" Megan asked.

"I heard your grandma tell your mother that if she didn't get some money by the end of this month she was going to have to make arrangements to sell the farm." May looked down at the floor.

Megan stood speechless. "I thought that grandpa left grandma well off. He always said he would take care of her and the farm, no matter what."

"That's not all. She said that if she has to sell the farm she will have to move to some old folks home and she knows that will just be the end of her," May spoke adding to the complications of the situation.

Megan went to sit down on the toilet not realizing the lid was up. She jumped up and put the lid down and took a seat.

"Megan," May spoke softly, "isn't there something we can do."

Megan just sat there for a few moments before she answered. "You are right. We must think of something to save the farm." She spoke as she looked up to meet May's eyes. "Go get your clothes and let's get a shower then we can talk this over."

When May returned to the bathroom, Megan was in the shower. It was one of those old tub showers and the tub itself was old as the hills. There was a plastic curtain that looped around the tub. May could hear the water running and the sound of Megan taking her shower. Megan had tossed her dirty clothes in the floor at May's feet. May got ready to take her shower. When Megan stepped out of the shower with her towel wrapped around her May told her, "I just overheard your grandma speaking to someone on the phone. I think she said it was a locksmith and she wanted him to come open the old safe upstairs. I heard her say that he couldn't be here until Monday and she said that would be all right."

"As if things weren't bad enough," Megan responded as she exchanged places with May.

"By the way, you might want to put this back where you found it," May instructed as she handed the old study key back to Megan.

Megan took the key and held it in her hand and suddenly a memory returned to her. "It's a skeleton key."

"What?" May called from the shower.

"Nothing," Megan answered for fear that grandma might hear her yelling. "It's just that this key can open or lock any door in this house, that's all." She continued in a whisper low enough that May couldn't even hear her talking over the sound of the shower.

Megan realized that if grandma was going to have someone come out and unlock the safe that she would soon realize someone had unlocked the door. She might even notice that certain things were no longer where they had been. The journal, for one, would be missing. She knew she had to re-lock the room and place the key back where grandma could find it.

The two girls got dressed and made their way back to their room.

"What are we going to do?" May asked.

"That key is a skeleton key. It can open any room in this house," Megan answered.

"So?" May asked.

"So, I know where there's another key just like it," Megan answered.

"Where?" May asked.

"In the old desk in the study. I saw one in the middle drawer last night under some papers," Megan answered as she peeked out her door to see where grandma was. "Keep an eye out for me," she told May. Not seeing grandma, she slipped back down the hall to the study, slipped in, got the key and sneaked back to her room.

"See," Megan told her as she held up the second key.

"So we have two keys to the study. So what do we do now?" May asked.

Megan smiled as she tucked the key in a pocket of her jeans. "Follow me," she said as she went out the door, down the steps and into the kitchen.

Martha was headed out the back door with her gloves on. "I'm going out to feed the chickens. Then I have to go into town to see someone, but I will be back by noon, I expect. You girls can find something to do, can't you?"

"Sure, grandma, we will be just fine," Megan said as she realized they were once again being left alone at the farm. This might just give them the extra time they needed to take another crack at that safe.

The moment Martha closed the door Megan reached up into a cupboard and removed a can of 3 in 1 oil. She shook the can to see how much oil was in it and then ran back upstairs.

"A can of oil? What are you going to do with that?" May asked.

Megan didn't reply but promptly oiled the hinges on her door and swung it back and forth a few times until it stopped squeaking. Then she ran to the study door and did the same thing. "If we are going to be sneaking around here, we can't afford to have a squeaking door give us away, can we?" she answered with a smile.

By the time she finished the second door Martha had returned to the house, gathered her purse, and was headed for the front door. "You girls be good while I'm gone," she called to them.

Megan stood at the top of the stairs, holding the oil can behind her back with one hand and waving good-bye with the other hand.

The moment the door closed behind Martha, Megan ran down the stairs and back into the kitchen. She replaced the oilcan where she had found it. "Got to put everything back where you find it around here, because, if you don't, it isn't long before someone notices it." Megan closed the cupboard door and then turned and looked at the phone. "Grandpa always used to tell me," changing her voice again to imitate her grandpa as she frequently did, "there's a place for everything and everything should be in its place." She spoke as she made her way over to the wall-phone beside the door that lead into the dining room.

"What are you looking at, Megan?" May asked.

"You know, a long time ago there used to be one of those old crank phones here," she spoke as she reached out and took the note tablet down from its hook and placed it on the table. The phone book and a pencil had been left on the table. It was evident that grandma Martha had made more than one phone call that morning.

It was also obvious to Megan that her grandmother was not following the house rules 'everything in its place.' This was a sign to Megan that whatever had occupied her grandmother's mind was on her mind at the time she made those calls. This is why she didn't replace the phone book on the shelf under the phone.

"What's a crank phone got to do with anything?" May asked.

"Nothing really. It's just where the new phone happened to end up and why there's a shelf there on the wall under it," Megan answered as she picked up the pencil and started rubbing it across the indentations on the tablet. Slowly some writing and numbers started to appear on the paper. Megan held the pad up, "We have to find out where grandma is going this morning."

"What does it say?" May asked.

"I can't really make it out. There is more than one message here. Wait, I see something here that might be what we are looking for." Megan placed the phone pad down and slowly ran the pencil over certain areas again. "Yes, we have I. M. Shyster."

May laughed out loud, "Sounds like a good name for a lawyer, if you ask me."

Megan looked up at her friend and then opened the phone book to the yellow pages.

"Get it, it's A Shyster Lawyer," May laughed.

Megan suddenly looked up from her search with a puzzled look, "This will take forever! Wait, I have a better idea, wait here I'll be right back." With that Megan ran from the room, back up the stairs and in moments returned with her laptop computer in one hand and a phone wire in the other hand. Quickly she disconnected the voice phone and hooked her wire into the phone line and then to her laptop. She turned the computer on and set to work.

"What are you doing? Going on line?" May asked.

"That's right," Megan answered. "Do you know a faster way to find out who a phone number belongs to than to log into the switchboard on line?"

In moments Megan was logged on the Internet and into the "Switchboard" where she did a search for that phone number and in seconds her screen displayed the owner of that number. A "Mr. Isaiah Morgan Shyster, Attorney at Law."

May threw one hand over her mouth in surprise that anyone, let alone a lawyer, would have a name like that. "Sounds like something you might see on one of those blooper shows."

Megan puzzled over the thought for a moment then answered, "It does, doesn't it? But that tells us that grandma is going to see a lawyer this morning and lawyers deal with legal matters, like contracts, selling farms. You know that kind of thing."

"She must be in deep trouble," May added as she watched Megan replace the tablet by the phone on the wall. "So what's the other number on there?"

"I would guess it's the locksmith," Megan answered as she ran a search on her computer for the second number and discovered that she was correct in her assumption. "Come on, we have got to find that combination quick." Quickly she logged off line and disconnected her computer. Then she replaced the phone wires and the two girls ran upstairs and back into the study.

Chapter 5
Safe Crackers and Ghosts

"What's this?" Megan said as she stopped dead in her tracks. There before them standing in front of the book case behind the old desk was Scratches. "How did Scratches get in here?"

"I didn't even realize that Scratches was missing this morning," May answered.

"Me either," Megan added, "but how did she get in here if there was no one to open the door for her?"

Both girls stood in amazement as they watched Scratches walking back and forth arching her back as she does when someone would pet her.

May looked around the room as a shiver came over her and then passed across Megan, "I don't know about you, but I have a real funny feeling we are not alone."

Both girls swallowed rather hard and took a deep breath. "Me either," Megan replied as she stood staring at Scratches on the floor sniffing around the base of the old bookcase. "She was there last night," Megan noted as she looked up at the bookcase above the cat. There were several old books on a shelf just about 4 feet from the floor that all looked alike. Megan removed one of the books and opened it.

"What is it?" May asked.

"It's another journal," Megan answered. She looked up and pulled out another one, looked in it and then up at May.

"Another journal?" May asked.

"Yes, looks like there must be 20 or so of them," she said as she flipped threw a few pages, looking at the dates. "These are older than the first one we found. Some of them are much older."

May turned and looked at the old safe. "Mosler, 1940"

Megan turned to look at May, wondering what she was talking about. Then she saw that May was looking at the safe, reading from the writing on the front of the safe, then an idea came to her. "What if he recorded the secret combination of the safe in one of the journals about the time or day that he bought the safe?"

May rolled her eyes and tipped her head, "Makes sense to me, but when did he get the safe?"

"We know he didn't get it before 1940, don't we?" Megan said with a smile. Then she reached out, took all the journals and placed them on the desk. Both girls started flipping through books until they found all the records dating later than 1940. They shoved all the other, older journals off to the side and started their search. What Megan hadn't noticed were the tiny numbers under her left thumb on the front cover of the first journal she started to search through. After searching for almost 20 minutes she looked up in frustration, realizing she had been that long on one book simply scanning through it for any clues to the combination of the safe. She tossed the journal down on the desk, looked up at May and said, "This is ridiculous. We are never going to find that combination." No sooner had she said that when Scratches jumped up on the desk, a gust of wind blew through the windows, the pages all flipped closed leaving the cover of the book open with Scratches right front paw resting only an inch from the tiny numbers.

"Look, the windows are open!" Megan said in surprise.

May walked over and looked at the windows and then across the south field toward the cemetery and the old house. "I would have sworn they were closed when we came in here."

"Me too," Megan said as she looked over at Scratches sitting there with her right front paw almost pointing at the numbers written inside the front cover of the journal. Scratches gave out a loud meow as if trying to attract Megan's attention. It wasn't the first time that Scratches had used this tone of meow. She always used that tone when she wanted something, like when her breakfast was 5 minutes late, or when she wanted her back scratched or a drink of water. The rest of the time she was fairly independent as cats usually are.

"What do you want, Scratches?" Megan asked, almost as if she expected the cat to answer.

"That's how the cat got in," May said.

"What?" Megan asked.

"Scratches must have come through the open window," May answered.

"But I was sure the windows were closed when we came in here," Megan argued.

"I was too, but were they really closed or did we just think they were," May said as she nodded her head toward the cat seated on the desk.

"I see your point," Megan said as she looked back at the cat and then unconsciously her gaze moved down to where Scratches' foot lay resting on the journal.

Her right hand moved up to cover her mouth as it fell open.

"What is it?" May asked as she walked over to see what it was that Megan had discovered. Like Megan, when she saw the numbers and saw Scratches seated there practically pointing at the numbers on the book, her hand also came up to cover her mouth. Both girls wanted to say something but did not know what to say.

"Could it be?" Megan said as she pulled the book out from under her cat.

"Let's find out," May answered.

Quickly, the girls took the book over to the safe, turned the dial to the numbers listed in the book, pulled the handle and the door of the safe swung open.

Megan fell backwards into a seated position as she looked inside the old safe. May pulled the door the rest of the way open so she could also see inside. Neither girl could believe all the things that had been stuffed into the safe.

"It's full of stuff!" May spoke in astonishment.

Megan reached in and pulled a few items out to see what they where, and several other things fell out of the safe onto the floor, including a small box. The lid fell off the box and several large gold coins rolled out onto the floor.

Both girls looked at the coins as they rolled to a stop, then at each other. "Gold coins," May said.

"Well, what did you expect?" Megan retorted with a laugh. "You keep valuable things in a safe, don't you?"

"Naturally," May answered with a smile.

Quickly, Megan looked at her watch to see how much time they had before grandma returned. Then as quickly as she could she started to pull things out of the safe and handed them to May, who then laid them all over the floor of the study.

"You know, I thought that was a big safe until I saw all the stuff we pulled out of it. Doesn't seem so big anymore, does it? How did all this stuff fit in it?" May proclaimed as she fumbled through some of the old items and coins laying on the floor.

Many of the coins were wrapped in single coin holders and labeled as to what they were, how old they were, and where they had come from. Some of the coins were in folders the size of a notebook page.

"Your grandma won't have to sell the farm now," May assured Megan that all would be well now.

Megan looked up at her friend for a moment, smiling, thinking that perhaps May was right. Perhaps all would be fine with the world now. She was then distracted as Scratches meowed loudly and started pushing a box all around on the floor, pawing at it and rolling over on it almost like a cat will with a bit of catnip.

"What is it, Scratches? What did you find?" Megan asked as she reached out and took the box in her hands and started to open it.

"You know, there are silver coins here, gold coins, and coins that I don't even know what they are. You know what I think?" May said as she fondled the coins in the wrappers and held one of the large gold coins in her hand. Megan listened but didn't answer right away because she had a question of her own. "I think your grandpa has been collecting coins for a long time, like this silver one here is dated 1870 and CC with a picture of Mrs. Liberty on it and this gold one here is dated 1992 with a 'W' on it. It looks to me like he was investing money into these coins every year for a long time."

May sat expecting Megan to respond, but when no answer came she looked up to see Megan holding some kind of circular thing with bright jewels around it in her hand.

"What is that?" May asked.

"I don't know," Megan answered as she looked over at Scratches, almost expecting the cat to answer the question for her. Scratches just sat there looking back and forth between the girls and the items scattered on the floor as if she could care less. Still there was something there, something that had to do with the strange things that were going on, and something Scratches knew that she couldn't exactly tell them. Megan knew it, May suspected it, but the answers were fleeting and the questions were too numerous to mention.

Megan looked down and pulled a folded piece of paper out of the box the jeweled band had been found in.

She unfolded the paper and started to read silently. On the paper was a note from her grandfather about the item.

"What's it say?" May asked as she fumbled through an old coin book that had come from the safe.

"It says that my grandfather bought this from a man in Mexico and that he suspected this object fit the description of an ancient Atlantian object used by Atlantian royalty believed to hold the key to great power." Megan looked at the object, back up at May and then back at the paper in her hand.

"Powwww-errrr!" May spoke in a deep ominous tone jokingly as Megan continued to read.

"He says the thing was like a crown but wasn't really a crown. It was a device of some kind. He said the legend said the object was made from some unknown material because it wasn't wood and it wasn't metal." Megan examined the object closely even so far as to inspect it with a magnifying glass she had removed from the safe. "They didn't have plastic back then but it wasn't plastic or jewel either." Megan looked back at the paper, "He says that some believed the thing to have been made out of bone and others believed it had been made out of the horn of a unicorn but no one knows for sure and even fewer had ever seen it." Megan stopped reading and examined the object again, turning it over every direction to take note of every part of the object. Under the magnifying glass she saw what appeared to be tiny little strands of wire imbedded in the inside of the headband.

"Unicorn?" May questioned. "That would have to mean that it was made before the flood of Noah."

"Why's that?" Megan asked.

"Because everyone knows the Unicorn only existed on earth before Adam and Eve were kicked out of the Garden of Eden," May answered.

Megan looked at May, turned her head sideways indicating curiosity with what May was saying. "I didn't know that."

"Yeah, and the Unicorn was the only animal in Eden that didn't eat that old fruit that got Adam and Eve kicked out of the garden," May spoke. "That makes me hungry just thinking about it," she added.

"Couldn't be," Megan spoke as she took another real close look at the headband. "I can't tell what it is made out of, but if it were that old, this thing would be, well, older than we could imagine."

"At least 12,000 years old, if not older," May spoke in a matter of fact tone.

"This thing can't be that old. It doesn't show signs of how old it might be, but it can't be that old, can it?" Megan questioned.

"Don't really know," May answered as she reached out and took the object from Megan. "If it is what he thought it was though, it's worth more than everything else in this room, including all the gold and silver."

"If it was, then how would you prove it?" Megan asked.

"I think that's just the point," May said as she closely examined the jewels that decorated the outside of the white head band, and then placed the band on her head. Instantly the band conformed to fit her head snugly, almost as if it was grabbing her head. May took hold of the band with both hands and gasped.

"What happened?" Megan asked as she leaned over toward her friend.

"It moved! It grabbed me!" May spoke as she struggled to remove the headband from her head. "The thing is alive or something!" she spoke desperately.

"Relax," Megan told her as she got up to help May remove the headband.

"Get it off!" May pleaded frantically.

"Is it hurting you?" Megan asked as she tugged away at the band on May's head.

"No, it's…" May stopped and realized the band wasn't really tight on her at all, just snug and that it should have come off with ease. "Wait," she said as she relaxed her arms and let them lay in her lap.

Megan moved back a step and just watched to see what May was up to.

A smile slowly creeped over May's face as she turned and looked up at her friend standing beside her.

"What is it?" Megan wondered.

"I don't know. I just have this really strange feeling all of a sudden. I can't explain it," May answered. She reached up then, took hold of the band and simply removed it.

"I've never seen anything like that before in my life," Megan told her as she reached out and took the object from her.

"Yeah, me too," May said still smiling.

"What was it like?" Megan asked.

"I don't know how to describe it. It's a feeling I got all of a sudden like..." May couldn't find the words to describe her experience since she had nothing from her past that she could relate it to. "I guess you will just have to try it yourself to find out," May told her as she shrugged her shoulders not knowing what else to say. "It's like, uh, magic."

Megan looked at the headband with doubt, concerned that some hidden danger may reside with the object. Megan took the object back over and took her seat on the floor. She picked up the paper and started to read again. May picked up her coin book and started looking up some of the coins that lay before her.

"He says right here that he paid that man in Mexico three special gold coins or the equivalent of $12,000 dollars," Megan remarked as she read the paper from the crown's box.

"Uh, Megan?" May spoke with surprise, holding one of the coins up before her.

Megan looked up. "This book says this one coin is worth from $27,000 to $50,000 dollars."

"You must be mistaken," Megan answered, "if that were so..."

May spoke, cutting Megan off short, "If that is so, your grandma has nothing else to worry about except maybe..." May stopped, reached down and picked up another coin. "Except maybe the thieves and sharks that would take it away from her."

Megan put a hand up over her mouth, "You're right. What if the wrong people should find out about these things. What if..." Megan stopped short of her thoughts, thinking the worst.

May jumped up and ran over to the desk where the old silver bonds were resting in their envelope. She pulled them out, took a seat at the desk with her book about the value of money and started going through them.

Megan returned to her notes about the object, the headband, she held in her hand. "It says here there is something else that goes with the Atlantian head band. Some kind of jewels that go on the front of it." She spoke softly, wondering what if this really was that ancient Atlantian treasure. If it were, that would explain some of the mysteries.

"Uh, Megan?" May spoke breaking Megan's trance. "You know these worthless pieces of paper over here?"

"Yeah," Megan answered.

"They aren't worthless," May informed her. "In fact, some of them are worth from $1,750 to $6,500 dollars each."

"They can't be," Megan disagreed.

"That's what the book says," May insisted. "Just face it. Your grandma is sitting on a gold mine here and evidently doesn't even know it."

Megan looked closely at the front of the headband and saw markings where it was evident that something was to be placed, but that something wasn't there. She looked down at all the objects lying on the floor in front of her. There were coins, things, do-dads she could not identify. There were stone objects, pot shards with strange markings on them, bones that might have been dinosaur bones, jeweled daggers, everything you could imagine but no sign of the jewel-like objects that went on the crown.

"It says the jewel things that go on the headband were triangular in shape," Megan spoke as she sifted through all the unopened boxes finding everything except what she was looking for.

"Megan," May said.

"What is it?" Megan asked.

"We better put these things back in the safe before your grandma gets home," May warned her.

Megan reached out and started to gather up the objects and put them back into the safe and then a thought came to her. "If we put all this stuff back in that safe, then when the locksmith comes on Monday, it's all gone. All this will be for nothing," Megan spoke in a tone of desperation.

"Not only that, but the locksmith will be aware of your grandmother's riches," May added.

"Yeah, and we won't be able to solve the mystery of the medallion either. That's what grandpa wanted me to do. If he had wanted grandma to do it he would have given the medallion to her."

"There must have been some reason why he left it for you to solve," May informed her.

"Grandma never understood the value of grandpa's archeological discoveries. She only understood when the bills got paid but never had to worry about any of that because Grandpa always made sure she had the money to pay the bills with." Megan placed the headband back in its box along with the note.

"We can't let the locksmith find any of these things. But what can we do with them?"

"We can't even let grandma find them. Not just yet." Megan spoke with determination, "because she won't know the value of these items and if she tries to sell them to someone they will most certainly take her to the cleaners."

Scratches stood up and started rubbing up against Megan. "What would you do, Scratches?" she asked. Scratches gave another loud meow and trotted straight over to the old bookcase behind the desk. Megan stood up and followed. May spun around in her chair and all of them stood looking at that book case again.

"You know, it might just be me but there's something really strange about that cat and that book case," May spoke softly.

Megan bent down to get a cat's eye view of the bookcase when she noticed that air was blowing around the bottom right hand corner of the book case.

"Megan," May called. Megan looked up, "Look at the floor in front of the book case." Megan looked down at the carpet and for the first time noticed the wear marks by the bookcase. There was a path worn in the carpet right to that section of the bookcase as if someone had been walking right through the bookcase into the wall. Megan stood up, reached out and touched the wooden frame of the bookcase.

"There's something behind this bookcase," she informed May as she started searching the bookcase for some hidden switch.

May smiled in amusement at her friend's actions as she also surveyed the situation. Then she stood up, walked over to the bookcase and simply pulled the right hand side of the frame toward her into the room. The bookcase swung open revealing a dark, dusty, cobweb-filled staircase that lead up into the attic of the old house.

Megan backed up, gave a stern look at May and said, "I could have done that. I could have done that."

Both girls moved over directly in front of the bookcase looking up into the ominous looking passage into the forbidden zone. Scratches was not hesitant however as she made haste up the stairs and out of sight.

The girls both watched the cat go up the steps leaving her tracks in the dust on the steps. This is what caused the girls to notice the single larger footprints in the dust also going up the stairs, but no return steps were visible. They both looked down at the steps and then back up at each other.

"You know what that looks like?" May asked.

"Looks like someone went up the stairs, but didn't come back down, is what it looks like to me," Megan answered.

"That's what it looks like to me, too," May agreed as the girls turned their attention back to the steps.

"Well, go on up there and see what's up there, Megan," May insisted.

"After you," Megan motioned with her left hand.

"No, that's all right. You go first," May insisted. "I'll be right behind you."

Megan, seeing she was not about to win the argument, picked up her courage, put one foot in front of another and headed up the staircase, brushing the cobwebs from her path as she walked.

"You're nuts, Megan," May mumbled in a whisper just loud enough that Megan could hear her. "And I must be nuts right along with you," she added as she proceeded to follow Megan up the dusty staircase.

Megan reached the top of the stairs and slowly peered over the flooring expecting the unexpected. All she saw were dusty boxes, trunks, things stacked upon things but no monsters, not even her cat. Slowly she stepped from the stairway into the semi-darkness of the attic. She ducked her head to keep from bumping the ceiling until she walked out into the center of the attic where she could stand. The only light that entered was through the louvers in the vents at each end of the attic.

May peeked up over the floorboards and, seeing Megan standing there, asked, "What's wrong?"

"It's dark up here," Megan answered.

May turned around and went back down the stairs while Megan looked around in the shadows of the attic. Moments later May returned with the old oil lamp and joined Megan in the attic.

"Scratches," Megan called softly as she looked around the attic.

"I take it your grandpa had plenty of years to collect all this stuff," May noted as she brushed a few cobwebs from the ceiling beams. She was referring to all the boxes and things stacked along both sides of a path the entire length of the attic.

Megan's attention moved from the many boxes and items piled in the attic down to the dust on the floor. There was what appeared to be a man's footprints in the dust, the ones that led up the stairs, but didn't come back down. Beside them were cat tracks leading to the darkness at the far end of the attic. "I don't like this," she whispered.

May moved up and stood slightly behind and beside Megan as she also noticed the tracks on the floor. "You don't think someone is up here, do you?"

"I honestly don't know," Megan answered as she held the light up trying to see into the darkness. "If there was someone up here, who would it be?" Suddenly something flashed in the darkness at the far end of the path. The two girls looked at each other wondering what it might have been.

At that moment they heard the familiar sound of Scratches' meow coming from the darkness. Slowly they moved in the direction of the sound. May saw an old ball bat lying across some boxes and she picked it up thinking, better safe than sorry. The girls followed the footprints the length of the attic to a point where the footprints simply vanished. There at the end of the hallway was a very old wooden baby crib. The crib was stacked full of things and there on top of a box in the crib sat Scratches, his eyes glowing in the darkness reflecting the light from the lamp.

The girls walked up and started looking around.

"You see those tracks are like the tracks of a man wearing work boots," Megan said as she bent down and took a closer look. "And they have tread in them that make a pattern."

"That's not all they have," May added. "They vanished right there. It's like they came out of nowhere and went back to nowhere."

Megan looked around and May was right. It just wasn't normal and that's all there was to that. But if someone had not made those tracks, then what did? There was only one explanation for that... "A ghost," Megan said as she stood up.

"Megan," May said softly as she tugged at Megan's arm.

Megan stood up and May pointed at the baby crib. "That's the crib we saw in the old house, the ghost crib," May told her.

Both girls stood in the dusty attic in front of this very old wooden crib in the dim light of their oil lamp. Then out of the blue Megan started digging things out of the old crib.

"What are you doing, Megan?" May asked.

"It's evident this crib is part of the solution to the puzzle," Megan answered.

"How's that?" May asked.

"We saw it in the old house when we saw that white mist float through the room, right?"

"Right," May agreed.

"But the crib wasn't really there was it?" Megan continued.

"Nope."

"And Scratches got into the study, but who let her in there?"

"I don't know," May answered.

"And then the windows were open, but we were both certain they had been closed when we came into the room, right?"

"Yes," May agreed.

"Then Scratches was the one who found the hidden staircase," Megan continued.

"All right," May answered.

"So, now we find these strange foot prints that lead up the staircase and right to this baby crib and where do we find Scratches?" Megan asked.

"On the baby crib," May answered.

Scratches jumped from her perch onto another box as both girls started digging the old baby crib out from under the piles of things that had been stacked on it.

In moments, they had the crib uncovered and stood there looking at, what? It was an old homemade wooden baby crib that had been made literally from tree branches and rough cut lumber. At one end of the crib was some kind of wooden object with some colored things on it that had evidently been made as a toy for the baby to play with.

"So, now what is so special about this thing anyway?" May spoke, doubting that anything was special about it at all. It was very old and it was homemade and that's all she could see in it.

Megan stood there for a few moments and in an act of desperation she bent down and looked up under the crib. Then she stood up and pulled the old mattress out of it, checking both the mattress and the area under the mattress. Then she pulled the crib out into the path away from the wall and turned it around, checking every aspect of the crib trying to find out what was so special about it, but found nothing. She looked up at May in despair and said, "I don't know. I just don't know."

May shook her head and checked her wristwatch by the dim glow of the lamp. "Well, I know something. We are running out of time fast. Your grandma will be back and we have a mess downstairs to clean up."

"Right," Megan agreed as she turned and started back for the staircase. As she reached the steps she realized that something was different and froze in her tracks.

"What?" May asked.

"The foot prints are gone," Megan noted.

May's eyes grew large as she looked behind her and along the floor where the footprints had been. "I think the place is haunted," she paused for a moment, "but we don't have time to worry about that. Let's get on with it," she said as she gently nudged Megan from behind.

Downstairs the girls stood before the items on the floor. "What will we do with it?" May asked.

"Simple," Megan answered, "we take it all up and hide it in the baby crib."

The girls started grabbing things, putting them in boxes, and taking them up stairs. When they arrived back at the crib, there sat Scratches playing with the mobile toy at one end of the crib. This caught Megan's attention. As she watched the circular object turning, she noticed the colored objects on the toy. She put her box in the crib and reached out to touch one of the objects. It was smooth like glass and had a metal frame. It seemed so out of place on this old homemade crib. Megan was so caught up in thought that she didn't even hear May come up and place a box on the floor behind her and then return to the study. "What are those things?" she asked herself as much as she did her cat, almost expecting Scratches to give her some clue to the puzzle. "It's the only thing that's left in the crib that might be what makes this crib of any value."

As Megan stood there puzzled over the object and the colored triangular objects, Scratches clawed at one of them and it fell from its place onto the crib mattress. Megan reached down, picked up the object and examined it. There on the back of the object was symbol writing like she had found on the back of her gold medallion. The realization that she had found what she was looking for thrilled her. Quickly she removed the other colored triangular objects and stuck them in a pocket.

"What are you doing Megan? We have work to do here," May insisted.

"Oh, nothing much. Just think I found what we were looking for, that's all," Megan answered as she turned and started putting the boxes into the crib.

When all the boxes were in the crib the girls covered it with an old blanket they had found in the attic.

"It's eleven. Grandma will be home soon," Megan said as they made their way down the staircase into the study, pausing a moment to allow Scratches to exit the stairs then closing the bookcase behind them.

May stood looking at the empty safe, with the door still open. "What are we going to do about that?"

Megan saw the empty safe and knew the items that had been in it actually did belong to her grandmother. Of course, the reason she had moved those things was to keep the locksmith from finding them first.

"What if we could convince grandma not to allow the locksmith to come out?"

May looked over at the empty safe and then back at Megan cocking her head sideways, "And how do you propose to do that?"

"I don't know unless..." Megan thought aloud. "Unless we open the safe for her."

"If we open the safe for her, she is going to know something is going on and she is going to want the answers."

"I know, but there must be some way we can pull this off." Megan's eyes moved about the room coming to rest on a small white box lying on the desk. She looked back at May. "I thought we put that in the crib upstairs."

"I was going to, but it occurred to me that if that headband is part of the puzzle you are going to need it. So I thought you might like to keep it until you figure it out," May replied.

Megan walked over, opened the box and removed the headband. She then pulled out the 5 triangular objects from her pocket and laid them on the desk. Each object had a metal clip on the backside of it.

She held the white one up in one hand and the headband in the other hand and examined them.

"From the crib?" May asked as she had remembered the objects from the mobile.

"Yeah, and if I don't miss my guess these things are the objects that fit on the front of this headband." Slowly she positioned the white triangular object over the front of the headband with the point up. Then she slipped it into place. It was a perfect fit.

"That's it!" May agreed.

"Now what do we do with it?" Megan wondered.

"Put it on."

Megan looked up at May hesitantly then she started to put it up to her head. Suddenly Scratches let out one of those loud meows and trotted out the study door into the hall and out of sight. "Grandma must be back."

Quickly the girls looked around the room to see what all had been left undone and wondering what they could do about it. May quickly closed the door on the old safe but did not latch it. Megan jumped from her seat as she gathered up the headband, box and jeweled triangular objects when she noticed the envelope with the silver certificates in it. "Here, put these in the safe," she called as she tossed the envelope to May.

Quickly Megan placed all the journals back on the shelf behind the desk, and out of the room they went just in the nick of time. They were just entering the door to their room when Martha entered the house. Megan peeked from around the corner of the hall watching Martha pass through the front room and out of sight in the direction of the kitchen hall. Scratches followed along behind her as she often did.

"Now what?" May asked as she peeked around Megan's shoulder.

"I don't know, but we have to find some way to help her without blowing our own cover."

The girls returned to their room and took a seat at the table. Megan fiddled with the box in her hand. It was evident to May that Megan was in very deep thought wondering what they could do. They wanted to help Martha but just didn't know how. They didn't know how the old woman would react if she knew all the things the girls had been up to. They didn't know how the truth at this time might affect their research into finding the answers to the mystery of the gold medallion. It was evident that her grandfather had given her that medallion for a reason, but what would Martha do if she knew that Megan had possession of it? Would she take it from her and sell it to help pay the bills on the farm? Little girls have virtually no say when it comes to adult business, Megan had been reminded many times of that old saying.

Megan's mind drifted back to the time right after her grandfather died when grandma decided to sell the ponies to the neighbor down the road. Martha said she simply had no need for ponies and she certainly had need of the money.

"I can take care of them, grandma," Megan pleaded.

"Nonsense, young lady, you aren't going to be here to take care of them all the time and Lord knows I can't do it every day." Martha flailed her arms about as she spoke, "Besides that, ponies have to eat and who's going to pay for it?"

Megan had no answers. She was just a little girl. What did she know about life in the real world? "Please, grandma, can't we at least keep Sparky. I'll try to help take care of him," Megan spoke in a last ditch effort to save her favorite pony.

Megan's words nearly brought Martha to tears. She remembered those ponies had been a gift to Megan and her older brother Gary, but Gary had lost interest in the farm, being completely caught up with his school activities and his new friends in high school.

"Grandpa bought that pony for me," she spoke, looking through her tears, reminding her grandma that pony wasn't hers to sell. It belonged to Megan and it had been a gift from her grandpa.

"I'm sorry, Megan," Martha told her as she placed the money she had received for the sale of the ponies in her purse.

Megan's sorrow turned to anger. "It's just not fair! It's just not fair!" she yelled as she ran from the house out to the loading ramp where a man was closing the tailgate on the pickup truck. Megan climbed up the wooden fence to get one last look at her beloved Sparky as the man drove away.

"I'm big, you're small. I'm right, and you have no say in the matter," Megan mumbled sarcastically though her tears. "Some day I won't be so small and some day I will make them listen to me."

Shortly after that, Martha sold all the cows and all but two of the pigs. She kept the chickens because they were basically cheap to keep, produced eggs which were handy to have and she could always sell a few on the side. Of course, chickens were always handy to have around during the holidays. She kept the pigs because she could always use them as a garbage disposal until they were big enough to butcher. Having a few piglets along on the side also helped bring in some extra cash since the neighbor who had bought the ponies was always willing to lend Martha a hand by taking the pigs to market.

"Megan, come back to us now. Back to the land of the living," May pleaded jokingly, waving a hand in front of Megan's face.

"Kids have no voice in the real world," Megan mumbled softly as she looked up at her friend.

It had been evident to May that Megan had wandered off into another world, but time was short. Decisions had to be made and things had to be done. "Oh, and guess what?"

"What?" Megan responded.

"We left the windows open in the study."

Megan shook her head and rubbed her face with one hand while her attention drifted from May down to the box on the table in front of her. She opened the box and removed the headband. She replaced the white jeweled object on the front of the band and once again started to place the object on her head. "If this thing…"

May closed the door to their room and locked it. "What's to worry about Megan? It's only a headband."

Megan took a deep breath and placed the object upon her head. Instantly the headband contracted around her forehead, not too tight but just enough to hold it in place. The fact that the thing appeared to be alive was more frightening than anything else at that moment.

The jewels in the headband began to glow. First a soft white light emitted from the white triangle mounted at the front. Then the diamond-like jewels around the edges also started to glow. A surprised expression came over Megan's face as she looked around the room. Everything looked different now. Things appeared and vanished in moments. Old things became newer, things and furniture moved around the room like a film being played in reverse at very high speed. When things slowed down and started moving forward again Megan turned toward the windows and saw standing looking out of a window a young girl about 5 years old.

There was something familiar about her. Megan stood up surprised at all the things she was seeing. She exclaimed, "Where did she come from?"

"Where did who come from?" May asked.

"The girl standing at the window?"

"There's no one standing at the window," May answered as she watched Megan's expressions, perhaps as amazed at what she saw in her friend's face as Megan was with the wonders she was observing. Megan's face had taken on a glow from the headband and her eyes had been replaced by a bright white glow. As May searched her mind for something she might compare it to, the only thing that came to mind was infinity. It was as if she could look into her friend's eyes and not see anything to focus on, there was just the white light.

Slowly Megan walked up beside the child she saw standing at the window. She reached out expecting to touch the girl on the shoulder but when her hand reached the child it passed right through her, like she was a ghost. Megan gasped for air as she saw the child standing in the window was her, when she was only 5 years old.

"Are you okay?" May asked.

"I don't know? I think so," she answered.

"What do you see?"

Megan didn't answer right away, but turned her attention out the window. There she saw her grandfather walking through the field toward the house. "I see grandpa walking in the field."

May moved over where she could see out the window but saw nothing more than the wind blowing the wheat in the field. She turned back toward Megan to see the glow that had originally been around her head had moved to include her entire body. May looked around the room to see if she could see anything different in the room but everything except for her friend was the same.

"Hum, Megan, you are glowing. Do you think that thing may be radioactive?" May asked.

Megan didn't answer, she just stood fixed on the man walking across the field.

"How do you feel?" May asked.

"As light as a feather."

May looked down to notice that Megan's feet were floating about 2 or 3 inches from the floor.

"In fact, I feel like I could just fly right out this window."

May, thinking that flying out the window might not be the best idea in the world, walked over and placed a hand through the glow to touch Megan on the shoulder.

The glow moved around Megan like a liquid as May's hand penetrated it. Then it moved up around May's arm, to her shoulders and soon engulfed her entire body as the power from the headband flowed through both the girls. In seconds, the images that Megan was seeing also became visible to May.

Megan and May literally floated away from the window turning their attention to a specific area of the wall. "Grandfather!" she gasped, as the ghost of her grandfather came through the wall in front of them.

May closed her eyes and trembled with fear but when she did the glow retreated from her causing her to lose her grasp on Megan's shoulder and settle to the floor.

"Hello, Megan," her grandfather said as he entered the room.

"Grandpa, is that really you?"

Fred smiled holding out both arms, "It's me, my little honey bee. In spirit, anyway."

Megan reached out to touch her grandfather but her hand passed right through him. "You're a ghost."

"Yes," he answered.

"Why are you still here?" she asked.

"Because my work is not yet finished here," he answered as he walked over to the table and looked at the box with the other triangular objects in it. "The answers were there in front of me all these years but I didn't realize the truth until I had passed on."

Megan looked down at her grandfather's feet and saw the new work boots that he was wearing. "Are you the one who has been helping us find things?"

"Yes, Megan. I don't have all the answers, only a few, but there were things I didn't have time to write down. Things that I hope I can tell you about now. If I can point you in the right direction, you can finish solving the mystery that your great grandfather and I have been trying to solve."

"Great grandfather," Megan said as she looked around the room.

May, hearing only what Megan was saying, quickly turned and looked about the room, fully expecting another ghost to show up. Megan saw her friend looking frantically around the room and smiled. "Relax, May. There is nothing here that's going to get you."

"I would have loved to introduce you to him, but when I passed over into the spirit my father was there to help me. When he had passed along a few things to me he passed into the light where he waits for us. He is the one who told me where to find the triangular jewels that fit on the headband. He also gave me a warning about them."

"Warning?" Megan questioned.

May, having regained her courage, moved silently around behind Megan and once again reached out and placed her hand on Megan's shoulder. Once again the light moved around her and she could see Grandpa Fred standing beside the table.

"Yes. When your great grandfather uncovered these jewels in Egypt, he was not sure what they were.

He also recovered hieroglyphic text on broken tablets that he pieced together and made a copy of on a parchment so that he could translate it later. He had recovered numerous items from his digs and, knowing that some of them had great value, he hid them in various places around the old house back in the woods. Some of the items he found he hid in plain sight like the triangular jewels. Some of the items he buried in jars and boxes around the old house. That crib was my baby crib and I played with these jewels as a toy when I was just a baby. I had no idea what they were and the thought never crossed my mind again until after my untimely death."

"I guess that gives us some idea of how long they have been there," May commented.

Fred looked over at May and nodded his head in agreement, then continued, "I promised that I would take care of Martha for the rest of her life, but I didn't expect to be leaving so soon. If she sells the house and property someone else will gain control over the objects which are still hidden on this land. She must never lose control of the old cemetery either. It holds secrets in the spirits of those family members who have passed on before. I don't understand all of these things but now that you have the Atlantian Crown you should have the ability to find the answers for yourself."

"What are the warnings about the Crown?" Megan asked.

"Each jewel has different properties. Each one has different powers and some of them may very well be dangerous."

May listened intently… "The parchment?"

"The parchment is hidden in two places, but it has not all been translated. You will find one hidden in the old roll top desk in the old house and the other…"

At that moment they heard footsteps coming up the stairs. Quickly Megan removed the crown from her head and the image of her grandfather vanished. The glow that surrounded the girls also faded quickly as the fear of being caught by grandma under these conditions swallowed it up.

"Megan?" called Martha as she tapped on the door. "Are you girls in there?"

"Yes, grandma," Megan answered as she tucked the crown back in the box and slipped it under her pillow. "We will be right out."

"I need to talk to you about something," Martha added.

The girls opened the door. Seeing the expression on Martha's face, they knew what Martha had to say wouldn't be the best of news. "Come with me dear," she said as she started off down the hall toward the study. "Megan, I went to see a lawyer this morning about my financial situation."

Megan noticed the key in her grandmother's right hand. She motioned to May and gestured so that May would understand what was going on. The moment that May saw the key she recalled the open windows in the study.

Martha stopped in front of the door to the study. "I have not been in this room in a very long time," she sighed as she put the key in the lock and turned it back and forth. She did not realize the door was already unlocked. She only turned the key until she heard a clicking sound and assumed the door had unlocked as a result of her efforts.

The old woman opened the door and entered the room. "Your grandfather spent countless hours in this room, Megan."

"I know, grandma. I remember."

The girls followed the old woman into the room. May's first thought was the open windows, but when she looked, the windows were once again closed. May and Megan exchanged glances indicating they had both noticed the same thing at the same time.

"Fred would come up here sometimes in the middle of the night to work on his archeological mysteries." Grandma spoke with a quiver in her voice as she ran her fingers across the edge of the old desk. "I sometimes resented him for that," she spoke soft and slow as she moved around the desk and placed her right hand on the back of the old wooden office chair. "And I'm so very sorry that I didn't take more of an interest in his work."

"Sometimes I would swear I can still here him knocking about up here in the night." Martha pulled a handkerchief from the pocket of her dress to blot the tears trying to escape her eyes.

Megan and May exchanged a knowing glance. It was highly likely the old woman may have just been dreaming. On the other hand, perhaps she really did here the ghost of her dead husband still working to solve the mystery of the medallion, an object that Martha evidently knew nothing about. Then again last night what she may have heard were the girls themselves sneaking about.

Megan wanted with all of her heart to tell her grandmother all the things that she had learned. She wanted to tell her how, only moments ago, she had spoken with Grandpa Fred in her room. She wanted to tell her that grandpa had made arrangements to provide for her and to preserve the farm. Some how she had to, but she had to find the right way and the right time. At the moment she was at a loss for words or thought. Perhaps if she could give her grandma reason to believe in her and then trust in someone other than herself. Yes, perhaps, Martha would listen then.

Megan shifted her attention toward the old safe. The silver certificates were in there and they were worth a good deal by themselves. In fact, if she could find the right buyer she could turn a fine profit from them. That would give her the extra time she needed to sort out more of the mystery. "Grandma, don't give up," Megan reached out touching her on the arm.

Martha looked at the child, wishing she could find some comfort in her words but Megan was still just a child after all and what do children know. Suddenly she took hold of the old chair almost in anger and shook it. "Why did you leave me, Fred? Why? You told me you would be here to take care of me and then you left me." She yelled, shoving the chair hard up under the desk.

Megan and May again glanced at each other as Megan worked up her courage. She felt now was the time but what to say was another question.

"I'm sorry, girls," Martha apologized dabbing the tears back once more with a hanky as she walked around the desk to the old safe. "I'm going to have a locksmith come out in the morning and open the old safe. I hope that Fred left me something in there that will help me."

'Something,' Megan thought. 'He left you a bloomin' gold mine, if you don't blow it.' She loved her grandma but knew very well she had no business sense and would probably just spend the money until it was gone and then where would that leave her? For the moment she had an option, a chance, even if she was not aware of it and it was up to Megan to sort it out and do the right thing.

Grandma did a lot around the farm when Fred was alive but now that he was gone she appeared to have lost her will to succeed. In the past there were very few things that stood between Martha and what had to be done. If she saw a problem she would deal with it, but those days were gone. She needed something, or someone, to believe in now that Fred was gone.

Megan was jolted from her thoughts by a swift shove from May who stood behind her. She looked back to see her friend motioning with her head toward the old safe. Perhaps May was right, perhaps now was the time to open the safe and give the bonds to Martha.

"Uh, grandma," she said hesitantly, afraid that her words might not be received with thanksgiving. Or that something worse might happen and Martha might become curious and start asking questions that would require complex answers.

"Yes, dear," Martha answered.

"If I could help you, I mean if we can help you," Megan motioned toward May with a hand indicating that May was a part of the effort.

"What could you do?" Martha questioned.

"I know you have always depended on your own judgment all these years and I'm just a kid, but if I could help you would you trust me to do some things on my own?"

"I don't understand," Martha answered.

Megan wasn't sure what she really wanted to say. She just couldn't find the right words, but perhaps actions would speak louder than words. "I'll show you." With that Megan walked over to the old safe, took a seat on the carpet and proceeded to turn the dial.

Martha gave a doubting look over at the other girl only to see a smile come across May's face.

"There," Megan spoke as she looked up at her grandmother. She took hold of the handle, twisted it and pulled the door of the safe open.

Chapter 5

Martha's lower jaw dropped down in astonishment. "But how?" She questioned with a trembling hand half covering her mouth.

Megan reached in, took the old envelope out of the safe and handed it to her grandmother.

"Guess you won't need that locksmith on Monday," May told her.

Megan stood as her grandmother removed the silver certificates from the envelope. "Is that all that's in there?" she spoke with much concern as she peered into the safe.

"I need you to trust me, grandma," Megan reassured her.

Martha held up the old paper money, "But these are..."

"Really old," May spoke cutting Martha off in mid-sentence.

"Really old and really valuable," Megan added with a smile.

Martha saw the expressions on the two girls' faces and it was now becoming evident these two children knew more than they were telling. "How do you know about these things? How did you open the safe?"

Megan thought for a moment before she spoke and realized it might be better if grandma didn't know the entire truth. If she had an answer she would be able to twist it around until she could find some excuse to dismiss it all as a fluke. If she didn't know what was going on though, it might buy the girls some extra time.

"If I told you, you would not believe me. But I will tell you that Grandpa Fred may be dead but he has not departed," Megan spoke as she walked toward the door. "And that's not all but in order for me to do what I need to do, I need you to give me the run of the farm without question."

97

"Not departed?" the old women spoke softly. "You aren't going to try to tell me that Fred is still here."

"A ghost," May said.

Megan cringed not knowing how grandma would take that, but May was only trying to help. She just needed to use a little tact once in awhile.

Martha fired a sharp look in May's direction and May quickly realized she had said the wrong thing. Perhaps a change of subject was called for. "Grandma, those old papers in your hands are worth several thousand dollars. If you don't believe me, call the coin dealer in the city and read this one off to him." Megan spoke as she pulled one of the bills from Martha's hands.

Martha walked from the room holding the papers in her hands as she proceeded to the kitchen with the girls following a few steps behind.

"A ghost," Megan whispered in a sarcastic tone at May as they followed along.

"I didn't know what else to say."

"I didn't either, but she all ready thinks we are one egg short of a basket. The last thing she needs to hear is that her dead husband is a ghost and still roams around the barn yard," Megan argued.

"I thought that's where you were headed with the conversation. I'm sorry. Okay?" May replied. "Besides that, you opened the safe for her. She has to know you are telling her the truth now."

"I hope you're right," Megan answered as they entered the kitchen to find Martha turning through the pages in the phone book.

The old woman looked up at the girls as they entered, but her expression still bore the weight of doubt. "Megan, dear, I really do hope you are right about this. God knows I need a miracle." With that she turned her attention back to the phone book, found the number for the coin dealer in the city and placed the call. She read off the information on the bill to the man at the other end of the line. Moments later her expression changed from one of doubt to that of hope.

"Thank you very much. What's that?" she said. "Yes, I might want to sell it... All right, I will call you back in a little while," she said as she hung up the phone.

"What did he say?" Megan asked.

The old woman picked up the bill she had been looking at. Holding it in her hand, she smiled. "He said that if it was in good condition that it could be worth a good deal. He said he couldn't pay me top dollar for it because he deals in resale mostly but he would make some calls and see what he could get me for it."

Megan pulled out a chair and took a seat at the table, "Grandma."

"Yes, dear"

"I want to help but..." Megan looked over at May for a sign of encouragement, then back at her grandmother, "...will you trust me now?"

The old woman looked down at the bill in her hand. "What do you want me to do, Megan?"

"First, I want you to call the locksmith and cancel the appointment. Just tell him you got the safe open all ready. Then I want you to let May and I have the run of the farm and plenty of time to read and work in the old study."

"Well, I guess so. But what do you hope to find?" The old woman turned her head as a thought occurred to her. "You found something in the old house, didn't you?"

"If I'm right, selling this farm could be the worst decision of your entire life." Megan got up from the table, turned to May and said, "Come on. We have work to do." With that they left Martha in the kitchen and proceeded back to their room at the top of the stairs.

"Close the door and lock it," Megan commanded.

"Now what?" May asked as she latched the door.

"Now I have to think what to do next."

"Having free access to the study is a big jump from sneaking around," May commented.

"Yes, but something tells me we are just getting to the hard part of this mystery." Megan pulled the little box with the crown in it out from under her pillow.

Chapter 6
Mental Images

It was three in the afternoon on a Saturday. The girls had accomplished far more already than they had ever hoped. They had a treasure of things they had recovered from the safe in the study. They had what for all purposes appeared to be the ancient Atlantian Crown of power. They could only wonder at what powers or dangers lay ahead of them.

Megan took a seat at the table as she instructed May to check to see where Martha was. "She's headed out toward the back fence," May spoke as she looked out a window.

"Good. We have a few moments here to find out what grandpa was trying to tell us when we were interrupted." Megan placed the crown on her head. Once again it tightened to fit her head and the light show started. Things started flashing around the room just as before but some how things were not the same. The objects, the things she saw, the color were different now.

She looked around the room hoping to see her grandfather but he was not to be found.

"What's wrong?" May asked as she observed the distressing expressions on her friend's face.

"I don't know. Everything is different now." She pulled the crown from her head and the glow lingered for a few moments then faded.

"Different? How?"

"I don't know how to explain it," Megan answered as she walked over to a window and looked back toward the old house.

"Oh, boy," May spoke seeing the same thing that Megan was seeing. Martha was headed across the field directly toward the old cemetery. "What if she goes to the old house?"

"She might, but then again I think she is going to pay her respects to grandpa."

"Oh, I see and perhaps that's why you can't see him right now," May suggested.

"Yeah, I guess that's it," Megan spoke as she looked at the crown in her hand. "I wonder what makes it work."

"The crown?"

"Yeah, there're no batteries in it anywhere," Megan spoke as she turned the crown all around giving it another close once or twice over.

May leaned against the windowsill watching Martha enter the cemetery. Then her attention drifted to the old house. She could only see the roof through the trees but she knew what had to be done. "We have to get into the roll top desk in the old house."

"It's locked, too. But I guess you knew that, didn't you?" Megan answered.

"It figures."

"Grandpa said the writings were in two locations. One was in the desk in the old house and the other one is somewhere else." Megan rethought what her grandfather's ghost had told them.

"I would be willing to bet the other piece is hidden in the old house. Not in the desk, maybe, but somewhere else."

"I agree," Megan spoke as she moved up beside May and placed the crown back on her head. As the glow of light started she reached out and placed one hand on May's shoulder. Looking out the window they saw days passing as if the sun were going from west to east.

They saw crops suddenly appear and then shrink before their eyes. Suddenly they were no longer standing in their room looking out the window, but they were standing in the field.

"Where are we?" May asked with concern.

Megan realized that if May became frightened she would lose contact with her. "Just stand still. We are still in the room. It's just our consciousness that is being relocated."

"Oh, well, that makes me feel better."

The girls turned and saw two children playing, riding ponies out through the field, past them and out to the pond at the southeast edge of the field. "Sparky," Megan said as the two passed them.

"They didn't see us."

"No, that's because what we are seeing has all ready happened. It's like watching a rerun on TV," Megan said.

"That was your brother on the other pony?"

"Yes," Megan answered as the girls watched the two pony back riders reach the far gate that led to the pond.

Suddenly, something changed. The wheat was gone and the girls found themselves surrounded by tall plants much higher than their heads. They smelled a different smell and the heat was bearing down between the stocks. May gasped and Megan was startled but quickly regained her composure. "Don't be afraid. Just remember we are still standing in the room."

"I hope to howdy we are!" May spoke with concern. "But what's going on?"

"It's corn. Grandpa planted corn this year." Megan reached out and touched one of the stocks of corn and then touched an ear of corn. "I can feel it. Look, May. You can touch them."

May followed her friend's example as she reached out and touched one of the stalks of corn. "It doesn't feel real, does it?" she proclaimed. As she spoke the sun moved in the sky, night fell and now it appeared to be early morning. The stocks changed from green to yellow right before their eyes. "What's that sound?"

The girls looked around. "I know that sound. That's the sound of the..." Megan turned quickly looking toward the big house just as a giant machine literally appeared out of nowhere. "...combine!"

In the blink of an eye the girls fell into the combine to find themselves laying on the floor of their room. Megan quickly pulled the crown from her head gasping for air. Huge drops of sweat dripped from both girls' foreheads. "Don't be afraid, she said," May spoke sarcastically. "There's nothing to be afraid of, she said."

Megan lay there for a moment assessing whether either one of them had actually been hurt. "Are you all right?"

"Sure, just fine as pumpkin pie. It's not every day I get run over by a corn picker."

Megan laughed, "It's just one of those things you need to experience once in a life time."

"It's just a good thing we didn't smack our heads on the table or something," May spoke as she stood up brushing herself off. She stood up straight looking at Megan as she started to stand. "It sure looked real, didn't it?" she added as a smile also crossed her face.

"Yeah, but I don't even remember falling. Do you?"

"Now that you mention it, no, I don't," May answered.

Megan took a seat at the table. Holding the crown in her hands, she shook her head.

"I think you need to learn how to use that thing."

"Yes, I think you're right. But the only way I know how to learn is to do it," Megan answered. "The darn thing didn't come with an instruction manual."

May looked out the window to reassure herself the corn was no longer there and that things were back the way they should be. She could see Martha standing in the cemetery at the gravestone of her dearly departed.

"I guess we wait until your grandma comes back to the house before we go out there to the house again."

"I guess I just put it on and it takes me where it wants to go." Megan remarked with a certain tone of despair thinking she had little if any control over what the crown would do.

May turned from the window to observe Megan puzzling over the headband she held in her hands. "I think there is more to it than that."

"What do you think?" Megan asked.

"I think your thoughts tell the thing where to take you. That's what I think."

"You mean, my memories tell it where to go?" Megan continued.

"I think that whatever you think of in your mind, the gizmo tunes into your thoughts and that's where you go," May suggested.

Megan looked back down at the headband in her hand. "If that's the case then I can prove it."

"Yeah, well go right ahead but I'll just wait here, if you don't mind."

Holding the headband in both hands, Megan thought about her room in the house where she lived in the city. Then she placed the object on her head. May sat across the table watching as the glow of light surrounded her friend. A smile came over Megan's face as she removed the object from her head. "You were right."

"And?" May responded.

"And I was just now in my room back home."

May sat not saying anything for a moment. She wanted to try it out for herself but was somewhat afraid of the thing. "So what is it really?"

"I don't know. I think it may be a kind of viewer that can focus your thoughts into the supernatural plane." Megan laid the device on the table and slowly started pushing it toward May. "I mean, we did see my grandpa and that was real time wasn't it? That wasn't a memory, was it?"

May reached out and picked the crown up, "I don't believe I am going to do this."

"Don't be afraid. Just picture some place you want to go see and put it on. When you see where you are, take it off again."

May closed her eyes, focused her thoughts, put the crown on her head and away she went. The glow of light came down around her as a smile came over her face.

"Where are you?" Megan asked.

May just sat there with a smile on her face. "It works like a charm."

"Where are you?" Megan was about to burst from curiosity.

May removed the device from her head but the glow of light lingered as well as her smile.

Megan leaned over, smiling along with her friend, still begging to know where she had been. "Well,

Chapter 6

I just proved that it can take you places you have never been to before."

"And?" Megan pleaded.

"And, would you believe the boys' locker room back at school."

"You're kidding!" Megan spoke placing one hand over her mouth. Watching May's expressions for clues to whether her friend was telling the truth. "You're not kidding, are you?"

"The forbidden zone." May nodded her head as she laid the crown back on the table.

"Too bad it's summer and the locker room was empty," Megan commented with a smile. "Do you know what this means? It means this thing can take us wherever we want to go. In spirit, anyway."

May sat there still nodding her head. "Anywhere you want to go."

Megan reached out, picked up the device, still thinking of all the possibilities. A sly smile creeped across May's face momentarily as another thought crossed her mind. "You know, though, if there is a destiny in all this and the spirits that be have brought this device into your hands, and yours alone, after all these thousands of years. Well, I don't think they gave it to you so you could peek into the boys' locker room at school. There has to be a higher purpose for all this."

Megan pondered on these words for a moment, then took the device and placed it back on her head. The glow once again enveloped her. May watched without saying a word. A few moments passed and Megan removed the object. This time she had a very solemn expression on her face. "The text that is great grandpa's original translation is in a book of some kind inside the roll top desk. I saw a corner of it sticking out from a dusty book."

Megan got up from the table. The glow of light still enveloped her. "No, I didn't see the key anywhere."

"What?" May asked, surprised.

"I just answered your question."

"But I didn't ask a question," May insisted with a curious expression on her face.

"Yes, you did. I heard you. You said, 'Did I happen to see the key anywhere?'"

May looked at the object in Megan's hand. "I was thinking it. I was going to ask you, but…"

Megan realized that somehow she had literally read her friend's thoughts. Perhaps not as much as reading her thoughts but having the ability to see a few moments into the future. It was as if she had actually heard her friend ask the question before the words were actually spoken.

"You read my mind."

Megan pondered for a moment. "I don't think that's what happened."

"What do you think happened?"

"I think this thing leaves some of its powers with me for a short while after I remove it. I think I was mentally displaced a few moments into the future and actually heard your question before you asked." Megan looked down at the floor for a moment pondering on the implications should her answer be correct. "Yes, that must be the answer."

May reached over and pulled the box containing the other jewels to her. "Is something bothering you?" Megan asked.

May looked up and then back at the objects before her. "I don't think you should try any more of these until you know what they do and how to use them."

Megan walked over, placing a hand on May's shoulder. "I will take that as good advice, my friend."

Megan then placed the headband back in the box and stashed it back under her pillow.

"So where's the key?" May asked.

"I look at it like this, either we find the key or we take a hammer and a screwdriver and open it the hard way. Either way we have got to find out what's on that paper."

"Wait." May stopped Megan as she was headed out the door. "You said you saw the paper in the book. How was that?"

"Elementary, my dear Watson. I imagined myself inside the desk," Megan answered as she proceeded out the door.

"Inside the desk. Why didn't I think of that?" May spoke waving her arms in the air. "So why didn't you just imagine yourself where the key was?"

"Because I don't know how to imagine myself where the key is, because I don't know where it is."

"I guess that makes sense," May argued with herself out loud as the girls made their way into the kitchen.

Megan stopped for a moment in the kitchen. "Hammer, screwdriver. Hummm, the shed." With that she departed through the kitchen door and went across the yard to an old shed at the backside of the fence just west of the chicken yard. She unlatched the wooden door and pulled it open. There before them was a tool shed but right in the doorway was a yellow and white riding lawn mower. There was just enough room to walk around it, so the girls made their way into the shed and set forth to find a hammer and a screwdriver.

"Neat little tractor," May commented as she took a seat behind the wheel. "My dad has a little riding lawn mower, but this one is like a regular little tractor." May pushed the pedal down on the left and moved the gear shift back and forth. "Must really be old, huh?" she asked as Megan made her way toward the door.

"I don't know how old it is. I just know it was here long before I was born and grandpa used it for lots of things. He mowed the yard with it, pulled a wagon to haul fire wood and pick up corn. Sometimes he used it to take hay to the cows back by the pond. Grandma still uses it to mow the yard." Megan reached over and pulled the hood up on the little tractor exposing the gas tank and engine. She unscrewed the gas cap to look inside, took a can of gas from the floor in the corner, and proceeded to fill the tank.

Megan continued to work on the little tractor as May watched. "I figured it had to be real old. The newer ones don't have a gearshift like this. They just have a chrome lever that comes out from under the steering wheel and a forward and backward lever. Oh yes and a gas lever with a little bunny and a turtle on it." When Megan checked the oil dipstick May realized she intended to use the little tractor. "What are you doing?"

"Why walk when we can ride?" she said with a smile. "Remember, we have the run of the farm at least for now." Megan motioned for May to get off so she could get the tractor started and out of the shed. The key was all ready in the ignition. Megan pushed the choke up and turned the key. The tractor started with a putt, putt, putt as she shut the choke off. May followed along behind as Megan pulled the little tractor around to the west side of the shed where she hitched a cute little red and yellow flat bed wagon on behind it.

"Your seat, my friend," Megan pointed at the wagon as she handed the tools to her friend.

"Why, thank you," May responded as she took her place on the wagon.

Chapter 6

Away they went, out the gate and down the path through the field, waving at grandma as they passed her on her way back to the house. Martha turned to watch as the girls went by. She didn't really care if they were using the tractor but she worried about the girls. It was her job, not to mention the fact that she knew where they were going and she knew that old house wasn't safe. Still she had given her word and it wouldn't do her any good to worry about it. She had to let the girls grow up sooner or later, that's just how life goes. That's what Fred would have said, if he had been there watching, and who was to say that he wasn't?

Chapter 7
More Pieces of the Puzzle

The girls reached the edge of the field where the path met the woods. The old path that parted the field was actually the old dirt road that led out to the main road where the new house was built. It was evident the path had not been used much since Fred had died. He always kept it mowed, right out to the old house. Seeing the path was grown up with some weeds and brush, Megan brought the little tractor to a stop to size up the situation.

"I think we can make it." Megan shifted into second gear and away they went into the woods.

Tree limbs hung down over the path causing both girls to duck to avoid the larger limbs while pushing the smaller ones aside. The smell of the weeds was strong in the heat of the afternoon sun. As the little wagon passed over them pollen rose up from them causing the girls to sneeze and their eyes to water. In moments they had passed through the worst of it and into the shaded path near the house where no weeds were growing. They approached the old house, hammer and screwdriver in hand.

"This place gives me the serious creeps," May protested.

"Why? Because it is haunted?"

"That and the fact I really hate bugs, spiders, snakes, and falling through rotten floor boards," May answered. "Not to mention it stinks in there."

"I can't argue with that," Megan told her as she stepped through the open door into the front room.

May waited, looking around through the door and listening to Megan's footsteps as she crossed the room. Peering down at the dirt at her feet she could see the opening under the house. "Snakes!" she said as she stepped quickly up onto the doorstep.

"What did you say?" Megan inquired.

"Nothing, just that there's probably snakes under this old house," May spoke as she looked back at the place where she had just been standing.

Megan worked away at the corroded brass latch on the desk, trying to find some way to open it without destroying it. May crossed the room to have a peek in the bedroom. She couldn't help herself as she looked over where they had seen the apparition of the old crib, but there was nothing there. Then there was the hole in the floor where she had fallen through the day before. "You know, somewhere around here is that other piece of the parchment? But where?"

Megan continued to work away at the latch making little progress. She pried away at the hardwood door lifting it a tiny bit and trying to see the nature of the latch hidden underneath. "I can say one thing for sure, this old desk is made out of better wood than the rest of the house."

May strolled over to the bed. Even though she was in the next room she was only a few steps away from Megan and they could see each other from where they were. "Wood," she spoke as she reached out to examine the wood the bed frame had been made of. "It must have been rough back then. I mean they had to make almost everything themselves." A round wooden ball like object had been carved at the top of each bedpost. The wood was very dried and cracked. The wooden balls sat

113

loosely on top of the posts. She reached out, took hold of one of the wooden balls, and pulled it from its resting-place. She then leaned over and looked into the hole where the ball had been seated. "Nothing."

"What?" Megan asked, still working at the latch on the desk. "Bobby pins! Why in the world don't I have a bobby pin?" Megan mumbled to herself as she continued to work at the latch.

May replaced the wooden ball in its resting-place. "I guess it was a long shot, but figured it was worth a try." She turned and there on the floor she saw the old rusty nail that Megan had stepped on as a child.

She had carried it into the house that first day, but when May had fallen through the floor she evidently dropped it on the floor. May reached down and picked the old rusty nail up. It didn't even look much like a nail anymore, just a sliver of rusty metal.

"That's it! I have had it!" Megan jumped up grabbed her hammer and was about to beat the desk to bits when May came in and stopped her.

"Whoa there, madam Hulkster," May yelled to get Megan's attention.

"What do you want?" Megan snapped back turning to see May standing there with a smirk on her face and shaking her head.

"You wanted a wire. Will this work?" May offered the rusty nail to her friend.

"The nail." Megan dropped her hammer. "It might work," she said as she took the nail and looked around the room for some way to bend it. "The floor is full of cracks," she whispered more to herself than to anyone. She kneeled down, placed the point of the nail between two of the boards. Then, taking the hammer in her right hand, she smacked the nail over sideways.

When she removed the nail from the crack it was bent over nearly 90 degrees.

"Well, that was inventive, I must say," the voice spoke from behind her.

"Yeah, but will it work?" she said as she turned and placed the bent nail in the keyhole of the old desk. "Will it work?" Megan turned and fiddled with the nail for a few moments and realized she was able to move the latch. However, she was not able to unlock the latch and lift the door at the same time.

Seeing Megan struggling with the desk, May pitched in and started to help. Pushing up on the old sliding roll top didn't work. It was stuck. She then took the screwdriver and pried under the lid as Megan worked at the latch. Suddenly the top came loose and slid up almost a foot before jamming again. Losing her balance, Megan fell back into a seated position on the floor. May stepped back and looked under the lid of the desk.

"Well?" Megan asked wanting to know what May was looking at.

"You were right," May spoke as she reached under the lid and pulled out an old book with a piece of paper hanging out of it and handed it to Megan who was now standing beside her.

Megan opened the old book. The edges of the paper and the bindings were falling apart. Some of the paper was so brittle that it went to dust under any stress at all. Megan looked up at May in desperation, wanting to open the book but afraid it would fall apart. "What am I going to do?"

May's heart sank. She had no answer for her friend. The only thing she was sure of was that they could not continue to move the pages of the old book. If they did, they might very well destroy everything they had worked for so far. "Close it, Megan. Let's take it to the house until we have time to think this over."

Megan agreed. She closed the book and took their precious cargo back toward the house.

"Did you find anything?" Martha asked as the girls came through the door.

"Just an old book, but we aren't done searching yet," Megan answered as she passed through the kitchen and the girls made their way back to their room.

Martha smiled. The girls were so cute when they were acting important. Of course she had to admit there was more to little Megan than what she had first thought. Perhaps they would discover something else of value on the farm. They had certainly bought her some extra time by opening the safe and handing over the contents of that brown envelope.

Having better light now back in the room, the girls seated themselves at the desk and both sat looking intently at the old book not sure what method might be best to acquire their treasured paper. "What do you think, May? Do we turn it up on edge, open it just a little bit and pull the paper out, or what?"

May sat there for a moment then answered, "Might be worth a try."

Megan tipped the book up on edge. The paper she wanted out of the book was sticking out just enough that she could get hold of it. She instructed May to take hold of the paper while she opened the book just enough to recover the paper from between the pages. The idea worked and only small pieces of paper were lost, not from the paper they recovered but from the pages of the book itself.

There before them laid the paper, having some hand drawn pictures on it and hand written words Megan started to read.

"Thou rollest up into the horizon, thou hast set light over the darkness, thou sendest forth air from thy plumes, and thou floodest the Two Lands like the Disk at daybreak. Thy crown penetrateth the height of heaven, thou art the companion of the stars, and the guide of every god. Thou art beneficent in decree and speech, the favoured one of the Great Company of the Gods, and the beloved of the Little Company of the Gods."

"Say what?" May asked wondering what this had to do with the object in the box.

Megan looked up from her reading for a moment, then returned. "It says 'Thy crown penetrateth the height of heaven, thou art the companion of the stars.' Then here under this it says, 'The Crown of all light having given insight and all knowledge to he who holds the key.'"

May cocked her head sideways as she sometimes did when something wasn't making a great deal of sense.

"'Thou art he whose White Crown is lofty,'" Megan read then pondered on the meaning of those words. "I think what it is saying is that the white jewel is the key to all insight and understanding, maybe." Even Megan wasn't sure she understood what she was reading.

"If that is correct then this white jewel and the crown give the one who wears it unlimited knowledge and truth. That is, if they know how to use it." May got up and fetched the box holding the crown and returned to the table. "And if that's true, the person who wears the crown is like a god, or at least they were like a god way back then."

"Yeah, either that or they really were gods."

"Or aliens maybe," May added.

Megan's eyes grew large at the implications of this thought. What if those gods way back when really were aliens? What if these items that her great grandpa

117

and Grandpa Fred had found were really some kind of alien device? It was possible, wasn't it? "Well, one thing I am sure of, those people really talked funny. I don't see how they could even understand each other talking like that."

May nodded her head in agreement. The language was certainly strange enough. "So does it tell you anywhere in there how to use the thing?"

Megan returned her attention to the page for a few moments then looked up shaking her head. "There really isn't that much here. Except this note at the bottom."

"What does it say?"

"It says 'the ancient text describing seven triangular objects is incomplete but what was found was written in three different languages, one in Atlantian symbol text and another in what was believed to be another Atlantian written dialect, the third being an unknown written language. What I have been able to decipher from several different texts evidently concerning this white jewel is something having to do with a crown like object worn on the head of the ruler of that land being referred to.'" Megan paused for a moment and, finding a new location on the page, started to read again. "'I believe the triangular jewel-like objects could not have been produced by ancient Egyptians, but must have in fact been the product of advanced technology. The metal frame that supports the jewel-like object is made of a metal unknown to mankind. The jewel itself is also constructed from unknown materials having a complex internal structure.'"

May rolled the crown like device around and, looking into the jewel-like object, realized the inside of the object was crisscrossed with tiny fibers and objects that she could not identify. "Yes, it's not just a jewel. It has lots of little things in it." May spoke as she continued to examine the object, pulling it from the band and examining the backside as well.

Megan watched for a moment then returned to her paper. Flipping it over, there was more writing on the back. "'The white jewel holds the key to all truth and knowledge, if the wearer is worthy.'"

"What ever that means," May commented.

"The white stone has been called by several names. The white fire crystal. It is also called the Capstone, the God Stone, and Cheops - which means the Light." Megan continued reading.

"White fire. I like that one," May commented as she picked up one of the other jewels and started to examine it.

Meanwhile Megan continued to read, "'This crystal allows the wearer of the head piece to enter into the spirit and into the God consciousness. It allows the user to use telepathy to communicate with other people as well as the spirits, to see into mystical places in the heavens and on earth. Because of the nature of this crystal having that of all knowledge and wisdom this device may also have combination powers that allow the user to accomplish many other things.'"

"Yes, and it has an after effect that let's the user read minds even after she takes it off," May spoke in an eerie voice trying to sound like someone on a spooky TV show.

"'The red crystal is the crystal of power, fire, lightning, sound, earthquakes, telekinesis and is sometimes called the crystal of war.'"

"And I was just getting ready to try the red one myself. What do you think?" May said, speaking more to herself than to Megan.

"'The blue crystal holds the power of the mystical doorways to other places and other worlds. It allows the user to see into the past and into the future and to walk through walls. This crystal also has the ability to give the user the power of invisibility. To walk among people and not be seen.'"

May giggled, "Now that's what I really need."

"'The green crystal holds the healing powers of the earth and spirit worlds. It will allow the user to call upon the spirits of the earth, to speak to both plant and animal life and to understand the language of nature.'"

"I think you should use that to ask my pine tree why it's dying. I never have any luck with pine trees for some reason." May sighed as she saw Megan look up at her from her paper. "It was just a thought."

"'The yellow crystal holds the power of metamorphosis allowing the user to transform themselves into different shapes from human to animal to liquid or solid objects.'"

"I could see how I could get in trouble with that one." May shook her head as she spoke.

"Here we have 5 different crystals for the crown like object, but it said in that one text that there were originally seven of them. Hummm." Megan laid the paper back on the table.

"So what color would you like to try next?" May asked as she held all the stones in her hands.

Megan studied the old book with the pages falling apart, "Paper is made out of wood. Usually, anyway."

"Plant fibers I guess," May agreed.

"And the white jewel has all knowledge."

"If you are worthy of it," May reminded her.

"So, if I asked the white one how to use the green one, do you think it would tell me?"

May smiled wondering why she hadn't thought of that first. She placed the white crystal back on the headband and passed it and the green crystal over to Megan.

"Lock the door," Megan told her as she put the device on her head. Her aura started to glow and the crown-like device lit up with a white light. Megan took the green jewel device in her hands and held it up where she could see it clearly.

May rejoined her friend, silently watching the light show. She walked around the table and took her seat across from Megan. She thought how strange it was that where Megan's eyes had once been was a kind of infinite light, a light with depth that defied description.

Not more than a minute passed before Megan removed the device, then exchanged the white and green jewel-like objects. "It doesn't look that hard to me."

"What did you see?"

"I don't know how to explain it. It's a feeling. It's like I was given the understanding of how to use the green stone." With that Megan placed the device on her head and in moments a light green light emitted from the device and enveloped her in a soft green glow. She reached out and took the old book from the table and held it up before her. The green glow moved from her hands onto the book until the entire book glowed a bright green. When the brightness dimmed back down to normal, Megan laid the book back on the table and removed the device from her head.

"That has to be the neatest thing I have ever seen!" May spoke, still amazed from the things she had been seeing.

Megan then reached down and opened the book and each page was like new. Even the cover of the book had been restored as if it were new. "Just like new,"

Megan smiled being filled with a sense of accomplishment. "I think we can figure the rest of this out even without the books now."

"The white one has the answers, doesn't it?"

Megan nodded her head as she turned around and looked at the old music box under her bed.

"The medallion. Is that what you are thinking?"

Megan nodded her head. "Let's give it a try." She fetched the music box from under the bed while May exchanged the green and white jewel devices on the headband. Seated once again at the table Megan removed the large gold medallion from the music box using the key from the back of her locket. Once in place, with the medallion before her on the table, she placed the device upon her head and once again the glow of the light enveloped her. She took the medallion in her hands and held it up before her. About a minute passed before she lay the medallion back upon the table and removed the device. She sat there with a rather confused expression on her face.

"Well, what is it? Where did it come from?" May pleaded.

"I don't know what I just saw. I don't understand," came the answer.

May sat perched on the edge of her chair bringing one leg up under the other and leaned out over the table. "Come on, tell me what you saw."

Megan took a deep breath. "It transported me to another place, like another world. At least it didn't look like the earth. I was on an island in the ocean and the sky looked just like water, waves and all. In the center of the island was a white pyramid as big as a mountain and on top of the white pyramid was a brilliant light, so bright that I couldn't even look into it to see what it was."

"All that and no answers?"

Chapter 7

Megan picked up the medallion again and realized the likeness of the pyramid with the capstone and the bright thing that was shaped like an eye. "It wasn't another planet. It was earth a very long time ago. A different kind of people who lived here."

May picked up the blue jewel and fumbled with it for a few moments. "Triangles. All triangles."

"Every one of them so similar, yet so different."

"Just like your pyramid," May added.

"We must have something here that will give us some idea what we are looking for."

"That's just the problem. We can't get the answers because we don't know the question." May had good ideas from time to time. Sometimes she hit the nail right on the head almost by accident.

"I think you are right. We don't know the question. We don't have a ghost of an idea what we are looking for, but grandpa did."

"Haven't seen grandpa lately, have we?" May got up from her seat, made her way over to the window and realized it was getting late. "Where has the day gone?" she spoke softly as she watched Scratches coming up the road from the direction of the old house. "I guess Scratches has been hunting in the field."

Megan pulled the old book over and opened the front page. The writing before her was her great grandfather's. After reading the first page, she realized this was a work in the making. Her great grandfather had been writing a book. From the looks of it, it was a fairly large book but because of his untimely death it was left incomplete.

May walked around the table and stood looking over Megan's shoulder. "Another journal?"

"A book, I think," Megan replied.

"What's it about?"

"I think it is about his archeological trips," Megan said as she flipped through several pages reading tiny bits on each page.

"Did he get it published?"

"I don't know." Megan continued to turn through the pages.

May stood there for a few moments thinking and watching Megan flipping pages and reading. She was still somewhat overwhelmed with the fact that just a few moments before the old book was falling apart and now it was like brand new. "Do you suppose it's worth anything?"

"What?" Megan asked as she looked up from the pages.

"You know if you could get that book published it might be worth something. Your grandma could use the money."

Megan looked back at the book considering what her friend had suggested. Perhaps she was right but, "The book isn't finished."

"So what's to keep you, or us, from finishing it?" May smiled as she reached out and moved the headband device around trying to attract Megan's attention. It worked. Megan looked up and saw what May was thinking. Maybe she was right, she had been having a streak of good ideas the past hour or so.

"Do you have any idea how long that might take us?" Megan wasn't exactly of a mind to start on such a huge project.

"Looks to me like he almost had it finished anyway."

Megan flipped through the pages and saw the book was nearly full. But was it nearly finished? That was the question. She didn't have a ghost of an idea what all was written in the book. She had no understanding of archeological subjects or anything like that. If she were to do anything at all in the direction of completing the book it would certainly be with the help of the device, and the white fire-stone.

"We could ask your grandfather to help us," May spoke trying to come up with a helpful solution.

"Do you think we could find him?" Megan asked. "What if he has moved on?"

"I don't think he would cross over without telling you good-bye. Do you?"

"I don't know. I don't know what makes a ghost do what ghosts do," Megan answered. Perhaps May was right. Perhaps it was a good idea but she didn't feel it was a decision that she wanted to make on her own. If she could find grandpa's ghost then she would consult with him about it. But where would grandpa's ghost be at this time of day? What if grandma walked in on them?

Their deep thought was broken by the sound of grandma calling them for supper. What she needed was time to think this over. It was evident she was confused as to what she should do now and answers were not coming as easy as the questions.

After having a good meal and a few hours of watching TV the girls were tired and went straight to bed. Along about midnight that night, Megan was awakened by Scratches licking her on the face. A cold feeling swept through the room causing her to pull the cover up close to her chin. Scratches wasn't giving up, she meowed loudly and started turning around in circles on Megan's bed. "Grandpa?"

Megan slowly rose up from her bed, reached under and pulled out the box with the device in it. She placed it on her head with the white jewel in place and there stood her grandfather.

"You wanted to talk to me about something?" he spoke softly and sounded distant.

"Yes. I wanted to ask you about this book we found in the desk in the old house." The two proceeded to the table where the old book was. Taking the book with them, their conversation continued from that room, down the hall toward the study. If a person had been standing in the front room looking up at the walkway at the top of the stairs they would have seen Megan's own ghostly form moving in the night. The dim glow of her own white aura was enhanced by the device making her appear more ghostly than physical. She was the only one who could see the form of her grandfather as they made their way to the study. Her footsteps made no sounds as she walked but she did not notice that her feet hardly touched the floor. Her thoughts were with the conversation she was having with her grandfather. Important things had to be discussed. She had many questions about what she needed to do and needed his guidance in these matters.

Once in the study her grandfather instructed her to sit in his chair, which she did. He placed his hand upon her shoulder and, though in ghostly form, she could feel his touch and his spiritual energy become one with her. Floods of images from his life started to rush through her mind. She saw one archeological adventure after another. She saw entire contents from books that he had read and books that he had written himself. She saw the entire contents of all of his journals and she understood the path he had followed trying to solve the mystery of both the medallion and the Atlantian Crown. He was answering her questions while giving her an understanding for his own questions.

Though they never actually spoke another word from the time he touched her until the time he broke contact, Megan understood every single word. The device had increased her ability to comprehend and to absorb huge quantities of information. For Megan, though, the duration of the event appeared to be hours yet in real time only a few minutes had passed.

"So you see, Megan, I had never seen the crown function for myself. I didn't realize my own father had discovered the keys to the crown even before I was born. He placed them in my own crib when I was a child and literally hid them there not understanding the real value or power they possessed. He didn't have the headband since it had been separated from the jewels perhaps thousands of years ago by tomb robbers who evidently didn't make the connection between the jewels and the headband. Who was to know the headband would be discovered ages later, a half a world apart?"

Megan listened intently as her grandfather related these things in words so there could be some interaction between them. During their link up before, the flood of information that came to her was so great, interaction and questions were not possible. "By the son of the man who originally recovered the key devices."

"What are the odds of that happening?"

"My thoughts exactly." Megan looked down at the book on the desk in front of her. "It's like some unseen force has brought us and this device all to this point in time for a reason."

"Yes, but for what reason?"

"If this is the case, then someone or something out there has the answers." Megan flipped through her great grandpa's book and when she got to the last page that he wrote she realized something in her conscious mind that had only been realized in her subconscious mind moments before. With the information she had received from her grandfather, and after reading the work that her great grandfather had written, it was now possible for her to do the impossible. "I can finish this book now." Megan reached out and took an ink pin from the top of the desk. The glow from her hand enveloped the pen as she began to write.

"I'll see you later, Megan." The voice of her grandfather drifted and faded away, as did his image from the room.

Chapter 8
In Search of Atlantis

Morning came as the girls were once again awakened by the sound of the old rooster crowing followed shortly by the voice of Martha calling the girls to go gather the eggs.

The two friends found themselves standing in the chicken pen that morning among the hens with the rooster keeping a close watch. The sky had turned gray. Low clouds were drifting over the farm. Some appeared to be close enough to touch. There was a smell in the wind, the familiar smell just before a storm. A big red barnyard squirrel scampered across the yard toward the oak tree that stood at the corner of the barn lot. His mate wasn't far away, still digging up nuts that had perhaps fallen in the yard during the previous year. The old squirrel feeder that hung on the side of the maple tree in the yard was old and brown. It appeared the brown corncob had been picked clean long ago. Evidently Martha had not noticed to replace it. But then it was summer and her little friends had plenty to eat.

May stood leaning against the chicken yard fence this morning while Megan gathered the eggs. She was looking across the fence at the mother pig and her babies all standing at the fence waiting for their breakfast. Megan threw some crushed corn and chicken feed to the chickens this morning. Martha fed the farm animals usually and she nearly always fed the pigs herself. The old corncrib stood at the edge of the pig lot. It wasn't a problem to throw some corn out the shed window for the pigs. Megan could have done it, but if Martha did it she knew it had been done right.

Megan tossed some feed out to the chickens and watched them pecking away at the feed. Two of the hens had chicks following them around the lot, but Megan was at least a thousand miles away in her mind. "I had the strangest dream last night," she spoke breaking her morning silence. "At least, I think it was a dream," she added as she tossed another handful of feed on the ground.

May looked back over her right shoulder. "You have been unusually quiet this morning."

"I don't know what's wrong with me. I feel really strange. I feel like I had dreams all night long about all kinds of things." She tossed more feed to the ground. "I dreamed my grandfather came back to talk to me."

May bent down and tried to pet one of the chicks, but they were old enough now to stay out of her reach. "I must have had the same dream." She stood up and brushed her hands off. "I thought I heard you talking to someone last night and when I looked you were not in your bed."

Megan tossed the can of feed on the ground and started for the gate, fetching her basket of eggs as she went. "Maybe it wasn't a dream."

"Ever catch one of them?"

Megan looked around. "You mean the chicks? Sure. They're not too hard to catch." She opened the gate and waited for May to catch up. "You just have to catch them in a corner and grab real quick." She smiled.

"Do they bite?" May questioned as she passed through the gate and Megan closed it behind her.

"Nah. The chicks usually don't peck. It's some of the old hens that peck the hardest," Megan spoke as they headed back toward the back door of the big house.

May saw the big red squirrel digging for something in the yard. It looked up and watched the girls as they passed within only a few yards of it. The squirrels in the city parks were fairly tame as well, so May didn't think much about it. Fact was these country squirrels were practically pets. If they had not been, they would have been out of sight in the blink of an eye. Of course this never occurred to May as her mind was on other things.

Martha was working in the kitchen as she always did in the mornings. She had a routine she kept fairly close to. In fact, normally you could just about set your watch by her. "Looks like the hens aren't laying quite as well as usual." She moved the basket over by the sink. "Must be the heat."

"I think a storm is coming, grandma," Megan told her.

Martha looked out the kitchen window above the sink. "Looks like you might be right." She took an egg from the basket, washed it and placed it in a bowl. "Mrs. Butler will be by this afternoon for some eggs. I wanted to have her a good dozen grade A."

Megan recognized the name. It was Mr. Butler's wife, the man who bought Sparky. "Does Mr. Butler still have Sparky?"

"I think he does. Least he did last month."

May, noticing the expression on Megan's face, said, "I think I hear gears grinding."

Megan smiled but never said a word as she slipped out the kitchen door and made straight for the shop. May followed along behind. "You know I know what you're thinking. You're thinking you are going to go over there and see your pony, aren't you?"

"Why not?" Megan opened the shop door, climbed into the seat of the little tractor, drove it out and hooked it up to the wagon. They didn't get far, however, because grandma met them in the yard and put a stop to their adventure.

"Just wait one minute, girls. You know it's Sunday morning and the Butlers always go to church on Sunday. Besides that, it's only 7 AM and you have not even had breakfast yet," Martha informed the girls shaking a finger at them.

Megan killed the engine on the little tractor near the kitchen door. "Well, maybe we can..."

"Come on back in here, girls. We will fix breakfast and talk about things," Martha insisted as she went back into the kitchen.

"Rats!" Megan mumbled to herself as she headed for the door.

"Besides that, it's about to come a storm and I don't want you out there running around on the tractor out there on the road in a storm," Martha told them as they both came back into the kitchen.

"Oh, grandma..." Megan protested.

"Don't you 'Oh, grandma' me, young lady. You know grandma knows best about things like this."

"I know. It's just that I haven't seen Sparky in a long time." Megan grabbed some plates and started setting the table.

May nudged up beside her. "Buy him back," she said with a wink as she pulled out the silverware drawer.

May was right, Megan thought. She had tons of money in the attic. Some of that money was hers. Her grandfather had saved it for her. Her heart leaped. That would be a dream come true. In fact, it was just too good

132

to be true. Grandma really stood between her and her heart's desires. Splitting atoms would be easier than convincing Martha to allow the pony to return to the farm. She swallowed her hopes as she finished setting the table.

During breakfast Martha could not contain her own curiosity. Not having much hope that two little girls could accomplish all that much, but still wondering what the girls had been doing, she asked, "What have you girls been up to?"

Megan pushed some of her scrambled eggs around on her plate. "We found a book that great grandpa had been working on when he died," she spoke as she dumped some ketchup across her eggs.

Upon seeing this May shook her head, "How can you eat them after you do that to them?"

Megan looked up at May wondering what she was talking about then she looked back at her plate. "Oh," she remarked as she realized what May was talking about. "Everything is better with a little ketchup on it." Quickly she grabbed up the bottle of ketchup and dumped some across a pile of cottage cheese on her plate.

May shook her head then looked to Martha. "We can show you if you want to see it," May added with enthusiasm.

"I would like to see it. Where did you find it?" Martha asked.

"In the old house, in the desk," Megan answered between bites.

"You say he was writing a book?" Martha asked quizzically.

"Yes, a book about the stuff he found on his trips," Megan told her.

Martha needed no explanation as to what Megan's statement implied. It was archeologically related. There was no doubt in her mind.

May finished her meal and ran upstairs to get the book. Not finding it on the table in her room, she called down from the stairs, "Where is it?"

"On the desk in the study," Megan answered without thinking until after the fact. She knew the book wasn't on the table, it was on the desk in the study. But if it was on the desk in the study, how did it get there? She realized then what she had observed the night before was real. It wasn't a dream.

In moments May returned with the book and placed it on the table in front of Martha. She started flipping through the book and realized it looked nearly new. "This can't be. It looks almost like new."

Megan finished her last bite, but when she heard Martha's comment she realized the implications. She couldn't explain why the old book looked nearly new, not to Martha, not to anyone, except May.

Catching Megan's expression May realized what was going on. "I guess the old desk preserved it really well, huh?"

"I guess so," Martha spoke in doubt as she flipped through the pages.

May stood looking at the book from the side when Martha flipped through the last few pages. Suddenly she realized something was different. There were new pages there written in another color of ink. She turned and looked at Megan. Her eyes grew large wondering what had really happened last night. Megan hadn't registered on the extra pages. In fact she had not even remembered writing them, at least not yet.

Martha flipped back and forth a few times realizing the handwriting at the end was not the same as in the rest of the book. "It looks like someone else finished the book recently." She read a page of the new entries.

Megan suddenly recalled everything from the night before, but contained herself very well. No, it had not been a dream and she knew that now. But why had it appeared to be so much like a dream to her? Was it because she had been awakened and placed the device on her head while still half asleep? Was it because she had not taken the object off until she went back to bed? Was it because she fell asleep instantly the moment her head had touched the pillow? Perhaps it was a combination of all of the above.

"Why this looks almost like," Martha looked up from the page, "Fred's handwriting."

Megan looked down at her empty plate on the table. "Grandpa did finish the book." She picked up her plate and glass and took them to the sink. May, following her lead, picked up the rest of the dishes.

Martha took the book and left the kitchen going through the hall to the front room.

"Great move, huh?" May mumbled as she watched the sink fill with water.

Megan didn't say a word as she put some dish soap into the water.

"I'm curious just how are you going to explain all that?" she continued.

"I told her the truth."

"Yeah, like telling her that her dead husband finished his own father's book," Megan said sarcastically. "Don't think it was enough that we told her the book was well preserved in that old desk. That book has to be 100 years old."

The girls were interrupted when Martha walked back into the kitchen. They turned to find her holding the book in one hand and the blue ink pen from the study in the other. Slowly she placed the items on the table and took a seat.

May was drying a plate as she watched. "You know you really should get a dishwasher."

Megan saw the pen. She knew where it came from. There was no need for grandma to ask the question because she knew what grandma was thinking.

"Megan," she spoke softly, "I don't really want to know how this happened, do I?"

"No, grandma," Megan answered as she turned back to finish washing the dishes.

"Megan thought you could sell that book. She thought that would help," May interjected, trying to break the tension and perhaps change the focus of thought in the room.

Martha sighed deeply as she picked up the blue ink pen. "This is Fred's ink pen. He never let anyone else use it." Her voice quivered as she held back the tears. "It's the same ink pen this manuscript was completed with." She pulled the book up to her breasts holding it tight in her arms.

"Finish up," Megan told May. She wiped her hands and joined Martha on the far side of the table. Placing her hands on Martha's shoulders, she said, "It's okay, grandma. Everything is going to be just fine. We are going to save the farm, but we are going to need your help."

"What do you want me to do, child?"

"I don't know the first thing about getting a book published, but May is right. This book could be worth some money if we can just find someone to sell it to."

"Honey, I wouldn't know the first thing to do," she answered.

Chapter 8

"It's simple. Just find some publishers and send out some letters, make some calls. You know, that kind of thing." May wiped her hands and faced the two at the table.

"The library might have information on how to get a book published," suggested Megan, thinking that might be the best place to start.

Martha looked down at the book and the pen. She desperately wanted to know how the book was finished in her dead husband's handwriting. Certainly these two little girls could not have done it, but the only other answer was too outrageous to even consider.

Megan patted Martha on the back. "Come on, May. We have more work to do." The girls left the kitchen and returned to their room to gather their thoughts.

Back in the room, May asked, "Now what do we do?" as she plopped down in one of the chairs at the table.

Megan strolled across to a window and pushed it open. Peering out across the wind swept field, her thoughts drifted. The storm wasn't far away. She could feel it. She could see it in the clouds and smell it in the wind. A soft meow came from behind as Scratches rolled over on Megan's bed. Megan unlatched the screen then pushed it out on its hinges. Leaning out the window she looked to the east. She could see the roof of Mr. Butler's house across the east field. Sparky just had to be there, he just had to be. Mr. Butler raised horses, trained them, and sold them. He also had cattle but he only had one old bull that was tame enough to actually ride and he was half-blind. What was his name she thought. She thought back to the day when grandpa took her to see Mr. Butler. She loved the horses but mostly she loved the ponies.

"Want to ride him?" Mr. Butler asked her.

"Cliff's a bull, Mr. Butler, not a horse," she protested laughing at such a silly thought.

"Yes, he may be a bull, but he's the best bull on the farm," he insisted. "My kids ride him every now and then."

"You can really ride on the bull?"

Mr. Butler smiled as he opened the gate and grandpa just stood there and smiled. Megan walked up and he placed the girl up on the bull's back. Ol' Cliff just stood there chewing his cud. He could have cared less if there was a child on his back.

"Say, I bet I know something you would like. I have a pony over in the pony pen that just had a new foal," Mr. Butler told her. Of course, that was the surprise that her grandpa wanted her to see that day. And, boy, what a surprise it was!

Megan's eyes grew as large as the smile on her face when she saw the tiny animal with its mother. "Oh, grandpa," was all she could say for several moments as she was all but speechless.

That little bundle of happiness was Sparky, her very own pony thanks to her grandfather.

"What?" May broke her train of thought once more. It was evident to May that Megan had a great deal of things on her mind. May brushed up against her from behind also trying to see what she was looking at out the window.

"We have to come up with some plan that will keep the farm afloat." Megan closed the screen.

"Just give her the money upstairs," May insisted. "No problem."

"It's more complicated than that," Megan insisted. "If we simply give her the money, she will spend it and in a few years she will be right back where she is now."

"So what do you have in mind?"

"I don't have a plan yet, but that's not all that's on my mind," she answered still standing and looking out the window.

"Does it have something to do with the gizmo?"

"Yeah." Megan looked down at the windowsill then over at May standing beside her. "It's like my mind is full of things that I don't really understand. It's a feeling that I have that I just can't figure out."

"Indigestion, huh?"

"Mental indigestion, I guess. Never thought about it like that," Megan answered with a smile. "I just didn't think it would make me feel strange all over." Megan shook herself as she looked back out the window at the clouds.

"Getting darker."

"Yeah," Megan agreed. "If it doesn't come a storm, it's going to miss a good chance."

"You left the little tractor out in the yard."

"Oh, great!" Megan turned and ran out the door, down the stairs and out to put the tractor away with May following close behind her.

Once on the tractor, however, Megan looked up again at the sky. She wanted to go see her pony so badly she was considering the risk. It's only about a mile down the road. How much trouble could a kid get into? A big sigh escaped her lips.

May stood there watching, wondering what Megan was about to do. She had literally grown up with Megan and many times they could almost read each other's minds. May looked up at the clouds, then at her wristwatch. "You really should wait until after church."

"Maybe your right," Megan reluctantly agreed as she started the engine and made her way back to park the wagon and return the tractor to the shed.

A loud clap of thunder caused the girls to jump, prompting them to return to the house, to their room and then to the study. "You said that grandpa finished the book?"

"Yes," came the answer. Megan pulled a book from one of the shelves.

"How did you pull that off?"

"I don't know how to explain it. It's like I let grandpa guide my hand to finish the work." Megan took a seat in the big chair behind the desk. "It's like that, but there was more to it than that."

May scanned the books on the shelves. "All that stuff is in your head, huh?"

"Yeah. It's like I read the entire book in just a few moments and I saw images in my mind as I touched the pages. Then grandpa touched me with his mind. I saw all the things that he had done in his research and I understood the work, so I finished the book. It was like magic."

"Ancient Mayans," May read on the back of one of the books. She pulled it from the shelf. "I have always been curious about certain ancient cultures." May dragged a dusty chair from the corner, brushed it off, and took a seat at the side of the desk. "So you say your head is full of strange things, huh?"

"Yeah, but it felt more like a dream to me after I removed the headband. I can't really remember everything. I just have a kind of feeling for it. It's like I understand it but couldn't really repeat much of it to you, well, not word for word anyway." Megan turned a page.

"You know it says here that in the digs of Samaria things were found that indicate the ancient Samaritans had a good understanding of the earth and stars."

"Samaria?" May, recalling something she had seen in the safe, looked that direction. "Who closed the safe?"

"I guess I did that last night."

"Why?" May asked. "There wasn't anything in it."

"I put all the stuff back in it from the attic. I didn't think it was a good idea to leave all that stuff up there. It needed to be locked up."

"I guess your right." May, remembering the combination from the book, went over to the old safe, spun the dial around a few times, and opened the safe.

Megan looked up but wasn't really concerned, just curious more than anything. In moments, May had rummaged around in the safe and pulled out a box that had the words 'From the Samaritan dig' written on top. She opened it and brought it to the desk. Inside the box was a six to seven inch long black rounded object. The object had lines carved in it that almost looked like snakes going up a stick. "Where have I seen something like this before?" May asked.

Megan looked over. "Looks kinda like that medical symbol with the snakes on it."

"Yeah, but it isn't exactly like that," May added as a sudden smile came over her face. She placed the object on the desk and hurried from the room. In seconds she returned with the box holding the crown device. She pulled it from the box. It still had the white key on it. She looked up at Megan. "So, can I try it?"

"Sure, but you know what it can do, so be careful," Megan cautioned.

"So what do I do if I want to find out what this thing is and where it came from?"

"You focus on the object you want to know about and don't take your mind off of it. If your thoughts drift the crown will follow them. Then you pick up the object and hold it right in front of your forehead. You should see images, pictures that will help you understand what the object is," Megan answered.

"Sounds simple enough." Of course, May had not forgotten her frightening experience as a result of the device either. Cautiously she placed the crown on her head. She picked up the object on the desk and the dim white glow came over her. She appeared to be in a trance for a few moments. Then she removed the device and placed it back in the box. Slowly the glow left her and a concerned expression came over her face.

"What did you see?" Megan asked.

"I think it's like a chain of DNA. It has a lot of codes and information in it, but you might not want to know what I saw."

Megan cocked her head sideways. "What's the ancient Samaritans doing with a DNA symbol?"

"It's not Samaritans. It's Seminarians, and I think I just saw the missing link on an operating table."

"What's that?" Megan asked.

"It's a table where they operate on you in the hospital, but I don't think this table was in a hospital," May answered.

Megan took a deep breath, "I know what an operating table is." She spoke with frustration. "Let me see that thing." Megan proceeded to do the same test with similar results, but catching something else in the background.

"It sure looks like an operating room, all right. But those aren't doctors, are they?"

"Not regular human doctors anyway," May answered.

"Aliens," Megan spoke softly as she placed the objects back on the desk. The two girls looked at each other wondering "what if."

Megan looked back at the crown. "If my grandpa had figured things out, he could have solved the puzzles and would have still been alive today."

May had an idea that she could not hold inside, even though she had second thoughts. "If he had the green thing on here, he might not have died either." She pondered for a moment. "Say you remember how you fixed the old book? I wonder if that works on people like that?"

"What are you saying, May? Dig up a dead body and see if I can bring someone back to life?" Megan spoke harshly. "That's just plain crazy."

"Somehow, I didn't think you would jump at the idea." She looked down, "Well his spirit's still here, I..."

"Forget it!" Megan cut her off. "I can't believe you would even suggest something like that."

"Bad idea, huh?"

"Bad idea, I guess! Besides that, have you forgotten about the curse?" Megan reminded her.

"I guess your right," May reluctantly agreed, as she looked down, smiling so that Megan couldn't see. It was evident she was just playing with her friend and wasn't really serious, but she didn't want her to know that. Still, it might have worked.

Megan sighed and shook her head as she returned to her book.

May picked up the object from the desk again. "DNA. Aliens. What next?" She placed the thing back in its box and replaced it in the safe, then returned to her book.

It started to rain so May got up and closed the windows in their room and in the study. Suddenly there came a bright flash and both girls started counting, "1001, 1002, 1003, 1004, 1005...5 miles," May said as she turned her attention back to the book.

Martha came into the study around nine with a tray of cookies and milk for the girls. She told them she had decided to go with the Butlers to church and she would be back around noon. The little church was only about two miles down the road toward the highway to the west. She left her present for them and left the room.

Another loud clap of thunder shook the windows in the house. The girls looked up at each other from their reading for a moment. "Big storm, huh?"

"I'd say," Megan answered.

"You know, I found a map in this book that looks kinda familiar." May held the book up for Megan to see.

"Where have I seen that map before?" Megan pondered.

"On the back of the medallion maybe?" May offered her suggestion.

Megan fetched the music box into the room and removed the medallion from it. She turned the object over to note the design on the backside. It did appear to be very much like a map, but it was a map of something she had never seen before. "It looks almost like it shows a continent between what might be North America and Europe." Megan turned the object around and examined it from all directions but soon returned to what appeared to be the upright position.

"Looks real similar to this map, if you ask me."

Megan compared the two. "It does, but this section that leads across toward the Caribbean, then up toward the Bahamas isn't the same. See this one shows an area of land and islands going all the way across..."

Megan got up to take an atlas from one of the shelves then returned to the desk. "See, it looks like there was a huge area of land between North and South America. The mountains run across Puerto Rico to Haiti and there's a large area that crosses from there to Jamaica and Cuba. Then from Cuba it goes all the way across to the Yucatan."

"The Southern tip of Mexico," May spoke softly. "Does that mean when this medallion was made that all that land was above the water?"

"I think that's exactly what it is showing."

"So where is Atlantis?" May asked.

"I don't know. Was it a city, a kingdom, perhaps, or a continent?"

"Maybe it's what they called the entire planet back then." May answered, puzzled.

"I never thought of that before. So instead of calling our world the Earth they might have called the entire planet Atlantis," Megan suggested.

"So, if they did, it's no wonder they can't find the lost city of Atlantis. They aren't looking from the right perspective," May added.

"Yeah, but then again that's just a theory and might not be the right answer."

"May not be the complete answer, you mean. But it is a worthy concept and I think we should keep it in mind," May insisted.

Megan looked at the map again and then at the medallion. "Either that or it was a city that sank along with all that land that no longer exists above water."

May picked up the headband. "I think you are ready."

Megan took the crown device and returned to her seat behind the desk. She paused for a moment looking at May and wondering exactly what she was looking for.

"Go to Atlantis, Megan. Find the answers. You have a specific question, you can find the answers."

Megan placed the device on her head and once again the glow of light engulfed her. Suddenly she found herself under the sea, waves moving overhead and some fish swimming here and there.

"What do you see?"

"I see water. I'm underwater. I see a mountain near me and piles and piles of rocks and silt."

"Go to the rocks," May instructed.

"There's something here, a hole that goes inside this place."

"A cave?"

"No, not like a cave. The hole goes straight down like a chimney shaft but the sides are square and hard like rock. Whatever this is, someone made it."

"Go on in," May instructed her.

Megan took a deep breath, concerned what she might encounter inside, but then continued down into the shaft. "I reached the bottom. I can still see light above me. I don't know how deep I am. There is a tunnel that leads away from here. I see more of these white looking rocks strewn about the floor. I am going into what appears to be a large rectangular room."

"Can you see anything? Objects, colors, anything like that?"

"There's broken things laying everywhere, like broken pots and statues. There are patterns on the floor and walls and some pictures on the walls." Megan moved on into the interior of the room.

"Do you feel like you are underground?"

"I can't tell. I do have the sensation that I am covered or buried under something."

"What else can you see?" said May, trying to guide her friend's focus into the vision she was seeing.

"I see two very large stone looking chairs at one end of this room." Megan's head turned as she looked around inside the room. "I see another..." she was going to say room. "No, this is a huge 'L' shaped room."

May could see Megan as if she were looking around the room so she sat quietly for a moment just watching.

"There's some broken stones in the floor here, and a hole in the floor." Megan talked as she viewed the far end of the longer, larger area of the room. "There's a door here on my left, and there is a door ahead of me." Moments passed. "Going to the left there is a smaller room. There is a stone table here and another door on my right."

May listened intently as she watched the movements and expressions of her friend. She watched as a puzzled expression came over Megan's face.

"The room here on my right has some things in it that are not made of stone or wood. They look like devices of some kind. They have controls on them, but I can't make out what they are."

"Take a guess," May told her.

"I guess they must be some kind of communication devices."

"Why is that?"

"Because they don't look like microwave ovens but they do appear to be electrical devices of some kind and they have controls on them," Megan answered.

Seeing the far door was blocked with fallen stones she returned to the large 'L' shaped room. She looked to the left. "There is another door here, a dark hallway." Megan moved toward it peering into the darkness. "I can't see very far. It's too dark."

"Go on in a little way. Perhaps you will be able to see something," May spoke trying to coax her friend to find out what hidden things might lurk in the darkness of the hallway.

Megan proceeded into the darkness a short distance then suddenly stopped. "What is it, Megan? What do you see?"

"I have the strangest feeling that I am no longer alone here." Megan turned looking all around. "I can't see anything but I feel that I am not alone."

"Come back out, Megan," May insisted.

"Headed out now." Megan moved back to the place where the broken floor stones were and thought to have just one quick look into the hole before departing. "There's a hole in the floor here that doesn't look normal. Why would they put a hole in the floor here?" She puzzled for a few moments as she came closer and closer to the hole trying to see into the darkness. "Oh, there's something in there! Something moving!" Megan's mouth fell open in surprise as she started to back up. "I hear growling sounds coming from there!" Megan started shaking her head back and forth. "There's great and ancient danger in there. I can see its eyes glowing red like fire."

"Time to come back, Megan!"

Megan moved away from the hole back toward the huge stone seats and noticed something she had not noticed before. "There's a design above the chairs." Megan might have pondered on it for a moment but at that moment the building started to tremble. The growling sound came from behind her and she moved quickly for the exit. The moment she entered into the open water she came from her trance-like state and removed the device. She instinctively reached for the medallion, picked it up and looked at the front side. "This is what I saw there above the big stone chairs."

"You saw another medallion?"

"No. I saw an image like this made into the wall. It wasn't a painting. It looked like it was made from stone and precious metals like gold and silver. Even jewels were in the eye-looking thing and what looked like a huge diamond in the center of the eye."

"What was the thing you saw in the hole?" May asked.

"I don't know. I saw it moving. I heard it and I saw its eyes. Very unnatural kind of creature."

"Are you sure it wasn't some kind of fish?" May asked in disbelief.

"A fish with glowing red eyes and growling like a lion?" Megan retorted.

"I guess not, huh? But if not, then what was it?"

"I'm not sure how to describe it but I did get an impression that I keep rejecting."

"What was it?" May begged.

"Promise not to laugh?"

"Sure I promise," May answered.

"I got impressions of some kind of dragon, maybe a dinosaur."

Megan saw May's mouth curled down as she did her best to repress a giggle. "You said you wouldn't laugh."

"Dragon?" May shook her head still holding back her emotions as best she could, but the expression on her face was a dead giveaway. It was obvious she did not believe there could be a dragon down there under the water in a hole in the floor of that room.

"You know I was wondering why there was a hole in the floor and it almost appeared that something had been buried down there and sealed up. Something that I can't explain but it was almost like they wanted to keep this thing sealed up, yet they wanted to keep it where they knew where it was."

A puzzled expression came over both girls' faces. "Buried it under the floor of the room?"

"It looked like an important room. A throne room, maybe," Megan commented.

"Where is this place?"

"I don't know. I only know it's on the bottom of the sea somewhere."

"How deep was it?" May asked.

"I don't know. I don't think it was all that deep. I could see the surface when I started up but the water was really clear," Megan answered holding the medallion in her hands. "Was it a building in Atlantis? Was it even Atlantis or was it another place that has something to do with the Medallion?"

"That may not be all it has to do with," May pointed out. " Maybe it has something to do with Egyptian history."

Megan let go a big sigh. "I have a feeling this mystery is going to take awhile to figure out."

"Even with the Atlantian Crown we still can't seem to find the answers." May shook her head.

"Well, we have learned a few things, I guess," Megan said, holding onto some fragment of hope. "And if these things were brought to us here at this point in time, one of these books or objects must hold the key to other parts of the mystery."

"I'm going with you next time," May insisted.

"It was kinda scary. Are you sure?"

KA-BOOM! Both girls jumped as a huge bolt of lightning struck very near by.

Chapter 9
Mysterious Being Arrival

A mysterious being stands in a void between light and darkness. He stretches forth his right hand and calls a name that can not be pronounced in human tongues. "Come forth!" he commands. A doorway of light forms before him and through that doorway floats a brilliant fluid shape that takes on a human form. The doorway closes behind him. "I have a job for you. Come with me," the first being commanded the second. He reaches out with his left hand and another doorway of light opens and both beings step through.

The two find themselves in a cave deep inside the earth. Cries of agony echo in the distance. From the cracks in the walls, eyes watch in the darkness. They float along above a muddy path, a path as old as the hills themselves. "The Crown of Knowledge and Power has been reactivated," the first being tells the second. "It is in the possession of two young girls on a farm in the United States of America."

"Does anything go on that you are not aware of?" the second asks as they enter into a large stone room. The first being continued on without answering. The second being, sensing something following them, turned quickly to see something move out of sight toward the ceiling of the passage. The sound of wings like that of a giant bat swished in the air.

The ceiling must have been 50 feet high. The stone walls appeared as if they had been carved by some strange and powerful force. Another passage led out the far side. High upon the wall to the right a stone window had been carved through the wall. A loud bellowing sound like that of a giant bull issued forth from that window. "What in heaven's name was that?"

"You have been on the other side now for over 13,000 years. Though some things remain the same, other things have changed," the first spoke.

The second being floated up to have a look through the window as another loud bellowing sound echoed forth from the other side. Standing inside this stone cell-like chamber was a huge beast, perhaps 30 feet tall. It had fiery red eyes and a head like a bull. It had the upper torso of a man, arms like a man covered with hair. It had legs like a bull and a very curious metallic-looking horn sticking straight out of the top of its head. The beast stood facing the northeast staring at one location on the wall almost as if it could see through the solid rock. Every so often it would let go with a bellow that would shake the earth.

The second being floated down and rejoined the first who was waiting at the entrance to the second tunnel. "Let me guess. A Minotaur version of a Unicorn, right?"

"It is one of the destructors. He shakes the earth and waits until that time when his cell can no longer hold him. He has only one purpose in his existence and his destruction will be great. Come with me," the first being commanded as he started off into the second tunnel.

"The girl who has possession of the crown is called Megan Martin. Her friend who also knows about the crown is called May Lynx. It is their task to help reveal the truth of past events to the modern world.

Truths that have been well hidden for thousands of years, but first they must discover these things on their own. In order for them to do this we have decided they will require some help and protection. This is why I have called you. You will be called 'Payah' because you will guard the doorway between the physical world and the underworld. You will prevent the powers of darkness from harming the girls or recovering the sacred and powerful device."

A sly smile crossed Payah's lips. There was nothing he liked better than a good fight with the minions of the underworld and this mission placed him once again in a position of battle. As far as he was concerned 13,000 or 14,000 years had been far too long. He was ready to once again stretch his legs, to touch the earth, and to breathe the air of the beautiful blue planet that he remembered from so long ago.

"Remember, don't go looking for a fight, but if you must you know what to do. You know which rules of contact with humans apply to you. If you are observed by humans you must keep our secret."

"You mean, if they see me, don't tell them who I am or why I am there?" Payah asked.

"Yes, but with Megan and her friend they have the device and it may be difficult if not impossible to remain hidden from them." The first being walked along for a few moments pondering upon what course of action might be taken under just these circumstances. He knew full well the device would reveal things to the girls that would not be apparent to others. Taking a long sigh he continued. "Try to stay out of sight as long as you can but if they do discover you as I think they will, you will just have to follow your heart and do the right thing."

The first being stretched out his hand again. A beam of fluid light traced a rectangular doorway though which a city could be seen. "May the Great One be with you," he said. "You will need Him," he whispered.

Payah stepped through the doorway longing to breathe the air, one of the pleasures he remembered from his last visit to earth. In a moment, he started coughing and gasping for air. "What is this place?" He turned to see the doorway of light starting to close behind him. "Wait, there must be a mistake! This can't be the right place!" His hopes vanished with the last glimmer of light from the portal. He looked around the area where he was standing to see many huge buildings with chimneys pumping out flames and smoke into the air. His eyes began to water. "This can't be the earth, can it?" A plume of toxic fumes passed over him with a gust of wind. "Judging by the look and smell of things, the devil himself must have won the last great battle here." He shook his head as he searched for some high point where he might overlook the area. Buildings, lots of tall buildings were here. He chose one. Then, pointing a finger at it, he said, "There," and was transferred to the top of a tall building in the distance.

A man was seated on top of the building enjoying his bottle of brandy along with the view of the city. When Payah appeared the man shook his head and looked at his bottle wondering what was going on. He sniffed the bottle, "Maybe it has gone bad," he thought.

Payah looked around over the city. Turning, he saw the man seated against the access building on top of the building. "Is this the planet earth?" he asked the man.

The man said nothing. He just sat there not sure if he was seeing something real or if it was a product of his own imagination mixed with bad brandy. He studied the situation for a moment then curiosity got the better of him. He stood and walked over to stand beside the apparition. Looking around to be sure no one else was standing behind him he worked up courage to speak. "Yep, it was the earth last time I checked," he said. "Say," he looked around. "Are you one of them there aliens I been hearing about on TV?"

Payah then noticed he was still wearing his white robe-like garment that stood out like a sore thumb at a blue grass festival. He studied the garments being worn by the other man and with the wave of his hand his own garment changed to become like that which he saw. "Hum, not much to look at, is it?"

Seeing this being now dressed identical to himself, the man stepped away. "Pod people!" the man proclaimed under his breath. "You ain't gonna try to eat my face or suck my brains out and eat them, are you, now?"

Payah's mouth fell open in surprise at hearing these words. "You have got to be kidding! Do they do that here now?"

"You ain't gonna take over my body and make me do all kinds of evil things now, are you?" the man spoke still inching his way toward the door.

"Ah, spiritual possession. Now that's something I am familiar with, but no I have no intention of harming you. It's just that I appear to have been dropped off at the wrong location," Payah answered.

The man puzzled over the answer for a moment and decided he was not in any mortal danger. "Where you from anyway, stranger?"

Payah looked up toward the sky. "Up there."

"Yeah, that's what I thought. I guess cab companies everywhere are like that. Thought you guys would have better service than we do in Long Beach." The man chuckled. "Guess when they screw up and drop someone in the wrong place, they do it in a big way, huh?" He laughed again as he stood there looking up into the sky almost expecting to see a space ship departing. Then he looked down at Payah's feet, "Looks like they lost your luggage too, buddy."

Payah turned his attention to the area around him. "This isn't suppose to happen."

"That's what they all tell you, but I'll bet someone is trying your suits on in some hotel on Mars right now," the man chuckled.

"Mars?" Payah asked.

"Yeah. You know, fourth planet from our sun. Mars," the man repeated.

"I have not been there in a very long time." A thoughtful expression came over his face. "Come to think of it, all the calendars were different. I don't even know what year this is." He thought for a moment as the man continued to walk around checking him out and talking to himself. "Let's see. I have been gone for about 13,000 years so that would make it..."

His thought was interrupted. "Say, can you teach me to do that trick you did with the clothes?"

"Clothes?"

"You know. The way you made your clothes change?" the man asked.

"Tell me, does everyone dress like this now?"

The man looked at the clothes. "Well, no, I guess not. Just some of us."

"If I wanted to get a good example of how people dress here on earth now, where would I go?"

The man placed a hand on his chin as he turned and looked toward LA. "I guess you could go to Hollywood and see how people dress there."

"You could show me around?" Payah asked.

"Well, I guess so. But it's going to cost you."

"What would you like in exchange for your help?"

156

"Oh, nothing much. Just teach me how to do that trick you did with the clothes. That ought to just about cover it," the man replied.

"Tell you what. I will fix you up with some nice clothes if you help me."

"Deal," the man said as he held out his hand.

Payah just stood there, looking at the man's hand for a moment. Then realized what the man was doing, so shook hands with him.

"Where to?" Payah asked.

"We go to Hollywood." The man pointed the way. "But you got to cover the cab fare," he added as he started for the door.

Payah reached out catching the man by the arm. "Those buildings over there. Is that Hollywood?"

"That's the general direction but you can't really see it from here. Too much smog in the air."

"Smog. I was wondering what you called this stuff we are breathing. It certainly couldn't be air," Payah said as he pointed toward some buildings in the distance and spoke, "There."

Instantly the two were transported to the top of another building several miles away. The man was astonished at the mode of transportation. "When I become familiar with your world, I will remember each location and will be able to go there instantly."

"Yeah, well there's something you better learn right now, mister. Cause if you go bopping around like that people are gonna talk and some of them don't take too kindly to aliens around these parts. Why, they will catch you and cut you up just to see what color your insides are. You got to learn to be more discrete."

"You mean I shouldn't let anyone see me, is that it?"

"You got that right, buddy," he answered.

"I can fix that." With the wave of a hand the two became invisible to the human eye and they continued their adventure into the city to try to find suitable attire. "You can call me Payah."

"Jake. You can call me Jake," the man replied.

The business of learning more about the modern world was an adventure in itself. While Payah was having a good time learning about the changes that had taken place during his absence, Jake was having a fantastic time showing his new friend around the city.

They observed many people, from the nearly normal to the completely bizarre, wearing platform high top shoes and leather with chains to various combinations of bright clashing colors. They saw hairstyles from the corporate conservative to the outrageous colorful designs that might have been inspired by tropical fish and birds. Finally he chose a combination arrangement that would allow him to blend right in with the 'average' humans whom he saw in this place. Now no one would suspect that he was anything but normal.

Upon the completion of their expedition into the dark city jungle each had picked out new attire more fitting their own desires. With a wave of a hand, Payah kept his bargain then returned them to the top of the original building where they had started out.

"Now what do we do?" Jake asked.

"I wait until she uses the device again. Once she accesses the powers of the cosmos, I will know where she is and I can go to her."

"Cosmos, hum. Girlfriend, huh?"

"She's my assignment on this mission."

"A Mission. I should have known that," Jake responded with a nod of his head. He was convinced this new friend of his was an alien all right. It wouldn't have

Chapter 9

made much difference to him anyway, angels or aliens, what's the real difference? Times were different now. Things had changed.

Payah fought with a spirit of depression. No one knew better than he that things had changed drastically over the years. The air was toxic and practically unbreatheable. The earth couldn't be seen in many places for the concrete and buildings that covered the land. The noise of the traffic in the city was enough to drive a person insane.

"Now all I can do is wait," Payah added, wishing he had thought of a better place to wait than on top of this building. But for all he knew the entire world was like this now. Had he realized that if he had been just a few miles to the east, the air was much better, he would have proclaimed his drop off point a cruel joke played on him by one of his superiors.

The two sat down and leaned up against the little access shelter on top of the building and began some small talk.

Payah pointed toward one of the flame belching smokestacks. "Why do they do this to the air here?"

"Those are fuel refineries. They take crude oil and make gas and other fuels there," Jake answered.

"Why would they want to do that?" Payah asked.

The puzzled expression came over Jake for a moment, "You don't use that stuff to power your vehicles do you?"

Payah looked down at the cars and trucks passing along the highway near the Navy base, then his gaze moved up to the harbor where the ships were docked. A Navy Frigate was pulling out heading west. "They use this same method of power?" he asked.

Jake looked around and, seeing what Payah was looking at, answered "Oh, those things. Yeah, most of

159

them use some kind of fuel like that. Some of them are nuclear though and they can go for a long way without stopping to gas up."

"Nuclear?" Payah asked.

"You know atomic powered," Jake answered.

"I see," Payah replied as he literally picked up on the thoughts and images in Jake's mind for a moment. Payah knew what the source of power was but was unfamiliar with the name being used to describe it. "So humans also use that for power here now." Turning to the old man, he said, "You know that it isn't safe for humans, don't you?"

Jake fished for a half-smoked cigar in his new shirt pocket. Not finding it he remarked, "I thought I put that in there somewhere." Then looked up toward the ships. "Yeah, I know it's not safe but it certainly doesn't smell as bad as some of these other things they use."

"I can't argue with that, Jake. It's just that I find it hard to believe that any intelligent race of beings would use fossil fuels for power and do this to their world." Payah motioned with his hands toward the smog clouds above them.

"Well, I never said the human race was intelligent, did I?" Jake answered as he made his way back over beside the little access building and took a seat.

Chapter 10
Payah Finds the Farm

Megan had not yet realized the thing she had seen hiding in the hole under the floor of the stone building in the ocean was something very evil and very old. It had lived in the castle when that building had been above water, before the demise of Atlantis and other cities that had met with similar fates. This happened during and after the battle of the lords of darkness against the Lord of Light. It was described as a time when the stars fell from the heavens to the earth. The thing is neither human nor animal. It is by definition the manifestation of pure evil, pure hate, and it now knows the crown-like device has once again accessed the power of the cosmos. The being was no longer confined to that location but had left its presence there. The powers of darkness do not know who has the crown or where they are but the minions of evil have been alerted and a search for the device has now begun.

The two girls had been reading books and pondering on the information they had been turning up. It appeared to them that for every answer came two more questions. Still there had to be some solution to all this and they were determined to get to the bottom of it. The answer or at least the key to the right question had to be there and the only thing they could think of was to read as many books as they could. Time slipped by, it was nearing 11:30AM and grandma would soon be home.

"So you say you can put the crown on and read a book simply by looking at the book and turning the pages?" May asked.

"Yes. It's really very easy."

"Speed reading at its best," May smiled. "Can I try it?"

"Sure." Megan handed her the crown. "Have you seen Scratches?"

"She was downstairs this morning, and I saw her outside when you put the tractor up. Maybe she is still outside."

Megan got up. "I'm going to go see if I can find her. Be very careful with that thing," Megan spoke as she left the room in search of her cat.

May looked through a few books and, choosing one, she took her seat with her back to the windows and facing the desk. When May placed the device on her head and started to read the cosmic continuum fluxed. If you could see it with the naked eye it would be very much like dropping a pebble into a pool of water then watching the waves extend outward from where the stone had entered the water. The powers of darkness may have found the crown quickly had it not been for the efforts of the other beings who were all ready doing their part to confuse them on the other side.

Deep inside the ground in a hidden, top secret military base, a man monitoring geomagnetic anomaly readings also noticed a change in the field energy of the earth. The satellite that was monitoring this disturbance was top secret and its actual purpose was shrouded in a mist of deceptions to hide the real truth of its purpose.

Halfway across the United States a very depressed being sat waiting for this very moment.

Megan, standing at the back door and calling for Scratches, was alerted by the terrified screams of her

friend upstairs. Quickly she ran through the front room
and up the stairs to find May standing in a corner of the
room holding thin air at bay with a large book.

"You, you just keep away from me or I'll lower
the boom on you!" May threatened.

Megan stood gasping at the sight before her.
"What's going on here?"

Payah had found the right place and was
invisible to Megan but not to May since she was wearing
the device on her head when he arrived. She could see
him clearly and was obviously distressed thinking that
she had perhaps unlocked a door or portal to another
dimension.

Payah looked over at the girl who still wore the
crown and was threatening to brain him with the book.
"Megan Martin?"

"Megan," May glanced over at Megan, then back
at the strange man. Megan walked up and placed her
hand on May's shoulder trying to calm her down when
her eyes beheld the form of the oddly dressed visitor
slowly appear before her.

There he stood with platform shoes just below
his bell bottom slacks that were covered with wild colors
in a geometric pattern. He wore a black leather jacket
with a heavy chrome chain draped across one shoulder.

Around each wrist he wore a leather spike-
studded band that lead into a matching fingerless glove.
His hair stood out and up at each side of his head like
wings with white undertones to accent his brown hair.
To the girls looking head on at him, his hair looked more
like horns than wings or hair.

"I'm Megan Martin," Megan answered. "Who
are you?"

"My name is Payah," he answered. Then he
turned toward May who still held the book between them

ready to throw at a moment's notice. "Then you must be May Lynx."

"How do you know who we are?" Megan asked.

"I am the guardian of the border from the place where you open the doors into the primal mainstream," he answered.

"Say what?" May asked, still holding her weapon in the air.

"You know, the cosmic continuum," Payah answered as he turned to look out the window. "Trees!" he exclaimed. "I love the trees."

"Who is this guy?" May spoke as much to herself as she did to Megan who was standing beside her.

"What have you done now?" Megan asked May, just figuring this stranger must have been the result of May's misuse of the device.

"I didn't do anything. I just started to read this book and that guy just appeared there out of thin air!" May motioned with the book as she spoke and made her way toward the door.

"What are you doing here?" Megan asked.

"My name is Payah and I am here to help you with your quest," Payah spoke looking over his shoulder from the window.

"Maybe we should ask, what are you?" May questioned.

"To help us with our quest," Megan spoke with disbelief. "You look like a reject from the circus if you ask me."

Payah looked at his attire. "I tried to adapt to your customs while I was waiting for one of you to access the power of the device again."

"Oh, well, that makes perfect sense," May said as she made her way back over and drug her chair a few feet from Payah who was still standing at the window.

"So where did you find that outfit? In LA?" Megan giggled.

"Yes, I believe the man said it was a place near 'L. A.'" Payah answered.

"Can you go visible?" Megan asked.

"I can do that as long as it is only you two who are here," Payah answered.

"L. A, or Hollywood. I might have known," May added as she opened her book once more and started to read. "Say, if I go ahead and read here, will any more of your friends show up to scare the by-jeepers out of me?"

"Nope, there's just me here with you now," he answered.

"You mean there's been someone else here with us all this time and we didn't know it?" Megan asked as she looked around the room.

"Not exactly, but not far away," he answered.

"Where is this other one at?" Megan continued.

"Standing between this world and the underworld keeping the powers of the darkness from knowing where you are."

"Powers of darkness? In the underworld?" May looked up from her reading as she finished the last few pages of the large book.

"I guess you might understand it better if I were to show you," Payah told them as he held out his hands to them.

The girls looked at each other, neither one of them trusting this magical stranger who had appeared out of thin air and frightened the wits out of them.

"How do we know we can trust you?" Megan asked.

"Ask the crown," came the answer.

As May sat still wearing the crown and looking at Payah she saw a soft white glow appear around him, quite angelic in appearance. "He looks like an angel."

"No he looks like a freak! Maybe it's a trick," Megan added as she touched her friend on the back so that she could also see. "We are evidently dealing with the supernatural world now that we have the crown. There may be things going on that we are not fully aware of."

Payah nodded his head. "You are exactly right and that's what I want to show you. But if you will not come with me to see into that world, I will bring the image of that world to you through the crown." He stretched his hands toward them. A radiant globe of light appeared hovering in the air in front of the crown. A fluid white light projected out from the triangular jewel on the front of the crown to the globe and soon an image of the dimensions appeared within.

"Each time you access the power of the crown it taps into the primal mainstream which leaves its signature in the continuum. A signature that can be detected by certain beings on either side of the continuum," he explained. As he spoke a picture of the crown appeared in the ball of light and waves moved away from it as a stone being dropped into a pool of water.

"I think what you're saying is the primal mainstream is the power source for the crown. Is that right?" Megan asked.

"Exactly," Payah answered.

"Batteries not included," May replied.

"No batteries required," Megan added. "If this primal mainstream is what I think it is, it is the very most basic power of the entire universe."

Payah was nodding his head, but May was in another world. "You're losing me here."

"It's really very simple. Everything in all of creation, things seen and things unseen, are held together and formed into shape by this power," Payah explained.

"By the direction of the powers that be," Megan added.

As they spoke, different images appeared since May was wearing the crown and her mind was searching for the understanding. Suddenly it all came to her like a rushing wind. "Oh, it's..." she hesitated for a moment, "...it's the power of God."

Payah smiled, "It's been called by many names but yes, you could call it that."

"Then who is God?" May asked and no sooner had she asked than she was given the answer in a flood of information and brilliant flash of light that caused both her and Megan to go limp and faint. Had it not been for Payah, they would have both fallen to the floor.

He removed the crown from May's head and laid her upon the floor. Both girls lay side by side on the carpet. Payah shook his head as he lay the crown upon the desk. "You had to ask a question the mortal mind cannot comprehend."

The sound of the front door closing alerted Payah to the presence of another being in the house. It was Martha returning from church. He looked around the room and knowing there were certain things he had to protect, he picked up the crown and the jewels and vanished.

Chapter 11
Revelations of a Time Long Ago

"Girls! Megan! I'm home!" Martha called in jovial tones. It was evident the sermon had been very uplifting for her.

Scratches ran to the top of the stairs. She had been laying unnoticed on one of the seats at the end of the upstairs hall all this time. "Meow," she called to Martha from the top of the stairs.

Martha looked up as she placed her umbrella in the catch on the tree style hat rack which stood beside the door. "What is it, Scratches? Is something wrong?"

Martha realized since it was storming now the girls most likely wouldn't be outside, yet they had not answered her call. She also remembered that Megan was insistent on going to see Sparky. She walked over, peeked out the kitchen door, and saw the wagon was beside the barn, indicating the tractor was still in the barn. "Megan? May?" she called as she walked back toward the staircase. Perhaps they had lain down and fallen asleep in their room since it was raining and there wasn't much else they could do. She climbed the steps and, not seeing the girls in their room, figured they might be reading in the study. When she looked through the open door of the study she smiled as she found both girls lying sound asleep on the floor.

"You girls must have wore yourselves out." She gently shook Megan awake. "What are you doing sleeping on the floor?"

Megan rubbed her eyes. "I guess we fell asleep," she said with a yawn as she sat up.

Martha coaxed May to awaken, but when May woke up she jumped. "What happened?" she yelled, not even realizing that Martha was standing in the room. She looked around then realizing Megan's grandmother was standing there, but still befuddled at what was going on.

"Did you have a bad dream, dear?" Martha asked.

"I guess I must have had a nightmare," May answered wondering if it had all just been a dream.

"Must have been a doosie," Megan chimed in, still rubbing her eyes and yawning again.

"Why don't you girls go to your room and rest a bit while I fix us some lunch," Martha instructed as she left the room.

"Ok, grandma," Megan answered.

The two girls looked at each other, then looked around the room. "The crown is gone!"

They both looked around the room frantically but no sign of the crown or the jewels could be found. "That Payah swiped the crown from us!" May spoke angrily as she searched the room.

Megan looked around the room. "Be very still," she said. "I don't think he left." She walked over and peeked out the door just as Scratches entered the room. "Payah, are you still here?"

"Right here," came the answer, yet no visible form was apparent.

"Where's the crown?" she asked.

A glow of light appeared on the desk and the familiar shapes appeared before them.

Megan laughed with a smirk. "Right there, I guess." She walked over and placed the objects back into their box. She covered it and headed for the door.

May stood there not saying anything until Megan reached the door. "Do you remember anything?"

"Yes, but don't ask me to explain it," Megan answered as she went out the door.

May, realizing she was standing in the study alone, jumped and ran to follow Megan to their room. She did have a recollection of the answer and fragments of things just before they passed out but that was all she could remember until Martha had awakened her. "Who is God?" she said softly as Megan placed the boxes back under her bed.

"He's the one who commands all the power of the primal mainstream. In fact, he is the primal mainstream," Megan answered as she started out the door. "I have a feeling for the understanding, but I can't seem to grasp it clearly or put it into words," she said as she stopped at the door looking at May.

"Me either," May answered as they both headed down the stairs with Scratches close behind. "Maybe that's not what's important right now."

Megan pondered on that thought for a moment. Maybe May was right. Perhaps knowing the exact identity of God wasn't the most important thing right now. Finding the truth that brought them all to this place at this time was foremost on the list of things that had to be done. Even so it would have to wait since Martha was waiting in the kitchen with lunch.

"Well, girls, have you found anything interesting that you can tell me about today?" Martha spoke in gleeful tones. She had a kind of glow about her since she had returned from church services.

"Grandma," Megan paused as she looked down at her plate. "Grandpa left you quite a bit more money, things of value and such." She picked up her sandwich, "It's just that we are trying to sort it all out before we can explain."

May sat at her place, unusually quiet as she ate. 'Sure go ahead and tell your grandma that grandpa is a ghost and he's still here with us. Tell her you have a crown like device that has untold powers. Tell her there's a real live angel in the house.' All these thoughts rushed through May's mind along with thoughts she had not realized. Suddenly her stomach turned, her face grew flush. "Please excuse me," she said as she left the table and hastened to the bathroom, closing the door behind her.

"I guess she must have developed an allergy to eggs." Megan also experienced the feelings and the nausea but it passed quickly for her.

"Goodness! I hope she isn't coming down with something." Martha shook her head. A certain amount of tension was in the air, which dampened their spirits some.

Megan ate quietly for a few moments. No one said anything until May returned to the table. "Grandma, if you had the money to keep the farm going for a few more years what would happen?"

"Oh, I don't know dear. I guess I would pay my bills with it and continue on for as long as I could," Martha answered.

It was the answer that Megan expected but it wasn't the right answer. The money would be spent rather than invested and sooner or later Martha would be right back where she was with the farm up for sale. A solution to the problem had to be found, but what?

Martha had always been a very active woman. She lived for helping others but when her husband died she lost her will to continue. If only Megan could find some way to restore her zest for life and once again give her a reason to live. She didn't have an answer yet but she was not ready to throw in the towel. If there was a solution she was determined to find it and set things right again.

After their lunch, the three retired to the den where they watched some Sunday afternoon TV programs. The picture wasn't as good as usual and sometimes faded out for several seconds at a time because of the storm. May sat on the built-in seat at the bay window in the den where she could see outside. She enjoyed the rain to some extent but was thinking she had had enough all ready. The TV fading in and out was starting to annoy them all when May noticed a satellite dish in the yard. "Does that still work?" she pointed.

"What is it dear?" Martha asked as she looked to see what May was referring to.

"The satellite dish. Does it still work?"

"Oh, no. Fred put that in about 15 years ago. He got it working real well but it stopped working the same day that he died. And hasn't worked since."

"Why don't you fix it?" May asked.

"I'm afraid I don't know anything about satellite dishes, hon. If it doesn't work when you plug it in and turn it on, I don't know what else to do about it."

Megan looked over at May sitting at the window. 'It stopped working the very day her grandfather died.' The thought hung in her mind like the old chandelier in the front room. Her gaze turned from the window to the old satellite receiver that sat atop the entertainment center to the left of the TV set.

172

"You know they have those little tiny satellite dishes now that work really well. They are really easy to use. You just turn them on like you would your TV set and punch up the channel you want to watch. They have lots of channels and even have a built in TV guide in them," May reported.

"I believe I have heard of those," Martha answered.

"You should think about getting one of them. I have a friend in the city who has one and they get lots of TV shows that you couldn't get here with your regular antenna," May informed her.

"I only get 5 channels when the weather is good and 3 when the weather is like it is now." Martha noticed Megan was messing around with the old satellite receiver. "Do you think you should be playing with that during the storm, Megan?"

Megan looked around. "No, I guess not." Megan walked over and joined May at the window. "It's letting up quite a bit now. I think the worst of it has passed."

Megan had always been interested in electronics. Her mother and father were both amateur radio operators and Megan had been studying to get her own HAM license. She was familiar with the concept of satellite TV and how it worked. 'It's just another kind of radio receiver anyway, so what's the problem?' she thought to herself. If it wasn't anything too complicated she might be able to fix it herself.

"I see that look in your eyes, Megan. What are you thinking?" May asked.

"Nothing really. It doesn't make any difference right now, anyway. It's too wet outside to do anything about it," she answered. Megan looked over at Martha seated in her chair watching TV and reading a book at the same time. She looked back at May and motioned with her eyes toward the door signaling that she wanted to leave the room now.

"Grandma, I think we are going to go back upstairs for awhile." With that the girls made their way back upstairs to their room.

"Do you think Payah is still here?" May asked as she laid down on her bed near the window.

"I would bet on it," Megan answered, closing the door. Pulling the pillow from the head of her bed and taking it to the other end she then laid down with her head at the foot of her bed facing May.

"You think you can fix the satellite receiver, don't you?"

"I don't know. Maybe. I know my dad could fix it if he would ever come out here," Megan spoke with resentment. Her father was always working, and seldom had time to spend with her. Come to think of it, her mother was always working. The girls were fortunate that Megan's mother took the time to bring them to the farm. There were times when Megan felt as if she had been abandoned. Her father worked for an electronics corporation and her mother was a computer programmer.

They normally worked regular business hours but they were always on call. When they got home after a hard day's work they didn't feel like doing much of anything. Dad would retreat to his radio room. Mom would fix dinner and sometimes help Megan with her homework. But when she settled down with one of her books, she didn't want to be disturbed. Megan thought it could be worse, but it was the same old thing day in and day out. Could it be that her entire family was in a rut?

When grandpa was alive at least dad would come to the farm for a visit. But since he died, her dad had only been to the farm twice and once was to go to his father's funeral.

Chapter 11

"Payah, are you here?" May called softly.

Megan looked up and smiled. The thought of having a real live paranormal being on call was somewhat thrilling. She could just imagine what the media would do with a story like this, 'spirits, proof of life after death, angels and aliens'. They would have a hey day with this, but then what? People would rush the place and hound them to death over it, so it wouldn't be worth it.

Seconds passed, then Payah's form appeared in the room. "Hello, girls." He took a seat at the table. "You called for me?"

"What have you been doing?" May asked.

"Just walking around the farm."

"You like it here?" Megan asked.

"I love it here."

"Don't get out much, do you?" May added.

"I've been on the other side for over 13,000 years now. Everything was different when I was here last."

Suddenly a light went on in Megan's mind. Quickly she pulled the music box from under her bed and removed the Medallion to show it to Payah. "Do you recognize this?" she asked as she handed him the object.

Payah looked at the object for a moment. "In your years, this is really old."

"Yes but what is it? What does it stand for? Where did it come from?" Megan pleaded anxiously.

Payah turned the medallion over. "Well, this looks like a map of the world..." He ran his fingers over the map as if recalling a time long past.

"You mean a map of the earth when you were here last, like 13,000 years ago?" May asked.

"Oh heavens, no," he answered.

"Yeah, I guess that was a long time ago," May spoke rejecting the idea.

"Actually, this is a map of the earth almost a million years ago before everything on earth changed dramatically. The land was different. The sky was different. There was a great vapor in the air like water hanging from the firmament. Volcanoes puffed fire and smoke into the air and the ash would be suspended in the vapor high above the earth. The rotation of the earth was somewhat different. Above the earth the poles were covered by this ash causing it to become very cold there. Snow and rain were common at the poles but the equator was quite warm, humid and it seldom ever rained there. At night the earth became cool and water would form in the air and a mist would cover the plants and the earth until water dripped from their leaves."

"Visibility wouldn't have been too good, I guess. It would make it hard to fly back then, I guess." May thought aloud.

"Foggy a lot of the time, huh?" Megan asked.

"I thought there wasn't anyone here until God made Adam and Eve," May interjected.

"No, actually there were other people on earth long before the Great One introduced Adam and Eve to this world. He had many different creations on this world before then but I see that many of them are gone now while some of the different races of people are still here even after the great disasters. Adam and Eve were a special creation whom the Great One favored," Payah answered.

"Disasters? Then the great flood came, right?" Megan asked.

"Oh, there actually more than one flood, here and there around the world, but this one was at the end of the last ice age." As he spoke he waved his arms in the air toward the center of the room and a large globe of light appeared showing images of the things he spoke about. The things he remembered when he was here so long ago.

"What happened then?" May asked as she sat up on the edge of her bed watching intently.

"That's when I left the earth and was taken back into my own world. What I can tell you about is before that flood. You see, it's a very long story but several races of people actually lived on the earth during that time. The earth was alive with living things of all kinds. There were huge beasts and animals that are long gone from the earth now. There were people who some called the Anah Naki who were among the last of their kind to come from the heavens and settle on earth and on Mars."

"You mean aliens?" May asked as Megan seated herself at the table.

"I guess you could call them that. They were not born here, but they set up residence here because their own world was dying. They were space travelers, sojourners in a dark universe, who crossed the vast dark sea of stars to find a new place to call home."

"Wow, that gives me goose bumps." May crossed her arms and shivered.

"The name Anah Naki was given to them by the people who were already living here on the earth at that time. It means literally 'they who came from the stars' or 'they who came from the heavens.' Their languages were very different from those being spoken by the people who lived here on earth. Some of the tribes of humans on the earth feared the newcomers. Some worshipped them as if they were gods."

"The people who were here then on the earth were Neanderthals, right?" Megan questioned, recalling her studies at school about the process of evolution.

"I don't know if I understand what you are saying," he answered.

"You know, like apes who were evolving into humans," she explained.

"Oh, no. Humans never evolved from apes," Payah spoke shaking his head. "Where did you ever get that idea from?"

"That's what they teach us in school," Megan informed him.

"Yeah, but that's not what they teach in the Bible," May added.

"The Bible?" he asked.

"Yeah, it's a collection of really old writings by the prophets of God," May said. "You have been gone a long time, haven't you?"

"You mean a holy record? We must talk about this further at a later time," Payah said as he continued his story about what life was like on earth thousands of years ago.

Payah showed the girls many things that afternoon. He told them how a race of human beings built a great city then by the power and magic of a god-like being named Kukla Khan, in one language. He literally took over and ruled the entire world with an iron fist. When the ruler of the heavens returned to check up on his creation on the earth, He was greatly angered because his representatives in this solar system had literally set up their own kingdom here. Payah told how they were doing all kinds of genetic research and manipulations to change certain life forms that the Great One had established in this solar system. They created mutations like cat-like beasts and horses with wings. They created great fur covered beasts half-man and half-ape along with many other various creatures. A message came to the Great King of the Heavens and designer of the original creations that all was not well, so He sent a messenger to check up on the situation. What they found on Mars angered the Creator and orders were given to destroy the perversions they had found and not to allow any of the mutations to survive. Then a Great War broke out in the heavens and the civilization along with all life on Mars was totally destroyed. Some of those creatures that had been released on earth were all rounded up and only God knows where they are now.

Payah paused for a moment as he thought, "Of course the Creator has some rather unconventional creations of His own but He has a purpose for all the things he creates and doesn't like it when someone else goes to messing with his designs."

Megan sensed there were things that Payah was not telling her. She picked up her device and looked directly at Payah. She also remembered how the crown was very helpful to her if she knew the right questions to ask. "What is this?"

Payah looked at the device then at Megan. "To some it was known as the Crown of the Shepherd King."

"I thought it was the Atlantian Crown of power," May interjected, tossing in her own thoughts.

"The device belonged to a certain group of mystics on the earth long ago. These men were chosen to carry out a certain mission on the earth at that time. They were representatives of the Great One and they followed the way of truth and of the spirit. To their leader, he gave the crown-like device, able to access the power of the cosmos so that he could accomplish his mission on the earth. These people were the bitter enemies of the king of the world because the king had become friends with another god. That other god however was not a god at all, but also had powers, knowledge and great influence. This being influenced a war-like tribe to attack the Shepherd kings during a time when they were not expecting a conflict. Had they been expecting trouble they would have been well able to defend themselves using the crown. But the crown was stolen and when the Shepherd king went to get it to defend his people it was gone. The people who took the object did not know what it was and they were influenced to deliver and sell the object to the king of the great city on the earth. The being that orchestrated this set of events presented himself as god and made a deal with the King of the world for the use of the crown. When the Great One returned to see what was going on He saw that all was not well, and many things that had been set in motion by His design had been changed. His people had been killed, and this other being had set up his own throne on Mars and on the Earth. That's when the war broke out and the Great One destroyed Mars and sank entire continents on the earth along with the great city from which the ruler of the world had ruled. These places are now upon the bottom of the ocean. The Great One had one of his own to take the crown and separate the parts and hide them so they could never again be used against the followers of truth."

"That follower's name wouldn't have been Payah, would it?" Megan asked, still feeling Payah was not telling the entire story.

"It would be," Payah replied, "It was the last thing I did on earth before crossing back to the other side."

"So you have been on the other side until now?" May asked.

"Yes, until now."

"You are connected to this device in some way." Megan held the object out toward him.

"It is my job to make sure that you are protected and that devious one cannot get his hands on the device again," he answered.

180

"So an angel made this device?" Megan asked, not particularly liking the term 'angel' and would more readily accept the term alien.

"It was constructed at the direction of the Great One, for a special purpose that you must discover in your own time," he answered.

May whistled in a descending tone, "And what else do you do?"

"I am here to protect and serve you as long as your requests are within my limitations."

"That being limited to what?" Megan asked.

"I am allowed to answer some of your questions, but I am not allowed to do your work for you. I can guide you and teach you how to use the device to some extent and I can help keep you from getting yourself into serious trouble with it."

"Doesn't appear you did the Shepherd King much good," May spoke somewhat sarcastically, believing it must have been Payah's job to protect the Shepherd King during the time he also used the crown.

Payah did not respond in his own defense.

"If this object was designed to help the people working for the Great One while on earth and it has been brought to us here at this time, the purpose must be similar to what the Shepherd Kings were doing thousands of years ago," Megan said, assessing the situation.

"You mean..." May started to speak but stopped in mid-sentence.

"Yes, we have evidently been selected to accomplish something for the Great One. Something similar to what the Shepherd Kings were doing thousands of years ago," Megan spoke as she turned her attention once again toward Payah expecting some acknowledgment.

Payah sat there for a moment looking at the floor. "Not exactly the same thing, but it is directly connected to your objective."

"And you can't tell me. We have to figure it out, is that it?" Megan asked angrily as she grabbed the medallion from Payah's hand and shook it at him. "And it all has something to do with this thing, I bet!"

"Shush," May cautioned placing a finger over her lips. "Your grandmother will hear you yelling and come up to see what's going on."

Megan pressed her lips together hard as she turned to look at her friend. "And we finish our mission and that's the end of us, just like what happened to the Shepherd Kings. We bite the bullet. We suck dust. We become a worm feast!" Megan spoke softer but was still very angry, waving the medallion in the air as she spoke. A very solemn expression came over May's face as she began to realize what Megan had been saying. She turned her gaze toward Payah, both girls waiting for some sign from him as to what the future held for them. Payah looked up at both girls then back at the floor.

"Well?" Megan demanded an answer.

"I can't make you complete your task here." He paused, stood up and looked in the direction of the graveyard across the field. "I can only say that your great grandfather and your grandfather have given their lives to bring this device to you at this point in time. It would be a shame for their efforts to be for nothing."

"See that, Megan? See that? He just admitted that thing killed your grandpas and now you have it." May looked down at her hands as panic overcame her emotions. "Oh, my God! I've touched the thing! I have used it! We are both doomed!"

Megan walked around and took a seat at the table. She looked at the objects she held in each hand.

Then she looked up at Payah still standing looking out the window. "We don't really know who you are, do we?"

"One thing we know is that he isn't telling us the full story here," May added.

With crown in one hand and medallion in the other, Megan said, "It's not the crown. It's the medallion, isn't it? That's what I am suppose to figure out. That's what my grandpa died for, isn't it?"

"Yes, partly," Payah replied.

"Then, if you are a messenger of the Great One then why didn't you save him?" Megan spoke harshly.

"I wasn't here then," he answered.

"Never an angel of God around when you need him, is there?" May said also with resentment.

"The crown and the seven keys are yours to use in order to solve the mysteries. The first mystery, which you hold in your hand, is connected to several things that date back to a time long ago. You must look to the past in order to find the answers to the future," Payah informed them. "Now if you will excuse me for a while." With that he faded and vanished from the room.

"Why do I have the feeling this is going to be one of those days?" May mumbled at the floor with her head in her hands.

"So what is it? The side with the pyramid and the eye, or the side with the map, or both?" Megan muttered in puzzled disgust.

Chapter 12
Learning the Keys

May joined Megan at the table and remembered something that Payah had said before he departed. "Did he say seven keys?"

Megan looked up at her. "I believe he did."

"We only have 5 of the keys."

Megan dumped the colored triangles out on the table. "White is for knowledge, green is for healing, red is fire from heaven, yellow is for metamorphosis. The blue crystal holds the power of the mystical doorways. There was no mention of any other keys."

"I think there was something about it in one of the journals, and Payah said there were seven keys," May insisted. "I wonder what color the other two are and what they do?"

Megan placed the device on her head with the white crystal. She held up the blue crystal before her forehead. The now familiar white glow of light surrounded her. In a few moments she placed the blue crystal on the table. "This one indicates that it can physically transport people from one place to another, even to other dimensions." She then picked up the yellow crystal and held it in front of her as she had the blue one before. She placed it back on the table. "This one indicates it can physically transform the user into an animal or perhaps what ever the person focuses their mind on."

"Cool," May said.

Megan picked up the red crystal and held it before her. When she laid it back on the table, she just sat there with an expression of deep thought.

"Well?" May asked.

"This crystal says it holds the power of the universe."

"What does that mean?" May asked.

"It means it holds enough power to destroy the world," Megan answered.

"I don't believe that God would allow someone to destroy the world with this thing," May insisted. "It wouldn't serve His purpose, I'm sure."

"You may be right but I have a very strong feeling that we only have a short time to learn how to use these devices correctly. Everything from here on out depends on it."

"Megan, are you thinking what I'm thinking?"

Megan looked, seeing a concerned expression on May's face, but waiting for her friend to answer the question.

"We found the medallion. Then we found the crown and the keys. Then we only used it a few times when this being shows up claiming to be here to help us. It appears to be that a set of events has been set in motion and…"

"That's what I was trying to say," Megan cut her off as she removed the device from her head and removed the white crystal. "We have to learn how to use this thing and all the keys correctly as soon as we can. Our lives may depend on it."

"Wonderful, I just can't wait to tell everyone back at school what I did on my summer vacation."

Megan picked up two of the colored triangular keys from the table. She studied first the yellow one and then the blue one. Unable to choose she looked up at May. "Pick one."

May pondered the thought for a moment then said, "I like blue. Let's see what it will do."

Megan placed the blue crystal on the crown. She held it in both hands ready to place it upon her head. "Ok, I have to focus on a place that I want to go to."

"Maybe you had better stand up," May pointed out. "We don't really understand all there is to know about these things and it's my theory that anything that is touching your aura will be transported with you."

Megan stood up. "I think you might be right, but I'm not going very far. Perhaps the old house, or even the attic."

May thought for a moment as Megan started to place the device on her head. "Wait, I want to go with you." She jumped up and ran to Megan's side and they clasped hands.

"We are going to try to go to the old house. I see myself in the front room of the old house." She placed the device on her head and continued to focus on the front room of the old house. The blue glow emitted out from the crystal through their bodies. It became brighter around them until only the soft blue light was visible. Then it faded away.

In the front room of the old house, the soft blue glow appeared and the forms of the two girls became visible. The blue glow faded as Megan removed the crown like device just in case something might go wrong. A feeling of exhilaration came over them as very large smiles crossed their faces. "Do you know what this means?"

"Yeah, it means there's no place in the world that we can't go," May answered.

"Yeah, we can use the white crystal to see where we want to go and use the blue one to actually transport ourselves to that place." What Megan didn't know was that she could also use the blue crystal to view into the place where she wanted to go, but she had not learned these things yet.

"Back to the house," Megan said as they held hands once again. She placed the device on her head and in seconds they found themselves standing back in their room.

"We can come to grandma's house any time we want, can't we?" May smiled as she returned to her seat at the table.

Megan removed the blue crystal and gazed into the sparkles of light that moved around inside it like a fluid. "It's like there are tiny little living lights inside the crystal." She handed the triangular object to May for inspection. "I never really noticed that before with the other ones."

Megan then picked up the yellow key and placed it on the crown. "What should I become today?" She spoke with much less concern now that she believed she was mastering the device and thought there was nothing to fear.

"I think perhaps I shall become a bird. An eagle." Megan placed the device on her head. At that same moment, May jumped up and started for the door.

"I'm going to go get us some drinks. I'll be right back." She walked to the door and paused to wait to see the transformation.

As the yellow glow engulfed Megan, a startling thing occurred. Suddenly she became totally fluid and splashed onto the floor. There was not a trace of her clothes or the device, just a puddle of silver fluid like liquid metal. May was so startled that she couldn't even

187

scream. She leaned toward the fluid on the floor. "Megan, you aren't a bird." At the mention of the word 'bird', the fluid rose up from the floor and took the form of an eagle. Then the color and feathers appeared. Megan had literally become an eagle and was setting there in the floor. The device was not visible, however. Yet for all practical appearances she was in fact a bird.

Megan stretched out her wings and examined them both. She hopped around on the floor and then jumped up on one of the beds. There was a yellow flash of light and once again Megan was in human form. "Oh, you have just got to try this one!"

May was still standing there with her hands over her mouth. Her eyes were very large not yet able to convince herself of what she had just witnessed. "That is…" she paused, "…the most amazing thing I have ever seen."

"Yeah, and something tells me this device can do a lot more than what we are aware of," Megan told her.

May's expression suddenly changed from glee to concern. "What if we were transported to the moon or to the bottom of the ocean? Would we be killed?"

"I never thought of that. I guess we are going to have to be very careful how we use these things until we find out."

"I bet Payah would know," May said.

"I bet he would, but we don't know if we can trust him."

"Can't the white key tell you if he is telling the truth or not?" May spoke trying to find a solution.

"I guess maybe it can." Megan took her seat at the table again and replaced the yellow stone with the white one and placed it on her head. A few moments later she removed it and looked over at May. "Yes, I guess maybe he is telling the truth."

"I hope so. We certainly could use his help."

"I saw something else." Megan reached out and picked up the medallion. "I saw that really huge white pyramid again with the bright white-fire capstone on top." Suddenly and unexpectedly, two tears rolled off her cheeks.

"What's wrong?" May asked.

"I don't know. It's like I'm filled with emotions that I can't understand."

"It's the pyramid shape and that medallion that is calling to you, isn't it?"

"I think you're right, but I just can't comprehend what it is trying to tell me," Megan answered.

"That's the answer to the mystery, if you ask me." May walked toward the door once again. "I'm going to go get us a snack and some drinks. I'll be right back." With that May left the room.

"All these years I thought the pyramids were built by the ancient Egyptians and now I find out that pyramids have been around far longer than that." Megan talked to herself as she held the medallion in her hands.

She recalled the TV show that her grandma had recently watched where the news of what appeared to be a human face and pyramids existed on Mars. One object near a group of pyramids on Mars looked like the picture of a lion and it had a large triangular shape around it. "Pyramids on Mars." Gathering her train of thought she reached for the device. With white key jewel in place she positioned the headpiece on her head.

When May returned with cookies and milk, she found Megan in a trance at the table. May closed the door behind her and proceeded to set her treat on the table.

"You know, a really long time ago there were people on Mars," Megan spoke while still viewing into the white light.

"Where are you?" May asked.

"Mars."

"Mars?" May whispered as she reached out and took hold of Megan's right arm. The glow engulfed her and she could then see what Megan was observing. "Those people look like..."

"Egyptians is the word I think you are looking for."

"Yeah, or Mayans maybe."

"Nope, I think these people look more like Egyptians, but the Mayans built pyramids, too." Megan turned her head and the two floated up away from the surface of the Martian image they were viewing.

"Oh, what's going on?" May spoke, being somewhat startled at Megan's sudden ascension.

"I want to show you something. I have been flying around this past image of Mars. It looks so much like the Earth did about 4000 years ago that it is almost frightening. There are civilizations scattered here and there. The people are different. They look different. They speak different languages." Megan pointed here and there at different cities, structures and villages as they passed over.

"What's that?" May asked, pointing toward a rather strange looking city made of stone.

Megan swooped down over the structure. "I think that's a shopping mall," she laughed.

May also thought the comment was funny but she had never ever seen a structure like this. "It's like an entire city all built into one big building."

"You would have at least thought they could walk a straight line when they built it." Megan referred to the fact that the structure wound around a valley between two hills and there weren't hardly any walls that were straight.

"Strange, huh?" May commented.

"Trees, air, flowing rivers, everything is so different here." Megan took to the sky again and had not flown very far when they saw another very huge pyramid. On the ground beside it was a bright dome-shaped object. Megan flew down to see what it was.

"It's a space ship. A flying saucer," May spoke excitedly.

"Jeez!" the word escaped from Megan's lips. She was astounded at the sheer size of the craft.

"Flying saucers and pyramids. This thing must be several miles across."

"What's wrong with this picture?" Megan asked.

May looked around. "There's no capstone on the pyramid."

"Right. Just like the Great Pyramid of Giza in Egypt." The two floated over to have a closer look. The structure was covered with brilliant smooth white stones all the way to the top. At the top of the structure there were huge notches at the corners. In the center of the capstone platform was a circle and inside the circle was a triangle. The two took a closer look still. "It looks like a landing pad for some kind of space ship."

"One thing is for sure, this is no tomb," May agreed with her friend as she looked around from high on top the structure.

"You know, back at that first place near the face there was a huge structure that had a triangle around it.

The thing was facing the west, I think. The thing inside looked like the face of a lion. A lion is the symbol of the constellation of Leo."

"So?" May asked curiously.

Megan turned looking off all four sides of this structure and noticed there was a clearing on each of the four sides. These were huge areas where people could come and gather around this pyramid structure. "They come here to worship their god."

"What about the lion?" May asked again.

"Oh, well, the Sphinx on earth faces the east and it has the head of a man and the body of a lion. It's kinda symbolic when you think about the features and courage of a lion and the head or mind of a man." Megan paused again as she observed several balls of light, smaller craft leaving the larger one.

"And?"

"And the hieroglyphics that were found inside one of the pyramids there in Egypt tells a story about the religion of the dead. It also shows the oldest zodiac in known existence. It is the first known record of a kind of map of the stars." Suddenly there was a flash of white light. Megan looked around and the two girls found themselves back on earth inside that place she had been talking about with the writings on the walls.

"This is kind of unnerving, if you ask me," May protested.

"Yeah, I know." Megan pointed toward the ceiling of the structure. "See that? It's like a kind of compass for the stars. A kind of star map."

"It's like a kind of universal calendar, isn't it?"

Megan turned toward May with a somewhat puzzled look on her face. Perhaps May had figured out the answer to the question she had been pondering on for the last few moments.

"You know, they watch the stars so they can tell what time of year it is and the stars are never in exactly the same place. It takes something like thirty some-odd thousand years for the same North Star to come around again," May told her.

"That may be what we are looking for." Another flash of light and the two girls found themselves as if they were standing on top of the Great Pyramid of Giza looking toward the east. "I saw this on TV the other day but never paid much attention to it. These two men were talking about how the Sphinx and Pyramids were like a clock. The men said that the sphinx was looking at its own image in the sky at sunrise during the time being referred to by these structures. They said the last time that happened was around 10,000 to 12,000 years ago."

"Ok. So, what are you thinking?"

"Well, if it's what I am thinking, that lion image I saw on Mars was west of the face on Mars. The pyramids were south and west of that." Again the girls appeared to relocate and were once again hovering in the sky over the Martian surface. "My question is this, if the people who directed the building of these structures were nothing more than cave men, why does it appear as if they were marking a date in time on both Mars and on Earth using similar symbols?"

"What?" May asked as she puzzled over what Megan had just said.

"I mean on earth we have a lion with a man's head and here we have a man's head in one place and the profile of a lion's head here." She pointed, "And over there the pyramids."

"You are saying this is no coincidence."

"That's exactly what I'm saying. Whoever was in charge of building these structures had more than a passing interest in the stars. Not only that, they had an extensive knowledge of the planets these structures were built on."

"Whoa there! So what you are trying to say is that if you stood at the lion's head here and backed time up until the constellation of Leo matched up with the sunset on Mars, the pyramids over there, and that one over there, all match up with a constellation as seen from Mars at a certain date in time?" May asked.

"And to put it bluntly our BC and AD calendars can't cover the range of dates that can be covered by the position of the stars at any given time in history. All we would have to do is put this data into a computer and start backing it up from now until a time when the constellation of Leo lines up with sunset on Mars."

"Why not sunrise?" May asked.

"The direction of rotation of the planet in relationship to the poles. You see you can't really tell which way is North can you?"

May looked around and realized that from where they were they could not tell which way north was on Mars without a compass. "I see what you are saying."

"And even if you had a compass and could tell which way was North here, it might not be the same as on the Earth. In which case the position of the constellations wouldn't be the same as on earth when the pyramid and sphinx were created there."

"Scientists just assume they know where the North Pole is on Mars. They figured it has to be, uh…"

"North Pole has to be UP, right?" Megan suggested with a question.

"Yeah, I never really thought about it, but that's right," May pondered as she looked around at the images floating in her mind. "So if the top of the head of the face on Mars was north, or what the Martians considered to be north, they would make their pyramids and other structures based on the same positions."

"So the pyramids they built here would also match up with certain stars in the Milky Way just as the Pyramids of Giza appear to match up with Orion's Belt and the Nile River with the Milky Way on Earth," Megan added.

The thoughts and information, ideas, questions, and theories flowed like the Nile River through the girls' minds as they viewed these things and images flowed around them as their thoughts moved through time. "Do you think that if the Pyramids of Giza represented Orion's belt at that time and the Great Pyramid of Giza represented a certain star in the heavens, could it be that Star in Orion's belt is a special star? Like maybe that's where that big space ship came from or something like that?"

"I think it means something. Maybe you're right, I don't know. But I would bet that if we can match up the constellation represented by the Pyramids on Mars we will have a good idea when in our solar system all these things took place. Maybe we will even figure out where some of these people came from," Megan said.

"This tells us something else loud and clear. It also tells us that the construction of these structures on Mars and on Earth were all under the direction of someone who traveled the stars. They weren't cave men, that's for sure," May spoke shaking her head.

As she spoke, Megan's thoughts drifted back to the top of the pyramid that had the circle and the triangle in it. Her thoughts transported them back to that place in time. The two looked down at the image. "It's the same kind of thing that's on the medallion. It's a circle represented by the medallion and there's a triangle in the center that's the pyramid. I feel like we are very close to solving this mystery."

"Yeah, it's like it is some kind of insignia or something" May said.

'An insignia,' Megan thought. They use designs like this to identify many things. Perhaps that's just what it was, but who or what was it the insignia of?

Chapter 13
An Act of Love

The day passed quickly. Around four in the afternoon, Mrs. Butler came by, dropped off a gallon of milk, and picked up a dozen eggs. Megan asked her if they still had her pony, Sparky. Mrs. Butler said they did in fact still have her pony but that he had taken ill and the vet wasn't due to be there to look at him until late Monday afternoon.

After dinner the threesome settled down for some Sunday night TV, watching all their favorite programs. But for Megan it was a matter of keeping her mind on something other than Sparky. Every now and then she would get up and pace the floor a few times out into the front room, then to the kitchen, back to the front room and return to the den. After the fifth or sixth time she did this May realized that her friend was troubled about something and followed her out of the room during one of her jaunts.

"What's wrong, Megan?" she asked as she paced along behind her.

"It's probably nothing," she answered.

"Maybe, maybe not. Tell me about it."

"Mrs. Butler said that Sparky was sick and they didn't know what was wrong with him."

"Did they call the vet?" May asked.

"Yeah, but he can't come until late tomorrow afternoon. She said he had to work at the livestock auction most of the day tomorrow."

May stood there for a few moments and realized they had not gone to see Sparky because of the storm earlier but the storm had passed bringing with it a nice cool front. Not to mention that even though it was starting to get dark, the girls had a method of transportation now that did not require the little tractor.

"I've got an idea. Follow me," May told her.

Back in their room May dragged out the box with the crown in it. "Here's the answer to all your problems."

"And just what do you have in mind?" Megan asked as she took the box and sat it on the table.

"Simple. You can transport over there to Mr. Butler's house, take the green stone with you and fix what ever is wrong with Sparky in short order."

It sounded too easy to be true. "Yeah, we might do that." Megan opened one of the windows and looked in the direction of the Butler farm. "But what if we zap in there right in front of Mr. Butler?"

May pondered on the thought for a moment. "Just use the white stone. Take a mental trip over there and find Sparky before you go. Make sure you know where he is and that no one is with him."

"Viewpoint you mean?"

"Why not?" May answered.

"Sounds simple enough. Let's give it a try." With that Megan placed the device on her head and with May holding her shoulder they both concentrated on the Butler farm. In seconds it was as if they were floating about above the buildings over the Butler farm.

"Watch out!" May insisted as they drifted into the limbs of a tree. "Keep your eyes and mind focused."

"Right," she answered.

"Why can't you just think about Sparky and go where he is?" May asked.

"It doesn't work like that all the time. It's like I have to find him first and then as long as he is near the same place the gizmo remembers where he is." Megan had learned that, along with the abilities the device provided for her, there were plenty of rules that had to be followed in order to produce the desired results.

Slowly they drifted down to the barn nearest the house. That was where Mr. Butler kept the ponies. All of the doors to the barn were opened since it had been hot this summer. Puddles of water and mud were all over the place since the storm. As they entered the barn they could here someone talking. They proceeded slowly to the stall where they heard a man's voice. Peering over the wall into the stall they could see Mr. Butler talking to something lying on the floor. On closer inspection they saw it was Sparky.

"Come on, boy. You just have to hold on. The vet will be here tomorrow." The man stroked the pony's head and sides with a wet towel. "Megan's visiting her grandmother. I know you will be happy to see her."

The two girls turned and looked at each other. "I knew he was sick, but I didn't think he was that sick," May said.

Megan was about to say something but suddenly Mr. Butler looked around in the general direction of where the girl's consciousness was hovering. This startled the girls for a moment but when Mr. Butler turned back to his task the feeling soon left them.

"He can't see us, can he?" May asked.

"I don't think so. If he had, he might have said something to us."

"It was almost like he heard us talking," May told her.

"I saw that. But how could he hear us?" Both girls were still observing the situation in the barn stall. "He's really sick." Megan shook her head trying to hold back the tears. "We have to do something about this if we can."

The two watched for a few moments until Mr. Butler looked at his watch, got up and left the barn.

"Now," Megan said. In a moment the two found themselves back in their room as Megan exchanged the white crystal for the blue one and stuffed the rest of them in a pocket. "Let's go."

The girls stood up and held hands and before they knew it they were physically standing in the barn about where they had been hovering a few moments before. "Watch the door for me," Megan ordered. May ran to the door and was looking around for signs of anyone headed for the barn. Megan approached Sparky speaking to him as she walked while exchanging the keys, the green one in place of the blue one. She stroked his little nose. "You're burning up with fever, old friend."

When Sparky heard the sound of his old master's voice, he opened his eyes. Seeing Megan, he tried to whinny but he was so very weak. "Hang on, Sparky. If there's a way in heaven or on earth you will be feeling better very soon." With that she reached out and laid both hands on the pony. A beautiful green glow enveloped Megan and flowed like a fluid down her arms to the pony lying on the stall floor.

A few moments had passed when May called to her from the barn door. "I can see Mr. Butler standing inside his back door. I think he is talking to someone on the phone."

Megan stroked her pony a few times as the green glow started to dissipate. Sparky tried to raise his head but he was still far too weak. "I'll have to be honest with you, Sparky. I really don't now what I am doing or how to use this thing to make you better." A tear dripped from a cheek as she talked. "But if love is the most powerful thing in this old world, you are going to be all right." With that Megan leaned down and hugged her pony and in a moment a brilliant green glow filled the stall until the entire inside of the barn was glowing like it was radioactive.

Mr. Butler was speaking to the vet on the phone trying to get him to come out that night when he looked out the door and saw the green light flowing from the windows and doors of the barn. "I'll have to call you right back, I think the barn's on fire or something." He hung up the phone and ran out the door.

Seeing Mr. Butler run from the house May ran toward the barn stall. "Megan! Mr. Butler's running this way. He saw the green light."

Megan grabbed May's hand and attempted to transport before she realized she had not exchanged the keys. When she looked she could not see what had become of the blue crystal. "I lost the blue crystal!" she said softly but urgently. "It's got to be here somewhere!" She searched frantically around in the straw that covered the floor in the stall until she located the crystal and exchanged them just as Mr. Butler came running through the barn door and slowed to a walk.

"What's going on in here?" he yelled, seeing the green glow was now gone and he had no idea what had caused it or what had become of it.

The two girls were kneeling on the far side of the wall a few yards from where Mr. Butler was standing. The tension was evident on May's face as Megan energized and the two vanished only a second before Mr. Butler walked into the barn stall. "Now that really is strange," he said as he lifted his hat with one hand and scratched his head with the other.

Meanwhile the two girls suddenly found themselves not back in their room where they had expected to be but standing in the barn loft in Megan's old secret hiding place on top of a pile of baled hay.

May looked around. It was very dark. "I mean, really, Megan."

Megan giggled, "Could have been worse. We could have landed in the hog lot."

"Yeah, right. Care to give it another try?"

The two clasp hands again and the moment before they transported they heard Martha calling their names from the direction of the house.

When they materialized in the room both girls were wondering how long Martha had been looking for them and where all she might have searched. "Now what?" May asked.

"Whenever I got upset or depressed or in trouble, I always went to my secret hiding place. It was the first thing that came to mind when Mr. Butler showed up."

"I don't mean that, I mean what if Grandma has all ready searched the house for us and now we suddenly show up back here in the room?" May asked.

"Oh that!" Quickly Megan removed the crown device from her head and tucked it along with the keys into their box then replaced them back under her bed. "I got it. Follow me." Quickly the two girls ran down the stairs, opened, then slammed the front door. "We're right here, grandma," she called out loud enough that Martha might hear her.

Martha was still outside in the back yard looking for them but faintly heard the sound of Megan calling and returned to the house. "My goodness, where have you girls been? I have searched high and low for you."

"Just walking around out in the yard," Megan answered.

"I was calling loud enough that the Butler's heard me all the way over at their house." Martha made her way back toward the den. "From now on, young ladies, when you hear me calling you answer me, don't worry an old woman like that." Martha shook her head as she seated herself back in her chair.

"I'm sorry, grandma. We went down to the corner barn west of the house and we didn't hear you calling until we were almost back," Megan replied, making up a little white lie to help soothe her grandma's nerves.

"You just stay away from that old barn. There's wild animals down there - coyotes and snakes and who knows what. Besides that the old barn is about to fall down and I don't want you in there."

"We didn't go inside," May said as Megan tugged at her sleeve.

"We're all right, grandma. I think we are going to turn it in early tonight."

Martha shook her head. "Kids! Wonder I've lived this long," she muttered to herself as the girls departed through the doorway.

Back in their room, the two girls landed on their beds with a sigh. "Been a very interesting day, hasn't it, Megan."

"I'll say. We've been to Mars, to Egypt, back to Mars…"

"And to Mr. Butler's barn and back to the barn loft," May laughed.

Megan smiled. "Yeah, well, it was only a little mistake."

"Yeah, I know. Could have landed in the pig pen." May laughed again.

"Where's Scratches?" May realized Scratches wasn't in the room.

"I think I saw her on the sofa in the den," Megan answered. "I'll go get her." Megan got up and left the room. A few moments later she returned holding the cat in her arms. Finding May all ready sound asleep she put the cat on the floor, closed the door and laid down on her own bed. The cat jumped up on the bed and curled up next to Megan.

"Scratches, you wouldn't believe the things we have seen today," Megan spoke softly, stroking Scratches on the head as she slid off to sleep.

Chapter 14
Sometimes Life Stinks

Monday morning came early as usual on the farm. The rooster crowed but they didn't hear it. Neither girl wanted to get out of bed even on the second call. Martha finally had to come knock on their door to get them to stir. Scratches jumped up on a windowsill and stood looking toward the chicken yard.

May rolled over in bed and looked toward the door. "Why do mornings have to come so early on the farm?"

Megan looked but had no reply to the question. Dragging herself out of bed she yawned, put on her shoes, and reached for the doorknob. "Eggs, got to go get the snake off the eggs." With that she stumbled out the door.

May, also yawning sat up and put on her shoes. Scratches jumped from the window and ran out the door following Megan. May stood and opened the window thinking the fresh morning air would help wake her. She watched as Megan crossed the back yard toward the chicken pen. "Walking around on the farm, gathering eggs this early in the morning. They have to be kidding." The fun of getting up early had already worn off. Her body was protesting, but she was not alone. The only three who really appeared to enjoy getting up at daylight were Martha, Scratches, and that darn rooster.

"Walking?" May thought as she saw Megan pass through the chicken yard gate. She could tell by the way she was walking she was still half-asleep. Then suddenly right out of the blue a thought occurred to her. She turned, and seeing the box under Megan's bed, she thought, "What if I didn't have to walk to the chicken yard?"

She grabbed the box, removed the crown, and sorted the 5 crystal keys in her hands. "Was it the blue one that transports people?" She thought for a few moments and decided that it must be right. She placed the blue crystal on top of the crown, stood at the window looking toward the chicken yard, and placed the device on her head. In a moment she found herself standing in the chicken yard. Thrilled with her accomplishment she ran into the chicken shed to find Megan moving an old hen off of the nest. Bud was no where to be seen but she looked around just to be sure. If there was one thing she liked to be careful of, it was snakes.

"Hi there, Megan," she spoke gleefully as she removed the device from her head.

Megan looked up and realized that May had used the device. She moved to the door and peeked toward the house to be sure that Martha wasn't anywhere in sight, then turned back to May. "You do know, of course, that thing could transport you to Mars or someplace else you don't really want to go, don't you?"

"Yeah, I know. But I was looking at the chicken yard when I put it on and that's where it brought me. Isn't that neat?"

"Yeah, it's neat all right. Only one problem - it's too early for me to have a sense of humor," Megan said as she returned to her task. She had not picked up more than 3 more eggs, though, when an onery streak hit her. She thought now might be a nice time to teach May a little lesson, one that she would not soon forget. She remembered how May had mentioned drinks the moment that she had put on the morphing key and how she had literally transformed into liquid instead of a bird. She also remembered how they had ended up in the loft instead of in their room when Mr. Butler had shown up in the barn. A sly smile came over her face but May could not see from where she was standing also gathering a few eggs.

When the two had finished gathering the eggs they started out the door. "Oh, say, you transported out of the room so you have to transport back to the room otherwise grandma might see the crown and figure something funny is going on."

"Right. Okay." May took the crown in her hands and closed her eyes for a moment to imagine herself in the room. This was the method they used to direct the device toward their target. "Going to the room now."

Just as she placed the crown upon her head Megan spoke, "Just be sure not to end up in the hog pond."

May vanished as Megan jumped up on the baseboard of the door to the chicken shed and looked toward the pig pond toward the southeast. Nothing happened. She looked toward the window to her room but didn't see May there either. Suddenly out of the blue she heard a scream from the hog pond. She turned and there stood May smack in the middle of the hog pond about knee deep in mud and water.

Hearing the screams, the old mother hog strolled up to the side of the wallow and grunted. As if things weren't bad enough, May soon learned she was more afraid of full-grown hogs than she was of snakes in the hen house. She screamed again just as she lost her footing and fell seat first into the mud.

Megan ran from the hen house and set the basket down just outside the gate. She ran quickly over to the hog fence and went over it in one quick motion. "I told you not to do that!" She said while trying to keep a serious look on her face. Seeing May sitting there in the mud was all she could stand. She simply couldn't hold it back anymore and she started to laugh right out loud. "That's got to be the funniest thing I have ever seen in my life!"

May made several attempts to stand in the mud, but each time she fell. "I'm going to get you for this!" she fumed in anger.

"May," Megan calmed her laughing. "May, listen to me!" At that moment she heard the back door slam at the house. Martha was on the way.

"Oh, no! May, listen! Just picture yourself..." But before Megan could finish May looked up and glared at her. In the next moment she vanished.

Megan slapped her forehead. "Now where did she go?" She looked up and there stood May in the window waving at her. "Oh, great." She turned to see Martha running for the hog lot.

"What's going on out here?" Martha yelled as she reached the gate.

"It's nothing, grandma." Megan reached out and scratched the hog on the back while trying to think of something to say. "I just fell down and thought I was going to fall into the hog wallow."

"I thought May was out here with you," Martha said.

"Oh, I don't even think she is up yet," Megan answered with a slight giggle as she gazed toward the window. She had all ready anticipated that all the mud and water that was on May when she warped out of the pond would be with her in the room. The mess would be there to clean up and certainly May would be more determined than ever to get even. What she didn't know, however, was that May had all ready made up her mind to do more than get even.

Megan placed the eggs on the table as she usually did and ran to the room expecting to find May there in a puddle of mud. All she saw was the puddle of mud in front of the window. The footprints were there, but May, the crown and all the keys were gone. "What's going on here?" she said as she assessed that May was no where to be found. By the look of the footprints on the floor she had warped out of the room. "Gee, May, I didn't mean to make you that mad."

Not far away May sat with the white crystal and crown on her head laughing as she watched her friend in distress wondering where in the world she had gone off to. "That should teach you!" she thought as she smiled and continued to watch.

Megan sat down on her bed pondering on the circumstances and what might be done about it, but the only thing she could conclude was that May had the crown and all the keys and could go anywhere and do just about anything she wanted to do. That is unless she got herself in trouble somewhere with it and then who knows what might happen. "What have I done?" she said as she propped her head up with her hands at the edge of her bed.

May saw all these things as she removed the headband and looked at the device and the keys. "Anything I want, right there in my reach, all I have to do is use it." As she thought aloud she realized the device belonged to her friend. There was no real doubt in her mind that Megan would allow her to use the device, even go with her, and all she had to do was ask. Perhaps the time to make up with her was at hand. Sure she had her mean streaks, her little white lies and from time to time a mean trick, but if there was one thing she wasn't, it was a thief, or one to betray a close friend. May thought for a moment and replaced the crown on her head. Again she saw Megan in the room. "Megan, can you hear me?"

Megan looked up. "I can hear you. Where are you?"

"I'm in the barn loft all covered with mud," she answered.

Megan jumped up and headed for the door. "Wait, bring me a towel and some clean clothes," May said.

Megan quickly grabbed a few items of clothing and ran out the door.

She clutched the clothing to her as she climbed the ladder into the loft. May reached out and took the towel from Megan as she reached the top of the ladder.

"Looks like I goofed, didn't I?" she said.

Megan climbed to her feet in the barn loft and seeing May she shook her head. "You are a mess."

"Yeah, I know," May answered.

"What happened?"

"I zapped out of the chicken yard back to the room and then before I could get the thing off my head I remembered what you said about not landing in the hog pen. I looked up and there was the hog pen in clear sight, and I thought boy I am glad I didn't land in the hog wallow. The next thing I knew I was standing in the middle of it," May told her.

"You mean sitting in the middle of it," Megan laughed.

"Yeah, that too," May spoke as she pulled off her muddy shorts and wiped herself off with the towel. "When I get back in the house, I'm going to take a shower."

Megan walked over and pushed the loft door open just in time to see a big black car pull up in front of the farmhouse. "Wonder who that is?" she said as May joined her.

"Looks like the Mafia, if you ask me."

Megan looked, glanced her direction for a moment with a concerned look on her face, then turned back to see two men get out of the car and walk toward the house. Both were dressed in suits and one of them was carrying a briefcase.

"I don't think I care much for the looks of this," Megan said. "Hand me the crown."

May fetched the crown and keys and soon Megan was at work trancing into the farmhouse to see what these two were up to. May reached out and touched Megan's shoulder so that she could also see into the house.

"Look at that. It's a banker and one of his henchmen," May said as they watched Martha lead the two men into the den.

"That's Mr. Simon Banister, the guy who's buying up all the farms in this area for his huge conglomerate. It looks like he is trying to buy the farm."

The two watched as the banker opened his briefcase and laid several papers on the coffee table. Then he picked out certain papers and handed them to Martha for her to read. Martha shook her head as she talked with the men.

"What did she say?" May asked. "What's wrong with the audio here?"

"She evidently borrowed a good sum of money from the bank and now the money is due. It looks like Mr. Banister is making her an offer to buy the farm and pay off the debts."

"Where will your grandma go if she sells the farm?"

"She can't sell the farm. We aren't done with our work and besides that Grandpa said not to let anything happen to the farm," Megan reminded her.

"What is she doing?" May saw Martha leave the room and return with the envelope with the silver certificates in it.

"Oh, great! Now they know she has the means to pay the debt off."

"That should solve the problem, right?" May asked.

"That depends," Megan answered as they watched the banker flip through the certificates, shake his head and tell Martha the things weren't worth the ink they were printed with.

Martha insisted she was going to sell the certificates and get the money to pay the debt with. The banker looked over at Mr. Banister shaking his head, and said "I'm very sorry, Martha, but if you don't have the money by the end of this month we will be forced to foreclose on your property and sell the farm to the highest bidder. You would be wise just to take the offer that Mr. Banister has given you now before it's too late."

The two got up and headed for the door.

"It's not fair! I'll have the money. You just wait and see," Martha scolded the two businessmen as they departed via the front door. "I'll have your money for you. You aren't going to get my farm," she yelled as she slammed the door behind them.

"You tell them, grandma," Megan said as she removed the device from her head.

Chapter 15
To Catch a Thief

The two men climbed back into the back seat of their limousine. "I want that farm," Simon yelled. "And I always get what I want, sooner or later," he reminded the banker as the car pulled out of the driveway and back onto the road.

"I'll have that farm and the Butler's by the end of this month and you are going to help me get them," Simon ordered the banker.

"Do you think that's wise? Putting the pressure on these farmers?" the banker asked.

"It's just business to me," Simon answered.

"These people have been here for years. They have been good customers of ours and it won't hurt to try to deal with them. When they see they can't pay, they will eventually give in and sell out." David Holland informed him.

"You just make sure they do," Simon told him as he toked on a big cigar. "You just make sure they do."

David Holland looked out the window as the car rolled along down the gravel road. He didn't like Simon Banister any more than the farmers who had lost their property to the land grabber. The main problem was that Banister had money, lots of money, which is what keeps the banks in business. Like it or not, Holland needed Banister and had to keep him appeased lest he should take his money to another bank and get the land anyway.

A thought kept haunting David Holland though, that being he was the president of an independent small town bank. One of the last of its kind and every time he saw a huge conglomerate swallow up an independent business it reminded him that small independent banks were on the endangered species list. He could just picture someone like Simon buying his bank, or another bank and then putting him out to pasture.

Mr. Banister picked up his car phone and made a phone call. David couldn't hear what all was being said but he did hear the words Martin house and certificates.

The big black car rolled past the little church by the pond and on out to the highway.

Back in the barn, May asked, "What are we going to do?"

Megan sat down on the floor of the loft with her feet hanging out the door. "You know something? Things weren't all ready complicated enough."

"Well, your grandma can sell those certificates and pay off the bank. Everything will be all right."

"Yeah, I guess there's really nothing to worry about there, but we have a mess to clean up in the room." Megan stood up and placed the device on her head to see what Martha was doing. "It looks like she's getting ready to leave. That means she will be calling us to tell us that she's leaving and she thinks we are in our room." Quickly she changed keys and both girls transported back into the room. Megan removed the device and placed it and the keys back in the box and slid them under her pillow. May hurried over and started mopping up the mud on the floor. She was thinking it was just a good thing the table was between the door and the window so that if Martha came to the door she wouldn't be able to see the mess on the floor.

"Girls! I'm going over to see how Sparky is doing. I need to see the Butlers for a bit. Do you want to come along?" Martha yelled up the stairs.

"Sparky! I can't believe I almost forgot about him in all the commotion." Megan jumped up and ran out the door. "Sure grandma we would love to go with you." And down the stairs she went with May following close behind when she realized she had not finished her clean up job, either on herself or in the room.

"Uh, Megan, tell her that I decided to stay here and uh..." May told her as she looked down to see the towel had not done all that good a job of cleaning off the hog mud from her legs. Not to mention she smelled to high heaven like a pig wallow.

"It's okay, May. Get cleaned up. It's not that far over to the Butler's. You know where it is and can walk over there in about ten minutes, five, if you run."

When they arrived at the Butler's house they got out and went into the house. "So how's that pony today?" Martha asked as she entered the kitchen area where Mr. and Mrs. Butler were seated at the table sipping on a hot cup of coffee.

Mr. Butler greeted the pair and offered them a seat. "You know, I think that pony is going to make it." He looked over at Megan and smiled, "And I expect he will be especially glad to see you, young lady."

Megan was bubbling all over at the good news and Mr. Butler could see she was not one for small talk this morning. Megan wanted to go see that pony right now. "Well, all right. Let's go," he said as he got up, took his hat from the rack by the door, and headed out across the back porch to the barnyard.

"You know, it's the strangest thing. Last night I was certain that Sparky was on his last leg and I came in and called the vet. When I was talking to the vet on the phone, all of a sudden I would have sworn the barn was on fire. So I hung up the phone and ran out here and there wasn't anything wrong. Then this morning, Sparky is standing and eating feed again. I never saw anything like that in my entire life."

"No kidding? What made you think the barn was on fire?" Megan asked as she walked along beside him.

"Well, see, it was a light I saw coming out of the barn. But, well, it wasn't like fire, it was a kind of green light. I didn't know what else it might be so I figured the barn was on fire." Mr. Butler shook his head as they walked into the barn to find Sparky standing at the stall door.

Megan breathed a sigh of relief seeing Sparky so full of life. She smiled as she patted the pony on the head and hugged his neck.

In the kitchen another kind of conversation was taking place. The two women were discussing the situation between the bank and Banister trying to foreclose on both their farms. Since Banister had moved in and started buying land, the Butler's business had gone from just barely making it to nearly non-existent. Then, right when they thought things couldn't get worse, several of their prized horses and several ponies took ill, including Sparky. It was like the bad luck bird of Peaceful Pond had dropped the egg of ill will and misfortune right on them.

"Did you ever find out what happened to the horses?" Martha asked.

"Evidently they wandered into some nightshade out there on the back side of the farm. Funny though, John has walked the entire area several times and says he can't find any signs of the plants." She got up to get Martha a cup of coffee. "Darn strange if you ask me. The horses get sick, several of them died, the people who were coming for riding lessons stopped coming. Even the guy we buy feed from raised the price of our feed so high we have to drive almost a 100 miles now to get feed from another feed store."

Martha sat stirring her coffee. "I can't prove anything but I'll bet you that Banister is behind all of this."

"If we can find a way to prove it we might have a chance. The way it is we will be forced to sell the farm at the end of the month. Either sell it or have them take it from us."

"You borrowed money from the bank too, didn't you?" Martha asked.

"Way too much, I reckon. Had to when the people quit calling and the buyers quit buying. Then all the horses got sick. You can't sell a dead horse for much, you know and now all the auctions and buyers think our horses are diseased or something. No one wants anything to do with them now."

Chapter 16
Wolf at the Door

Back at the house, May had finished cleaning the floor in the room and took a shower. She went back up to the room to finish brushing her hair and was getting dressed when she heard the front door slam. Someone was in the house, but who? She opened the door and was about to call for Megan when she saw a man's head moving through the front room toward the den. She crawled over to the banister and peeked down to see where the man had gone. She could hear him shuffling through things in the den. Moments later he came out and stood in the hallway looking all around. Then he went into the kitchen where May could no longer see him, but she could hear him going through drawers. "Burglar," she whispered to herself as she returned to her room. "What if he catches me here?" she thought. "The window," she thought as she moved quickly but quietly. "Wait, the crown. I can't let him get that," she thought as she hurried back over to look under the bed. Not finding the box there she dragged the music box out from under the bed and removed the medallion. Then she remembered that Megan had placed the box with the device in it under the pillow. She grabbed it and quickly put in the teleportation key, then with box in hand, "Back to the loft, back to the loft," she said over and over.

Finding herself standing once again in the barn loft, she looked out to see an old pickup truck parked in the driveway. "License number. Got to get the license number." She fumbled as she placed the items she held under some hay. "Nothing to write with." She was so excited she couldn't think clearly as she searched her pockets for anything she might scratch a number down with but came up empty-handed.

"Payah," she called, unable to think of what she might do in this situation. She wasn't sure who the guy was or what he was after, but she was certain he shouldn't be there.

In moments, Payah appeared in the barn loft with her. "You called?"

"Do something!" she commanded.

"Do what?" he asked actually unaware of the situation since he had been preoccupied with another matter.

"There's some guy in the house and I don't know who he is or what he is doing there."

"So use the crown and look to see what he's doing," Payah advised.

"Can't you do something?" she asked in desperation.

"Sorry. Not my department."

May fumed at him and if looks could have killed that would have been the look that would have done the job. Seeing her frustration, he said, "You see, I can advise on the use of the thing but my main purpose in being here is to see to it the crown doesn't fall into the wrong hands. Beyond that I am afraid you are pretty much on your own."

Seeing that Payah wasn't going to be much help, May turned and, using the white key, she focused into the house. She saw the man going through drawers and papers until he came to the phone drawer hanging on the wall. There he removed the envelope with the silver certificates in it. Seeing he had found what he was looking for, he headed for the door. "He went straight for the silver certificates, like he knew what he was looking for."

"License plate." She zoomed in on the license on the back of the beat up old pickup truck but was discouraged to find it caked with mud and having a trailer ball sticking up right in front of it didn't help, but wouldn't have made any difference. "Mud! I can't read it!" she said now even more frustrated.

Payah watched as the man left the house, wondering what he might do to help that would not be against the rules of his duties here. "Each key has several powers. Some of them even have similar abilities. For example, the white key, the blue and the red all have the power of telekinesis. You can touch things and move things with the power of your thoughts. The white, the green, and the blue all have the power of telepathy. You can speak to people over any distance using only your mind. Of course, you could just use the red key and blow the guy's truck to bits so he can't leave." Payah continued to throw ideas into the air but May was only catching a few of them and the ones she did hear she wondered how that might help. Of course that last idea with the red key wasn't such a bad idea, but she had no idea how to use it without blowing the entire farm up. Then she realized that if she did something drastic like that it would only serve to attract attention to the farm and to her, so perhaps it wasn't that good of an idea after all. Now if she could just let the air out of the guy's tires that would slow him down. She watched as the man got into his truck, turned around and started down the road.

"The tires. That's worth a try." She focused on one of the truck tires and thought to let the air out of it. Suddenly there was a loud rush of air from the tire and the valve stem was broken off. Still the truck went on down the road a short distance and around the corner until it was in a low place out of sight from the house.

"Ok. Now to tell Megan what's going on." May focused on the Butler farm and found Megan standing with Mr. Butler at the horse barn where two of the sick horses were laying in their stalls. "More sick horses. What's going on here?" she thought out loud. "Megan, can you hear me?" Megan recognized the voice and turned around but May was not there. She realized then that May was using the crown and she had only heard the voice in her head. "There was a man at the house and he stole your grandma's Certificates."

"What are you looking for, Megan?" Mr. Butler asked seeing Megan looking around.

"It's nothing. I just remembered I forgot to do something back at the farm." Megan turned and ran to the door, stopping for a moment to wish him well with his sick horses and promising she would return soon.

Once outside of the barn where no one but a few horses could see, she called May. "Can you transport me, or come get me or something?"

"Can I transport her from here with the blue crystal?" May asked Payah.

"You must be in contact with the subject or thing you wish to transport." Payah rubbed his chin then added, "You can view a place with the blue crystal before you transport to it though. It was a feature that was added to help prevent a person from transporting into a solid object."

"You mean to tell me we didn't have to use the white crystal before we used the blue one?"

"No, I guess not, but still you did the right thing. Best to understand how the device works before using each feature," he answered.

"Right!" Quickly May exchanged crystals, the blue for the white and looked up at Payah.

"Just tell the crystal something like 'look before I leap'. Then focus your mind where you want to go. Then when you are ready you just think 'Engage' and…" May turned her head sideways as her eyes narrowed. "Or you could just think 'go', if that's easier to remember."

"I think we need to have a talk when I get back," May said as she turned and closed her eyes to relocate Megan at the Butler's farm. Finding her, she zapped in, grabbed Megan's hand, and zapped back to the barn. "I'm getting better at this."

"Where's the guy who broke into the house?" Megan commanded.

"He's just around that corner, but we can't see him from here." They couldn't see the truck for two reasons - the low place in the road and the barn they were in both blocked their view. "Wait," May told her as she focused on the truck. "Look before I leap," she said.

"Look before I leap?" Megan asked as she turned around to see Payah standing a few steps away shrugging his shoulders with a silly smile on his face.

May found the pickup truck. "Ok, just touch me and close your eyes. You can see this guy."

Megan touched her friend on the shoulder and closed her eyes. "So that's the no good weasel that swiped my grandma's certificates."

"That's him and there they are laying in the seat of his truck."

"We have to get them back," Megan insisted. When she realized that May was viewing the target area with the blue crystal she turned loose abruptly and stepped away. "May, you still have the blue crystal on the headpiece!" She exclaimed, breaking May's trance.

"What if we just zapped in there and got them and returned here?" May asked.

"What if the guy sees us?"

"You could use the transparent or invisible entity mode if you like," Payah interjected.

"What is going on here?" Megan turned around to look at Payah. "Did you change clothes or something? You look different some how."

"Transparent mode?" May questioned as she also turned to look at Payah.

"Yeah, this guy talks like he knows a lot about this gizmo."

"He knows more than we do, that's for sure," May added. "You can view things and places with the blue crystal kinda like you can with the white one. That's not all, you can move things around with it like..." she said as she turned to Payah

"You call it telekinesis in English," Payah told them.

"And several of the keys have some of the same abilities like that," May told her friend.

Megan turned to Payah. "It is evident to me that you have been around this device before, to know so much about it."

While Megan spoke with Payah for a moment, May was changing back to the white key and focusing in on the pickup truck that was now moving down the road again. "Megan, watch this," May told her. Megan turned and placed a hand on May's shoulder. Closing her eyes she could see the same things that May was seeing. Just as the pickup truck reached Pleasant Pond near the church and cemetery all four tires exploded. The truck swerved this way and that and finally landed nose first in a ditch right in front of the graveyard.

"That was pretty good," Megan laughed.

"Not bad, even if I do say so myself," May added with a smile as she polished her fingernails on the front of her shirt.

The driver of the truck pried himself from the steering wheel, opened the door and fell promptly into the ditch. Mumbling something along the lines of having some awfully rotten luck. He got up to find all 4 tires beyond repair and threw his hat on the ground cursing.

He looked up and saw a gravestone standing in front of his truck on the far side of the cemetery fence. "Nah, couldn't be?" he thought out loud. "I hate grave yards." He reached into his truck to use his cell phone. "Mr. B. isn't going to like this."

"Ok, now what do we do? How do we go about getting the certificates back?" May asked.

"We can't just zap in there and get them can we?" Megan turned to Payah. "The guy would see us."

"Invisible, you said?" May asked Payah. He nodded his head.

"Wait! If we do this, we get the certificates back, but the guy goes free. Right?" Megan thought as she spoke. "I'll bet you just about anything that's the guy who poisoned Sparky and Mr. Butler's other horses."

The three stood there contemplating what the results might be and what course of action would be better.

"So, if we get the certificates back the guy will go free for poisoning the horses." May pondered aloud, "And if we don't catch him handing the certificates to Banister we can't connect the two?" May assessed aloud.

Several moments of silence passed while the three were thinking, then Megan realized the odds of catching him with the horses would be slim anyway. "No, let's just deal with this right now and worry about the rest later. The first thing we need to do is call the sheriff and tell him we saw the guy steal the certificates and tell where he is so the sheriff can pick him up." Megan picked up the items lying on the loft floor. "Beam us over to our room May." She said as she took hold of May's hand.

Once back in the house Megan called the Sheriff while May used the white crystal to keep an eye on the thief as he was walking down the road toward the gas station. Then she called her grandma over at the Butler's to tell her she had returned to the farm house and discovered that May had seen the man come into the house and steal the certificates. "Yes, grandma, we called the sheriff and told him what kind of truck the guy was driving and which way he went."

May was thinking how nice it would be to frighten the guy just a little in order to be sure he didn't show his face around the farm again. Using the white jewel she tranced in on the man as he was walking. "You have made a terrible mistake by taking things that do not belong to you." She spoke in an eerie voice. The man looked around. Not seeing anyone there he started to walk a little bit faster. "You must pay for your crimes," she continued. Again the man looked around but there was no one there. "I'm going to get you!" she yelled. With that the man broke into a run but had not gone far when the Sheriff's deputy turned off the main highway onto the gravel road. The deputy knew who the guy was from the description of his truck and by the clothes he was wearing.

"Going somewhere in a big hurry there, Slim?" The deputy spoke as he got out of his police car.

"No, just headed for the station, had a flat tire back by the cemetery," the man answered.

"Yeah, well just step over here and put your hands on the car and spread 'em." The deputy took the man by the arm and guided him forcefully over to the patrol car.

"You don't have anything on me!" the man protested.

"I guess we will see about that, won't we?" the officer answered.

As the officer was searching the man he found the certificates and just as this was taking place the long black car with Mr. Banister drove by but did not stop. The deputy looked up as the car passed. "No doubt Banister is out evicting women and children from their homes today." It was evident Mr. Banister didn't have many friends on the police force either since he was pulling the same tactics on some of their families.

Holding the envelope where the man could see, "I guess you just happened to find these along side the road."

The man made a quick glance at the envelope "I want to see my lawyer."

"Yeah, I'll just bet you do." The officer put the thief into the back seat of his car and took one last look at the black car in the distance as it rounded the corner down the road. "One of these days, Mr. Banister, you are going to make a mistake and I will catch you."

May and Megan had been watching viewpoint during this entire ordeal and heard the officer's words. They both smiled. "Perhaps we can help," Megan said, not realizing she had been focused on the officer at the time.

The deputy hearing what sounded like a voice looked around to see who had said these words. Not seeing anyone, he said, "Must be the wind," as he smiled and got into his car and headed toward the man's truck that was in the ditch by the cemetery.

May removed the headpiece from her head and with a smile she turned to Megan. "You know this little gizmo could be invaluable to us."

"Not to mention we have only learned a few things that we can do with it," Megan agreed.

"Put that thing back in the room," Megan instructed as she looked up to see Martha headed back toward the house.

A few minutes later the deputy drove up to the house where the girls were standing and had them identify the man and the contents of the envelope.

"That's him all right," May told the deputy.

"That's not possible, there wasn't anyone here when I was here." The man blatantly incriminated himself without realizing what he had said until it was too late.

"Martha, I'm sorry but I must keep these certificates as evidence until the trial," the deputy told her.

"How long do you think that will be?" she asked.

"County Court is running about 3 months behind."

"But I need that money to save my farm from Banister," she pleaded.

The deputy looked at the envelope and pondered for a moment. He realized what was going on and if there was one thing he hated to see it was Banister taking another farm from the landowners in the area. Not to mention that Martha and Fred had been good friends of his for many years. "I can't promise anything, but I will speak with the judge about it and give you a call as soon as I can." The deputy got back into his car and placed the envelope beside him in the seat. Pushing his hat back on his head he looked back up at Martha, "How soon?"

"By the end of the month."

The officer shook his head, started his car and drove off down the road.

A sigh escaped her lips as Martha and the girls stood watching as the deputy drove away. "What am I going to do now?"

"It will be all right grandma, I won't let that evil blood sucker take the farm, I promise," Megan assured her as they all went back into the house.

Back inside the house, Martha was in great despair wondering what she might do about saving the farm. The sheriff had the certificates now and she would not be able to sell them to save the farm until they were returned to her.

"It's all right, Grandma Martha," May said trying to comfort her, "but you really don't have to worry about it. Megan knows what to do." May looked up at Megan as she nodded her head indicating to her that it was time to tell Martha about the valuable coins that were in the safe.

"Children," Martha said, "you are so very young. What could you do to help me now?"

"We found the certificates, didn't we?" Megan asked her. "You don't honestly think that was the only card we had up our sleeve, did you?"

Martha looked into Megan's eyes wondering what she was implying by that. Could it be that Megan knew a lot more than she was telling?

"Follow me," Megan told them as she started up the stairs toward the study. "Before I show you this I want you to listen to me carefully. If we simply pay off the debt how long would it be before you were right back in a financial mess again?"

Martha listened but made no comments as they walked up the stairs into the study. Megan opened the safe, as Martha's eyes grew large. "What, where did all this come from?"

"It's been here all along" Megan told her.

"We hid it," May added with a happy smile on her face until she caught Megan shaking her head.

"You hid it, but what on earth for?" Martha asked.

"Because you had called the locksmith to open the safe and we didn't want him to see what was in here." Megan informed her as she reached in to remove some of the most valuable coins and the coin book.

"This coin book is like really, uh, 6 or 7 years old so it's not real up to date," May told her.

"Yes, but it shows some of these coins as being worth quite a lot of money. Some of them worth thousands of dollars," Megan added.

Martha reached out to take one of the gold coins from Megan to take a closer look.

"It's real gold," May said.

"Why didn't you just tell me you knew the combination to the safe?" Martha asked.

"We didn't want you to know we had been in the study. We were afraid we would be in trouble," May answered.

Martha looked up and May then turned to Megan. Megan was nodding her head in agreement with May.

May was flipping through the coin book. "Some of these coins were worth quite a lot just 6 and 7 years ago and this book is out of date, we need a new one."

"They could be worth quite a lot more than that now," Megan added.

May handed the book to Martha, then she looked up at Megan. She tilted her head in a motioning gesture that she wanted to talk to Megan alone.

"Go ahead and look through it, I'm sure there's enough here to more than pay the farm out of debt." She started for the door. "In fact you should have plenty left over."

"We think you should invest the money in something that will make more money," May insisted once again with that happy, almost silly, smile on her face.

"Oh, and there's a box in there with my name on it. Grandpa had some coins and things tucked away for me," Megan added as they went out the door.

Back in their room the girls talked the situation over. "Now what do we do?" May asked.

"I don't know about you, but I have work to do. If you can stay here, I have to take the green key and pay a visit to some sick horses over at the Butler's barn. If I don't do something quick the horses will die." With that Megan grabbed the box with the device in it and all the keys. She positioned the blue stone on the device and put it on her head. "You keep grandma occupied and out of this room until I get back." With that and a flash of blue light Megan was gone.

"Right, keep granny busy," she tightened her lips with determination and away she went back toward the study.

Chapter 17
Angel of Mercy

Although she had not first scanned the area before she made the jump she lucked out and no one was in the horse barn where the sick horses were. Several of them were knocking on death's door and there was no time to waste. Quickly Megan changed to the green jewel and went to work with the horses. Once again the green glow of light filtered through the windows and cracks in the barn and was visible to the house on the hill where the Butler's lived.

Megan spoke to the horses as she touched them and the green glow of light flowed down her arms to the animals. "I will find out who did this to you and I will make them pay for what they have done."

As she finished up with the last horse she heard something behind her, she turned to discover Mr. Butler standing in the doorway with his mouth wide open in astonishment. Chills ran through her as she wondered what she might tell him, how she might explain what he was seeing. No sooner had fear overcome her than courage took its place. There was no time to be concerned. Mr Butler was about the finest man she had ever known. He was like her new grandpa and if she couldn't trust him with her secret then she couldn't trust anyone. She took a deep breath as she turned and stood removing the device from her head and replacing the green jewel with the blue one once again.

"Mr. Butler, it would be very difficult for me to explain what I am doing here, but just trust me. Your horses are going to be just fine." She turned to have another look at the animals, as some of them had even been able to stand just moments after she had treated them.

"Megan, is that really you?" he asked.

"It's me," she answered.

"But how?"

"I can't explain that now. I don't know if I ever can," she spoke as she walked toward him and toward the door with her crown still in her hand.

"I know someone poisoned your horses and I think it was the same man who robbed grandma's house today. I think he is working for Simon Banister and I think he has been doing everything he can to put the farmers out of business here." She turned again to look at one of the horses that was still laying on the stall floor as it raised its head. "The trouble is I can't prove it yet."

John pondered on this for a moment as he also observed the horses starting to show signs of improvement. "You know that makes perfect sense. I knew he was low but I didn't think he was that low, but you may be right."

"Yeah, I get lucky sometimes. But even if we can prove that he had something to do with this, we still have a problem," she told him.

"What? Paying off the debts that low life has forced us into?"

"Yes," she answered as a thought crossed her mind. "How about this, if you had a larger area to say, set up a dude ranch, do you think you could get your business back on track again and pay off your debts?"

John pondered on the thought for a moment as he looked around and out the door. His little farm was built on a narrow hilltop and his pasture was not all that large. "What do you have in mind?"

"Grandma has a fairly large farm and you rent the south pasture each year for planting, right?" she asked.

"Yes."

"Well, how about you and her go into business and you have the horses and she has the land, you could run a dude ranch right here. You could have campfires, cookouts, camping and riding and all that right here. People would come from all around to spend a week or a weekend on the farm. My grandma's house is large enough she could run a bed and breakfast right there.

"Might work," John said as he rubbed his hand across his chin. "It just might work. But we don't have the money to get it all set up. It would be very expensive to get everything in order and pay for the insurance and all that. I don't see any way we can do that unless..."

"Unless you could get a very large business loan right?" Megan asked.

"Exactly," came the answer.

Megan walked near the door and peeked out to see if Mrs. Butler was anywhere in sight. Not seeing anyone, she placed the crown on her head again and turned back toward Mr. Butler. "Look, Mr. Butler, I really need you to keep my little secret and don't tell a living soul what you saw here just now. If anyone finds out about me, I'll be, well, they might just cut me up to see what my insides look like. You keep my secret and I promise you I will get the money and I will set things right again."

"Does your grandma know about this," John asked. "I mean does she know about you and the..."

"No, and don't tell her, she has enough problems on her mind these days." Megan looked out the door again then back toward the horses in the barn. "You know, I never really realized until now what it was like to be grown up and to think like an adult."

"Something has happened to you, hasn't it?" he asked.

"It seems like just yesterday I was a kid playing with my friend, in search of the answers to a mystery and today I don't really know who I am. But I'm not the same and I'll never be the same again." With that she turned to look back out the door and as the flow of liquid blue light covered her she said, "I'll be back." With that the blue light faded away taking Megan with it.

John stood there scratching his head under his hat and shaking his head. He wasn't at all sure what he had seen. But the one thing that he did know was that his horses were going to live and that was the best news he could think of. For that he could keep Megan's secret and then some. A smile slowly appeared on his face as he considered the possibilities. If she could make his horses well again and then vanish in a blue light perhaps she could get the money and perhaps she was his angel in disguise.

Chapter 18
Phase Two

The soft blue light filled the girls' room back at the farm spilling out into the hallway. May was standing beside the desk and Martha was seated at the desk going through the old coins and checking the value the out of date coin book had listed for those they could find in it.

May, seeing the light, stood up and headed out the door hoping to block Martha's view for a moment. It wasn't that hard to do since the blue light only lasted for 2 or 3 seconds and it was gone.

Back in their room, Megan was once again hiding the device under her pillow when May entered the room. "What's up?"

"The horses that are left are going to be just fine. But now we have to do something about pinning the blame on the guilty party," Megan remarked. "And..."

"And just how are we going to do that?" May asked.

"And, Mr. Butler caught me in the horse barn."

May's hand quickly came up to cover her mouth as her eyes grew large. "OH, NO!"

"I think he will keep our secret. He's a nice man, and I had an idea while I was over there that I can tell you about." Quickly she reviewed her ideas with May and they discussed the possibilities. It would be fantastic if they had their very own dude ranch and grandma and the Butler's could save their farms.

They walked into the study where Martha was still looking at some of the coins. Looking down at the desk and seeing the old coin book she knew they had to get a new more up to date one, but the closest bookstore to the farm was back in the city where Megan lived. Megan looked up at May and May could almost read her mind. "Want me to go this time?" May asked.

Megan turned around and walked back out into the hallway with May right behind her. "Do you think you could get in and out of the bookstore without being seen warping in and out?"

"Absolutely. I know one of the book stores real well and I am sure I can get in and out without any questions asked," she answered.

"And what if someone sees the light?" Megan questioned.

May hadn't thought of that. It could present a problem. She took a deep breath and let it out slowly. "Well, I could warp in behind the book store by the dumpster."

"That might work," Megan said as she was thinking about the possibilities. "And how about I just transport you in there and wait for you to get the book then you come back and we warp out?"

May agreed. It would be better if she didn't have to be totally responsible for the device. She would have had to take it off, hide it, go in and buy a book, then come back out, put it on and then leave again. Slowly they walked into their room wondering what they might do to get quick access to an up to date book about coins. And when should they go? Megan had just made one trip with it and grandma was no doubt tired and about to give up searching through the coins for the time being.

"We could go in after dark, then perhaps no one would see us." Megan suggested.

"The light is more visible at night," May said.

"Yes, but there are less people to notice it," Megan argued.

May pondered for a moment then a sly smile came across her face. "I have it," she said. "We can scan the restroom and if no one is in there we can just warp in and out of there and no one will know the difference."

"Good idea," Megan agreed, "but perhaps we should wait until after grandma goes to bed," she continued as she looked at her wristwatch. "It's almost dinner time," she added. Where had the day gone?

After dinner, the girls cleaned the dishes and went into the den. Out of curiosity, Megan started playing with the old satellite receiver. She turned it on and pushed the buttons to move the dish east and west while looking out the window watching the dish move back and forth. She then examined the wires on the back of the unit and in a few moments she had figured out which wires did what. She changed all through the channels moving the dish back and forth and for a moment thought she had found something. The screen went from rastor to black with white spots.

"Look, Megan," May pointed. "I think you almost had something there."

Megan played with it a little while longer but the picture didn't really get any better. It was evident to her that she was picking up something though and if something was there all she had to do was figure out why she couldn't get it in better.

Digging around in a drawer under the unit she discovered the owner's manual and an old satellite guide that showed where the satellites where located.

"Man, you are really into this, aren't you?" May asked.

"No, actually, I am thinking about getting a new coin book so we can see what those coins are really worth," she answered.

May looked around to see Martha knitting something on the couch while reading a book. She appeared to be miles away at the moment.

Megan let out a sigh, "Ok, if the dish isn't pointed right at the satellites, it won't work."

"Right," May nodded.

"And if the wires get broke or messed up on the ends it won't work right either," Megan continued reading in the book.

"Wires, right," May chimed in again as if she were actually helping.

"It says here it has something called polarities in it and if they are not lined up it won't work right either," Megan stated as her lips tightened and another larger sigh escaped her lips.

May noticed her friend's expressions and it was evident they were not about to get any help from Martha. "We need help, don't we?"

Megan nodded her head. "We could use some, I would say." With that she reached up and turned the receiver off and unplugged it. Then she removed the coaxial cable from the back of the receiver and looked at it. "Hum, that doesn't look right."

May strained to see what Megan was looking at. "What doesn't look right?"

"I think there's suppose to be a wire inside this thing that goes into that little hole in the back of the, you know where this wire goes," she said. Then looking closer she saw it. "Needle nose pliers," she commanded.

May handed her the pliers and Megan worked at the end of the wire for a few moments. "There," she said as she held it up to examine it. "I wonder why that wire was so short. It was like it pulled up inside the rubber stuff." With that she screwed the wire back on the unit and turned it back on.

"Look, I can see something in the picture now," May proclaimed. She was right but it was not a very good picture.

Megan moved the dish back and forth a little bit and, finding the position where she had the best picture, she left the dish position and started adjusting the polarity until the picture improved quite a bit more. "Still looks really bad, doesn't it?"

Martha looked up over her glasses at the girls working on the satellite receiver. She also let out a small sigh as she shook her head and went back to her knitting. What were the odds those two little girls could ever get that thing working correctly again?

"Well look at it like this," Megan said. "It wasn't working at all before we started on it and now we have a picture." She made a face at it. "Well, it's almost a picture anyway," she added.

Then she jumped up and headed out the door toward the satellite dish with manual in hand and May close behind her.

"Well?" May asked.

"Well what?" Megan answered.

"When are we going to go to town?" May asked.

"Can't just yet. Grandma is up and she knows what we are up to. If we do anything out of the way just now we will get caught for sure. We have to wait until we find the right opportunity to zap out and get the book," Megan answered. It was evident she had been thinking about the project all the while.

The girls came to stand in front of the big satellite dish. Megan stood there just looking at it for a few moments then she walked around it slowly looking everything over. She looked at the dish then at the manual and the pictures and drawings in the manual. "Trouble shooting." She started flipping though the pages again to the back of the book.

"You know, it's a wonder this thing doesn't fall over on its face," May informed her as she touched the large dish with a hand. "It's awfully heavy." She looked around at the relatively small post holding the large metal dish up. "And just look at that little pipe that has to hold it up there."

Megan looked up for a moment and realized it did look a little bit odd that such a large dish was being held up by such a small pipe sticking in the ground. "It says in the book that some dishes will settle over the years and no longer be lined up exactly right with the satellites and you have to crank this adjustment under the dish to get it lined back up again."

May looked under the dish at the adjustment. "Well anyone knows that," she remarked with sarcasm.

In a few moments, the girls, working together, had managed to lengthen the adjustment a full turn. Then they returned to the house and discovered their picture had cleared up considerably. In fact it looked like a TV picture once again. "See there," Megan said. "I knew we could fix it."

Martha looked up at the TV for a moment and was somewhat surprised to actually see a picture on it.

Seeing her opportunity to return to the room upstairs and make a trip to town Megan shut the satellite system off and turned the regular antenna back on. "I'm going to turn it in, grandma. It's late and I'm tired."

"All right girls, sleep tight," Martha answered. "I'll not be up much longer myself."

With that the girls returned to their room. "Pencil and pad," Megan called to May as she pointed at the table.

May took her place and was ready to write.

"We need the book," Megan said as she pointed at the pad.

May wrote it down. "And a new satellite guide," she added with a smile.

"We need our money," she said as she pulled her backpack from under the bed to recover her purse from it.

"Money, check," May said as she wrote.

"It's going to be a big day tomorrow," Megan considered as she took a seat at the table.

"Big day tomorrow," May called off as she wrote.

Megan's eyebrows came down over her eyes and one corner of her mouth curled up as she gave May one of those "what do you think you are doing" looks.

May looked up at Megan. "What?" she asked once again sarcastically.

Megan shook her head, placed the purse in a pocket and retrieved the device from under her pillow before returning to her seat at the table. "I mean we are running out of time to get a lot of things done, and I mean done right," she spoke very seriously.

"Ok, you want to build a dude ranch here so your grandma will have steady income and let Mr. Butler run the dude ranch and grandma run the bed and breakfast, right?" May asked.

"Right, but first we have to find out what the coins are worth and sell them for as much as we can get out of them," Megan spoke as she waved a knowing finger in the air.

May reached out and, taking the device from the box, handed it to Megan. "Let's do it."

Megan placed the device on her head and walked to an open place in the room. "Lock the door, May."

May locked the door and then, taking Megan's hand, they turned around in the room this way and that. Megan was tuning in on the restroom in the bookstore 60 miles away. "You know this will be a long jump."

"The longest actual jump we have ever made," May added.

"Yes, and it looks like the coast is clear. Let's go." The blue light flowed over them and in a moment they appeared in the restroom exactly where Megan had intended them to be.

"Let's get those books," May said as she started out the door, then realized that Megan was just standing there.

"I can't go out there with this thing," Megan said as she held the device in her hand and looked for a place to hide it.

"Ah, well just tell them you've been to a Halloween party," May told her. "No problem."

"Some how I just don't think that will work at this time of the year," Megan said as she shook her head still looking for some place she could hide the device without it being noticeable.

May looked around the bathroom. "You could find some place to hide it in here I guess."

"What and run the risk of someone else finding it? I don't think so," Megan spoke in a commanding tone. "You go get the books, you know what to get and I'll just wait here for you."

"Oh, Megan, no one will notice you. Listen, you can look at the magazines in the back of the store and just wear it or hold it in your hand until I get the books and come back." Suddenly a puzzled expression came over May's face. "The check-out is in the front of the store and they put the books in a bag and they expect you to leave through the front door."

"Yeah," Megan answered.

"But I'm not leaving through the front door, I have to come back here."

"So just tell them you..." at that moment a woman opened the bathroom door and, seeing the two girls standing there talking, gave them a dirty look.

"Yeah I know, or get off the pot," May said as both girls walked out of the restroom into the back of the book store.

"Must be a lady truck driver," Megan whispered.

"HA! Woman truck driver, but that woman is no lady," May responded.

"Right, let's find those books and get out of here ASAP," Megan commanded. If she had to go around in the store with her device it might look better if she just wore it like a hat, so she put it right back on her head. It was better than being questioned about it by one of the clerks. If they saw her wearing it then perhaps they would understand it was hers and she couldn't help it if she was just a strange kid.

Searching the magazine rack in the back they found the satellite guide very quickly then set out to find the book on coins. A woman passing them in one of the isles noticed Megan's crown-like device and smiled at her.

"She thinks I'm nuts, May," Megan whispered.

May looked up at Megan for a moment. "No, she doesn't think your nuts," she said as a soft giggle escaped her lips.

"You think I look silly too, don't you?" Megan asked.

May shook her head as she continued down an aisle not having any idea where to go to find a book about coins. Seeing one of the people who worked in the store she asked them for directions and in moments had found the books on coins. They flipped through some of the books until they decided on one then headed for the checkout.

"Cute," the check out boy said with a smile as he eyed Megan and her device.

Megan felt like she could just about die. The guy was handsome and couldn't have been more than 16 or 17 and now she stood there looking like a fool in front of him.

May giggle and leaned into Megan, bumping her softly. "Ah."

Megan turned to see what May was doing and found May was looking up at the device. The blue jewel was glowing, so was Megan's face. Quickly May grabbed the device from Megan's head.

"Say that's neat. How did you do that?" The boy asked.

"Ah, it's a new thing," May said as she gathered up the change and reached for the bag. "Her dad made it."

"Yeah, my dad, he's an inventor," Megan agreed as she grabbed the device from May's hand and headed out the door. She felt so humiliated she could just die.

"So, you go to school around here?" May asked as she picked up the bag with the books in it.

"Yeah, we just moved here last week. I'll be going to school over at Southside," he answered.

"Really, that's where we go to school. Maybe we will see you there sometime," May answered with a smile. She turned to see Megan standing outside looking in. She had her arms crossed and was standing there patting one foot hard against the ground.

"Name's Matt," the voice came from behind her.

May turned, "What?"

"My name's Matt. I hope to see you two in school. You have a good day," he said.

"Yeah, I'm May and that's Megan," she said as she turned and walked out the door.

"What have you done now, May?" Megan spoke in an angry tone.

"Nothin'. I just..."

"Nothin'? You told him who we are, didn't you?" Megan asked.

"Well," May answered in a long drawn out high pitch tone.

"Don't you know that we aren't suppose to even be in the city now?" Megan informed her in a stern tone.

"I think you worry too much. He doesn't know where we are suppose to be but..." Suddenly her eyes grew large as she looked up and saw someone walking toward them in the parking lot. Quickly grabbing Megan's arm she pointed them toward the side of the building. "Walk, walk," she told Megan.

Megan tried to look back over her shoulder, "What is it?"

"It's our English teacher, Mrs. Abrey, and believe me she will know we aren't suppose to be here"

"That's right because we had to give that report on what we were going to do on our summer vacation." The girls hurried all the way to the back of the bookstore where the trash dumpster was. With a quick look around the corner, they saw they had not been followed. "Do you think she saw us?" Megan asked.

"I don't know, but get us out of here quick," May commanded.

They were lucky. The bookstore was on the edge of town not far from the airport and there was nothing behind it but a field and a fence. Megan placed the device on her head once again and they held hands. In a glow of blue light the two vanished and reappeared back in their room to find Scratches curled up on Megan's bed.

Megan took the device off, removed the blue jewel and put it all in the little box which she stuck in her backpack this time. "That was close enough for me."

"You said it," May agreed.

"At least we got what we went after," Megan said.

"There's only one problem with that," May said as Megan looked up at her. "How do we explain how we got the books?"

Megan had so many other things on her mind she had not even considered that. "I don't know, but I guess we can figure that out tomorrow." Megan tossed herself on her bed next to Scratches. "Tomorrow. I'll worry about it tomorrow."

The next morning arrived as usual, too early. The sound of the rooster awakened the girls. They pried their now aching bodies up out of bed and on to their chores. With only one exception, everything went as usual. They discovered old Bud the snake in the hen house again but this time Megan did something May didn't expect. Without hesitation and having her gloves on she simply walked up took the big snake by the neck in one hand and body in the other and carried him out of the hen house to turn him loose in the south forty. The big snake never offered any resistance. It was a trip that he may have remembered in the past when Megan's grandfather was still alive. The old gloves had the same scent on them as they always have had and perhaps the old snake didn't know the difference and thought it was Fred. Or perhaps he just didn't care.

May stood inside the chicken yard fence holding the basket of eggs and watched as Megan returned. "Ohhh, I don't believe you just did that?" May shook all over making a rather unpleasant expression as she turned around and headed for the gate.

As Megan arrived back at the gate it was as if she suddenly realized what she had just done. She had just physically removed old Bud, the huge black rat snake from the chicken shed without even realizing it, and without a thought or concern about doing it. Slowly she took a deep breath and, exhaling, she shook her head. She closed the gate and both girls started back toward the house.

"What ever possessed you to do that?" May asked.

"I don't know, it's like I think of things differently now. It's like I have changed inside and I don't really know who I am anymore," Megan answered.

"I'll say! Just two days ago you wouldn't have touched a wild snake like that and today it was like you were someone else. You walked in there and took that snake out of there like your grandpa would have," May responded.

An expression of curiosity came over Megan's face. Perhaps that was the answer. "You know every since I started using that crown thing I have noticed that something about me is different. I feel different. I think different."

"No kidding, and you even walk different," May reported as she noticed Megan's stride.

"You know I didn't even think for a moment about taking old Bud out to the field. It was like I was my grandpa or something," Megan added.

"Or perhaps you have been in contact with his spirit and you are starting to think more like him," May suggested.

It seemed logical when they thought about it. Perhaps that was the answer.

Chapter 19
Where Evil Lurks

In a dimly lit office room in his luxurious mansion, Simon Banister sat behind his desk chewing the end off of an expensive cigar. In his right hand was a red ink pen that he sat flipping over and over in his hand as he pushed each end against the table as it flipped over. Before him laid several papers and a map of the countryside where Megan's grandmother lived. Several areas of land had been marked off in red. These were property plots. Each one had a name and acreage marked on it telling how large it was and who it belonged to. Many of the farms all ready had the word "Banister" marked across them in red ink. These were farms that Banister had managed to buy out one way or another.

The phone rang and Banister answered it. It was his lawyer. "Yeah!" he barked into the receiver. "Listen, I don't care how you do it, but get him out of the slammer and don't leave any paper trails to lead him back to me."

"I can't believe the idiot got arrested and lost the certificates," he growled into the phone. "If I can buy out the Butler's, and the Martin farm I will have one entire quarter section of the land I need for my new development project. I have them where I want them, and I'm not going to give up now."

Banister hung up the phone. By the expression on his face, he was in deep thought. Then he picked up the phone again and dialed someone else. "Say, what's the status on the Butler's?" he asked, then listened for a moment. "I heard the Butler's horses were all sick with some unknown disease and there was nothing that could be done for them." A few moments passed as he listened to the voice at the other end. "Really? Well, you check on that and get back to me on it by morning, no later than nine o'clock, you hear." Banister slammed the phone down with a thud.

"If that vet gets in the way again I'll give him a plague on the other side of the county that will keep him busy for a month." A sly laugh escaped his lips as he crushed out his cigar in a very large ashtray on his desk. "Yes, I will."

The next morning rolled around to find a black Lincoln in Mr. Banister's driveway and a man in a suit standing at his door at 8:30 AM. Banister came to the door to speak with his visitor.

"I got Jordan Gilmore out of jail last night, but it's going to cost you a hundred grand," Don Lowrey informed Mr. Banister.

"Really?" Banister replied as he lit up one of his rather large cigars. "Pocket change," he added as he looked toward the western sky testing the wind to decide what kind of day it was going to be.

"Uh," Lowrey cleared his throat, "you know that's not his first offense."

"Why do you think I hired him?"

"Yes, well, I understand that but you should know the police have an eye on him and if he gets picked up again there's no telling what might happen." Lowrey watched Banister's expressions as he toked on his cigar. Banister took his time responding as he took another puff on his cigar. Then he turned and, poking Lowrey with a finger, said, "That's why you make dead sure there's no way that Jordan Gilmore can be traced back to me," with emphasis on the 'dead' to be sure Lowrey understood him.

"Yes, well, you know there's a good chance that 100 grand will go to pay the fines and he will most likely even do time for breaking and entering and stealing those certificates," Lowrey informed him.

Banister looked Lowrey straight in the face and never said a word as he climbed into the back seat of the big black car.

"I just hope it's worth it," Lowrey added as he closed the car door and proceeded around to the driver's seat.

Lowrey was also a businessman. He had a past history of both good and bad deals. It was nothing new to the man to make an investment that would bring him over 100 grand or more and then turn right around and make a bad investment that would cost him everything he had just made. He didn't have the highest morals either and perhaps that's why he frequently worked jobs for Banister. Still there were some things that were beyond him that Banister wouldn't think twice about, and having someone 'put out of the way' was one of them. While for the moment the only person who knew both Lowrey and Gilmore was the middleman, if the link could be made back to Lowrey, the investigation would soon discover Simon Banister was behind it all.

In the backseat of the big black car Banister made several phone calls and one of them was to his lawyer. Mr. Shyster was his name - perhaps a cruel trick of fate or perhaps the fates just named him correctly. He had links inside the local sheriff's department. If anything was going on that might affect Banister's illegal business ventures, Mr. Shyster was soon to inform him about it. That's part of what he was on the payroll for.

Banister hung up the phone and leaned forward, "Did you know that Butler's horses are not only not sick but doing well today?"

Lowrey paused for a moment then answered, "I haven't heard anything about it."

"Well, they are and that's not what I was paying for. I want that man crushed and out of my way for good. I want all those people out of there. That land is mine and I always get what I want." Banister leaned back in his seat, pulled up a newspaper, and shook it. "He only lost 3 horses out of that entire deal. What am I paying for?"

Lowrey shook his head. It wasn't his idea to have Butler's horses poisoned. But if Banister could secure the land he wanted, then Lowrey stood to gain a good deal in the long run. Lowrey would have chosen another method to secure the land perhaps, but for now he was in too deep to change much of anything.

"Listen, I want Gilmore back in there tonight and tell him he had better do the job right this time!" Banister shouted.

"Yes, Mr. Banister. I'll see to it," Lowrey responded.

"Or they'll find him floating face down in the river. Then let them try to figure out what happened." Banister mumbled mostly to himself, but Lowery heard every word and he knew Banister was quite capable of doing just that. Besides, once he had what he wanted, Gilmore was expendable and if he was dead then he couldn't tell anyone whom he had been working for. Then the sheriff would have no solid link to the middleman who might trace the path back to him.

Chapter 20
Investing in the Future

Back on the farm the girls had gathered their eggs, had breakfast, and were going through the coins again using the new coin book. When Martha had asked them where they found the new book, May simply told her she was interested in coins and had forgotten that she had her book in her backpack. Martha suspected the girl wasn't telling all the truth about it, but still it was partly true since she had taken a sudden interest in coins the moment they had opened the safe.

"You know, some of these coins are, like, worth a lot of money," May informed them as she jotted some numbers down on a piece of paper.

Megan smiled as she thought things were finally starting to look up. Having enough money to pay off the twenty thousand dollar debt against the farm plus what ever interest had been charged shouldn't be any problem at all providing they could get the best price on even a few of the coins. If they had enough money left over, they could help Mr. Butler out of his mess by loaning him some money to pay off his debt. Then, last but not least, to make some improvements on the farm itself and start making preparations to build a dude ranch out of it.

Of course, she still had to convince grandma that it was a good idea or most of this planning would be for nothing.

While thinking about how grandma was going to receive the idea of building a dude ranch and having hundreds of people passing through her house and across her farm, Megan turned and realized there were some archeological artifacts laying on the floor near the safe. Perhaps they were worth something to someone but to whom and how much was another question.

Megan walked over and took a seat on the floor with the objects before her. Slowly she picked up each item and examined it. Then she would lay them back on the floor where they had been. What if there was a good reason why grandpa had kept these items? What if they were still part of the puzzle that she had to solve?

May looked up and noticed what Megan was doing. She knew by the expression on her friend's face that she was in deep thought about something.

Just then there was a knock at the door. Megan jumped from her position to answer the door. "Don't let anything happen to these things," she instructed them and down the stairs she went.

John and Alma Butler were standing at the front door with Sparky. "I didn't think you would mind if I brought an old friend along with us," John told her.

A very large smile came across Megan's face and she ran out to greet them, especially Sparky. "Oh, Mr. Butler, I can't tell you how much I appreciate you and everything you have done."

Mrs. Butler entered the house, leaving the three standing at the door. "What's Martha doing this morning?" she asked Megan as she went in.

"She's upstairs in the study," Megan answered.

Mrs. Butler nodded her head and went on inside the house.

Once they were alone, John smiled, seeing how happy Megan was. "You know, I think he really is happy to see you."

"I know I'm happy to see him," she said, putting her arms around his neck to give him a big hug. Then she looked up at Mr. Butler. "Is our secret still safe?"

"Secret?" he smiled. "You know I had the strangest dream yesterday afternoon."

A curious expression came over Megan's face as she listened, "Really?"

"Yeah, I thought I dreamed that a beautiful young guardian angel came to my farm and saved all of my horses," he continued. "What do you say about that, Sparky? Did you see an angel the other day?"

A huge smile crossed Megan's lips. She knew what Mr. Butler was doing and her secret was quite safe with him. "What do you think, Sparky? Did you see an angel the other day?" she asked the pony. She glanced up to see Mr. Butler wink at her.

"Anyway, I was thinking that since Sparky is feeling much better today that he might like to come spend a few days with you. So, if it's all right with Martha, I bought some fresh hay and things and I can fix up his place in the barn," Mr. Butler suggested.

"Oh, I'm sure it's all right with grandma," Megan insisted.

They were walking toward the barn when Mr. Butler placed a hand on Megan's shoulder. "I don't know how you did it, or if I was just hallucinating, but if that was you in my barn yesterday, I'd be curious to know what you have in mind to help us save these farms."

Megan looked at the ground for a moment as they walked, thinking how she might answer. "I have some ideas but I don't know how grandma will take it."

"You mentioned something about setting up a dude ranch and said you would find a way to get the money," he reminded her.

"Yes, I know. And we have the space and I think we are going to have the money real soon because grandpa had saved a bunch of very valuable old coins over the years. We can sell some of the coins and pay off the debts for both of our places if we can convince grandma to go along with the idea. Then we can start fixing the place up into a dude ranch. You run the ranch, grandma and Mrs. Butler can run the bed and breakfast and May and I can help you during the summer," she said.

John leaned against the side of his pickup truck pondering on the idea. "You know it just might work."

John had parked his pickup in front of the barn at the loading shoot. The hay was in the back of the truck and it was no problem to move a bale into the first animal stall for Sparky. As he worked he was thinking and sometimes talking with Megan about the possibilities and complications of just such a venture. He examined the old barn, which could use a coat of paint and some fixing up but over all it wasn't in that bad of shape.

The barn had 4 full stalls for animals and it would be an easy thing to keep horses handy for the visitors. Not only that, some of the visitors would pay them to come live and work on a farm for a weekend or a week at a time. Of course, they would ride horses around the farm and learn what it's like to live on a farm. They could pasture a few cows on the land and have a round up just to make things interesting for the visitors.

There were a few old buildings on the farm that should be torn down and removed, and perhaps the pond in the south forty could be dug out some. Maybe they could make it into a large recreation area for fishing, swimming or something. The pond beyond the hog lot needed to be dug out and the building near that pond needed to be removed. Quite a lot of things went through Mr. Butler's mind in just a few minutes as he prepared the stall for Sparky.

Megan helped and even went to draw water into the large horse tank near the fence that bordered the yard to the house. While she was sitting on the old concrete box that housed the water tank watching the water run, Mr. Butler walked up and leaned against the box.

"I've been thinking it over and if we can get the money and if Martha will go for the idea, I'm willing to give it a try. It could be the best thing in the world for my business, not to mention it could provide a fair income for Martha," Mr. Butler said.

"All we have to do now is convince grandma," Megan said with a sigh as she looked up toward the house.

At that moment, an old pickup truck went whizzing by followed by a cloud of dust. Megan looked up and recognized the truck. It was Jordan Gilmore, the man who had robbed the house only the day before. "Holy rust buckets!" Megan yelled as she stood on the concrete wall of the water tank. "It's the man who broke into the house and stole the certificates yesterday!"

John looked up to see the old truck going off down the road in the direction of his house. "That's Jordan Gilmore," he shook his head.

"He has to be the one who poisoned the horses too," she said. "Wonder how he got out of jail so quick?"

"Yeah, might be. He's bad news," John said as he moved away from the water tank and headed for his truck, "and he's headed toward my house."

"Going with me," he called back at Megan.

"No, I think I'll wait here," she called as she followed along behind him to the truck. "You go check your house and make sure he doesn't go there. I won't be far away," she added as she pointed to her head. "If you know what I mean."

Mr. Butler drove away quickly as Megan ran for the house. She took two steps at a time going up the stairs and then in a moment she entered her room and locked the door behind her. May had heard Megan's footsteps and, wondering what was going on, left Mrs. Butler and Martha in the study. "I'll be back in a little bit," she told them.

Upon reaching the room and finding the door locked, she knew something was going on but she didn't know what. She knocked on the door and called for Megan.

"Yes?" Megan answered.

"It's me," May responded through the door. "Let me in."

The door clicked and May entered locking the door behind her. "What's going on," she asked.

"That guy who was here yesterday is out of jail all ready and we saw him headed toward Mr. Butler's house. Then Mr. Butler took off down the road to check and see if the guy went to his house." Megan said all that in one breath while putting the white stone in the device, then positioned it on her head. With that she gasped for a large breath of air and went into a trance. The white glow flowed over her body as her eyes became brilliant white.

May shivered as she watched the transformation of her friend into the light. "That gives me cold chills," she said as she reached out to touch Megan on the shoulder to join her and see what Megan was seeing.

Inside the vision, Megan and May could see Mr. Butler as he pulled into his driveway. He was looking off down the road toward the dust cloud that was moving away toward the east. "That's him going on down the road," Megan told May.

"Where's he going?" May asked.

"I guess we missed it. Looks like he is going on down the road," Megan said as she watched from a floating position about 50 feet above the Butler's house. She certainly had a better view of the path of the vehicle than Mr. Butler had.

"Uh, oh," May said excitedly. "Zoom in on that guy's truck. I have an idea."

Megan quickly flew over the trees and down the road to catch the pickup truck just as it turned to the right taking another road that paralleled the Butler's farm.

"Inside," she commanded. "I want to see him."

Megan positioned the view inside Gilmore's truck where both girls could see his face clearly. "What are you thinking?"

"Oh just a little, uh, message," May answered. "Watch this."

"Hello, dirt bag," May called to the man. When she saw the expression come over the man's face like he had heard a ghost, she knew she had made contact. "You know, your time is running out don't you?" she added.

Gilmore looked all around wondering where the voice was coming from. Then suddenly he made the connection from the last time he had heard that voice. It was yesterday, right after all of his tires blew out leaving him stranded, and just before the sheriff's deputy showed up to haul him to jail. The last thing he needed was to have another run in with whatever that was. "Hey, who is that?" he yelled. "Just leave me alone!"

May laughed as she saw the frightened expression on the man's face. As they moved away from the truck they could see that Gilmore's driving suddenly left quite a lot to be desired. He swerved this way and that on the narrow dirt road nearly landing in a ditch before he managed to get his truck back under control.

Quickly Megan flew up over the trees returning to Mr. Butler's truck and in the process heard the sound of something falling on the floor beside her. "It's all right Mr. Butler. He's gone for now."

Upon hearing Megan's voice Mr. Butler looked all around to see where the voice had come from. Not seeing her he called out, "Megan, is that you?"

"Yes, it's me. You can come back now," she told him.

Mr. Butler shook his head as he turned around and headed back toward the Martin farm. He was starting to get the idea that Megan had more tricks up her sleeve than he could have imagined.

Megan removed the device from her head and turned to see May laying on the floor looking up at her. "What are you doing down there?"

"You heard that thump on the floor awhile ago, right?"

"Yeah," Megan answered

"That was me falling"

"Oh"

"Next time you are going to spin around and fly off like that you should signal or at least give fair warning," May insisted.

Megan laughed a soft laugh as she smiled 'sorry about that.' Megan put a hand up over her mouth as she realized what had happened. If spinning around like that in a person's mind wasn't enough to cause them to lose their balance, sometimes she actually did turn physically while viewing things mentally. She had turned around very quickly and knocked May flat on the floor in the process.

"Oh! I left the water on at the barn," Megan said as she tossed the device back in the box and shoved it back in her backpack. Out the door she ran, down the stairs out the front door and across the yard. May ran after her and Scratches, taking notice of the commotion, decided to follow.

Mr. Butler was pulling back into the driveway by the barn just as Megan arrived at the water tank. "Tank's full now," she said as she closed the valve on the old pump.

Mr. Butler approached the girls and, seeing May standing there, wondered if May knew about Megan's special abilities. Megan realized this just by his expression and answered him. "It's ok, she knows," she answered, even though he had not said anything.

"So now what?" May asked the two.

"Now we go talk to grandma and see if she likes our idea," Megan answered.

John nodded his head and they all set out for the house. Scratches turned and watched them for a few moments as they walked away. He didn't seem to understand what the big deal was. They run out of the house and then they return to the house. It didn't make sense. He looked up to see Sparky standing there getting a drink and perhaps wondered if he and the pony were the only sane ones on the farm.

Inside, the five of them held a meeting and discussed the possibility of starting a dude ranch. Martha was for the idea until she realized she would be in charge of the bed and breakfast there in her house. "It's too much work for an old woman. I would have to clean and cook and..."

"And do all the things that you do every day anyway," Megan cut in.

The two sat there at the kitchen table just looking at each other for a moment. "Grandma, I know it's tough, but you won't be alone. You will have the Butler's here to help you and I'll come in the summer and whenever I can to help."

Martha looked over at Alma to see her nod her head in agreement.

"You know, if we don't stick together, that Simon Banister is going to run us off our land and out of our homes to the poor farm," Alma said.

Well, she certainly had that much right, and they all knew the battle wasn't over. The fun was just about to get started.

"Listen, you all talk this over. May and I have some things to do," Megan said as the two left the kitchen and returned to the upstairs room.

Megan locked the door behind them, retrieved her crown device and they took a seat at the table. The pencil and pad were still lying there from May working on a list of things that needed to be done.

"What are you thinking?" May asked.

"I think they will work it all out and soon we will be the proud owners of a dude ranch. Then the hard works starts," Megan answered.

"There's still the problem with Banister," May reminded her.

"Yes, but when the debt is paid off, Banister will no longer be a problem."

"What about that guy, what's his name?" May asked.

"Gilmore," Megan said. "You scared the mashed potatoes right out of him. I doubt he will come back anytime soon."

"Yeah, I did, didn't I?" May smiled.

"Only problem with that is now we won't be able to actually catch him in the act and send him up the river for it." Megan considered the likelihood of putting Gilmore out of the way for a very long time might be slim. It appeared that he wasn't going to get what he deserved for what he had done. "The thought of that guy walking away scott free really grinds me."

In the distance they could hear the phone ring downstairs. It was the Sheriff calling to say they had taken photographs of the certificates and signed some kind of documents stating they were the items stolen from Martha's house. The Sheriff, knowing just how badly Martha needed the money, was making an extra effort to get them back to her so she could sell them.

Martha told Megan what was going on and the girls went back to work trying to find a buyer that would pay the highest price for the certificates. They called several buyers back in the city but not one of them would offer to pay them even the lowest dollar listed for the certificates.

It wasn't very long before a sheriff's deputy showed up at the house with the envelope with the certificates in it and returned them to Martha.

The girls were still making phone calls in the kitchen but not having much luck getting the answer they were wanting to hear.

"What did he say?" May asked.

Megan hung up the phone and the expression on her face indicated the news wasn't what she wanted to hear. "He said he was interested in them but even if they were top notch he wasn't willing to pay the bottom dollar price on it. And they are top notch. Like new even."

"I know that guy. I think they call him Crazy Bob. He owns the pawn shop just a few blocks over from the bookstore." May sat there at the kitchen table and stewed over the dilemma for a few moments. Then suddenly she took a deep breath and let out a huge sigh. "Listen, I know you would rather not influence regular people on things like this but..."

"But you have an idea, don't you?" Megan interrupted.

A sly smile came across May's face. "The guy owns the pawn shop. He deals in all kinds of strange things and I happen to know that he is very superstitious." She paused, "And I hear he has quite a lot of money stashed away."

"Really?" Megan asked.

"Yeah, he has all kinds of good luck charms laying around the place. He even carries a rabbit's foot key chain and some kind of Indian MoJo pouch on a leather strap."

Megan tilted her head sideways and smiled but didn't respond.

May sat there for a moment without saying anything, just thinking about it. "I know a guy who took a special collector's edition of one of those old "Hiss" dolls over to see what it was worth and the guy like totally freaked out. Said 'get that thing out of here right now, it's of the devil' or something like that."

"You mean the rock star that painted himself up like some kind of clown to do his shows?" Megan asked.

"That's the one. The guy with the big snake & long tongue trick," May answered.

Megan looked down at the envelope and certificates that Martha had left on the table only a few minutes before. She picked up one of the most valuable certificates and looked at. "Get me some clear cellophane from the drawer over there," she pointed.

Chapter 20

Megan then carefully cut a section of cellophane that fit quite well over the certificate then she got a new envelope from the drawer under the phone and placed the certificate into it. Then she looked up at May as a small but sly smile came over her face.

"We are going to make a little trip, aren't we?" May smiled a similar smile.

"We are," Megan answered. "Follow me."

Back in the room, Megan and May both hatched out a plan that they felt would work on old Crazy Bob.

"Ok, here's what we will do," Megan instructed. "We will go up into the attic and get some of those really old clothes. Then we will get dressed up and make ourselves look like we came right out of the history books."

As she spoke a huge sly smile came over May's face. "The history books. Hum." May was somewhat superstitious herself, but Halloween was without a doubt her most favorite holiday. Well next to Christmas, anyway. Playing practical jokes on people was something these two girls were good at. If they were not in trouble for it back home, they were hatching a new plan to pull on someone at school or the boys who lived on the block.

Quickly they made their way into the attic and dragged several boxes of old clothing down and into their room. Throwing out certain other old things like old newspapers, they started sorting through and picking their dresses out with care trying to get the right look and correct size. Then a touch of makeup to make them look different and to disguise their looks.

"Go heavy on the powder," Megan instructed. "We might even look like ghosts or zombies or something."

May was packing the powder on her face in front of the dresser. "What if Crazy Bob dies of a heart attack?" May stopped and looked toward Megan.

Megan considered that might not be the best way to get top dollar out of the certificate. "Ok, lighten up on it some and we will leave room for him to wonder who we are."

Faster than one might expect, the two girls had made themselves up to look like they were 20 years old and had walked right out of the history books - not really ghost-like, but somewhat unnatural looking. Lipstick, earrings, eye shadow and liner, really old jewelry they had found in the old house. The plan had them all excited and once again feeling like the teenagers they were. In fact, for the time being, the plan had become more important to them than the money was. Could they pull it off?

"Now here's what we can do," Megan suggested. "We view in on ol' Crazy Bob and watch until no one else is in the shop. Then we can wait for him to go into the back room and we can just appear in the front room. What do you think?"

May bit her lip, "What if someone sees us from outside?"

"We will just have to keep that in mind and make sure someone doesn't see us," Megan agreed.

May stood there thinking for a moment when she noticed an old camera laying on the dresser. It gave her an idea. "Oh, boy, did I just have an idea!"

A look of curiosity came across Megan's face. "What?"

"The blue stone transports us, right?" she asked.

"Yes," Megan answered.

"Can it take us back through time?" May continued.

"I don't know, I think so," Megan answered. "But even if it can, I don't know how to do it."

May looked down at one of the old newspapers. "You concentrate on the place you want to go and the thing takes us there, right?"

Megan nodded her head in agreement.

"So, if you had like a picture of a place you wanted to go back in time to, why couldn't you just think about the picture and the time the picture was taken and go there?' May suggested.

"It might work," Megan thought as she picked up one of the old newspapers and looked at the front-page photos. It was a paper from April of 1912 and showed a picture of the passengers standing at the handrail of a huge ship and waving to the people on the docks. The article was about the tragic sinking of the Titanic. No doubt the paper alone was worth some money, but selling it was not what the girls had in mind.

The old newspapers had been saved because they more or less documented historical events. Her grandfather had saved as many of them as he could. In fact, there were numerous old newspapers in the attic, everything from the sinking of the Titanic & Edmund Fitzgerald to the landing of men on the moon. If you could remember it, chances are it was in the attic in one of those old newspapers. In fact, Grandpa Fred had collected all kinds of valuable, as well as not so valuable, things over the years and so had his dad before him. The next interesting thing to note was that old Crazy Bob was in the business of buying up things like that at less than bottom dollar and then selling them to some unnamed source for top dollar. That's how he made his living and, without some special inspiration, he wasn't likely to change old habits.

Megan suddenly laughed aloud when she realized what May had in mind. She wanted to transport back to the past, get their pictures into one of the major headline photos and then zap back to the present. It would make their little adventure prospect even more exciting than it was. Then to make sure that Crazy Bob had the newspaper, or at least managed to get a copy of it in order to top off the plan with some style.

"So how would you get him a copy of the paper with our pictures in it?" Megan asked.

"Let's cross that bridge when we get to it," May said as she pulled the crown device from Megan's backpack. Then she paused "I think he actually has that one in a display hanging on the wall of the pawn shop. I'm almost sure of it."

Chapter 21
An Adventure Through Time

Megan positioned the crown with the blue crystal on her head as May held on tightly to Megan's left hand. She held the newspaper up in front of her face directly in front of the blue crystal as she focused all of her thoughts toward that picture and that point in time. The blue glow of light engulfed the two just as Payah appeared across the room from them. Then they were gone into a black mist dotted with images of time flowing backwards around them.

"Look at that, and that," May pointed as the images moved quickly around them.

"I don't think I like this very much," Megan told her friend. A very uneasy feeling had come over her and the thought that they might never be able to return home once they got where they were going.

"What's wrong?" May asked. "I think it's neat, like, real Galactic."

"What if we can't get back?" Megan told her. "You know, in a way, we will be changing history."

May had not thought of those things but was quick to come up with an answer. "Then we just have to make sure we don't do anything more than get our pictures taken."

Megan thought for a moment then decided it couldn't change history very much if all they did was have their pictures taken.

Suddenly the images started to slow down and in a flash of blue light they found themselves standing on the deck of a very large ship. Before them stood a large number of people standing waving to their friends and loved ones on the shore. Streamers were being tossed into the air off the side of the ship and people were yelling. In the confusion, only one person, a ship's mate, standing only a few feet away had observed the arrival of the two girls and, being in a state of shock, had nothing to say about it.

Megan was in shock herself as she stood looking back and forth from the picture in the paper she held in her hand to the group of people crowding together at the hand rail only a few steps in front of her. She was finding it difficult enough to believe the two had actually passed through time to arrive on the deck of this large ship.

"Quick, quick!" May repeated herself while shaking Megan's arm. She glanced first at the paper then turned to the young man standing to her left. "What time is it?"

The young man came out of his trance as May reached over and shook his arm. "What time is it?"

The young man pulled a pocket watch from his pocket and showed her the time.

Leaving him standing there, she pulled Megan toward the hand rail of the ship and both of them looked down on the shore to see several photographers with very large box-looking cameras taking pictures of the people on the ship.

"Oh," May said as she looked at them all taking pictures, "which one took this picture?" She pointed at the picture in Megan's hand. Then, looking at the position of the picture, she judged there was only one photographer who could have taken it and he was positioned on a rooftop on the docks.

"There, that's him!" she said as she nudged Megan's arm to look that direction. The girls watched until the man had taken several photos then they moved back to where they had started. The young man was still standing there and had not taken his eyes off of them for one moment since they had appeared.

"What's wrong with you? You look like you saw a ghost or something," May told him as they walked up to him.

"He saw us," Megan said softly in May's ear.

"Yeah, but he's not going to tell anyone, are you?" May said as she reached out and straightened the young man's rather short odd-looking tie. The young man stood there with very large eyes and mouth wide open. He wasn't sure who or what he was looking at, but he knew these girls were not part of the regular passenger list.

May took her position right near the young man with him to her left and Megan then took her position to the right of May. Suddenly May realized she was standing on a doomed ship among people who were soon to be dead and wondered if they had made a mistake. Words left her. Her expression suddenly went from being excited that they had accomplished the impossible to morbid fear. Megan had been in shock from the onset of the adventure and didn't like the idea from the start, but May's insistence on going had pushed her into the adventure.

"We can't do this," May said as she looked at the expression on the young man's face. "You know you really should reconsider..." Suddenly she was distracted by Megan's elbow striking her in the side.

"We can't, May. It would change history," Megan reminded her.

"Take us home," May said. The young man watched in amazement as the blue light came around the girls and they vanished into thin air.

After watching images flash around them for what appeared to be several minutes, the girls reappeared in their room. May looked down to see what time it was, thinking they must have used up most of the day, but to her astonishment not one minute had passed. Thinking something must be wrong with her watch, she turned to check the old black cat clock on the wall but it read within a minute of the same time as her wristwatch.

"Look, Megan. No time has passed since we left!" May showed her friend.

Megan checked her watch then the clock on the wall. "Do you know what this means, May? We can go anywhere and do almost anything in time and come back right to the moment we left."

"Exactly, just think of the possibilities," May said looking at the picture in the paper that Megan still held in her hand. They watched as the image of the two girls appeared standing at the handrail and waving directly at the photographer. "Wow, this is really Galactic," which was her way of saying it was really 'huge' or 'cool' as the case may be. Still the sadness lingered. Something from the past had touched the present because of what they had done and now once again something inside both girls had changed. The realization of things that once were so far beyond them in history that it was nothing more than a history lesson, had reached into their hearts and minds and had become real to them. They had stood on the deck of the Titanic next to many people who lived back then and actually spoken to the young man. May had actually touched him, held his arm and fixed his tie. As these thoughts ran through her mind, a tear ran down her cheek. She realized that perhaps time-tripping to disaster sites wasn't such a hot idea after all, because now she knew that if she could change history she would. She would have done her best to warn everyone about the impending disaster. Still who would have believed her? Perhaps the young man on the deck would have since he had seen the girls appear and then vanish into thin air.

Megan also noticed the picture's transformation. "It worked. Ok, now we have to make a trip to see Crazy Bob down at the pawn shop." Megan nodded her head, satisfied the plan had started to come together, even though she saw the tear that May wiped from her cheek.

"It's all right, May. We didn't hurt anyone and we didn't change history and we didn't cause them to hit the iceberg either. It was just one of those things that God alone understands." Megan paused for a moment. Realizing they were not alone, she turned and saw Payah standing behind them near the dresser. He had his arms and legs crossed leaning up against the wall. He nodded his head in agreement with what Megan had just said.

May mustered her courage and with that she stood straight and said, "All right. Let's get on with it."

Megan checked her pocket for the envelope and with that she stood facing the east wall as May took her hand. Slowly the blue light engulfed her head and they started to turn around in a circle as they viewed the inside of the pawnshop.

Chapter 22
Trip to the Pawn Shop

Across the front of the building was a sign that read "Bob's Coin and Pawn." The pawnshop was an old wood frame building that had managed to sustain the onslaught of progress in the civilized world that had sprung up around it. The old wooden floors showed the wear of many footsteps across it. Nearly everything in the place was an antique, including the old display cabinets that were made of varnished wood. Old newspapers in rough cut wooden frames decorated the walls and nearly all of them had a price written on masking tape stuck to the bottom of the frame. The glass in the display case in front of Bob's desk had a crack all the way across one corner with duct tape over it and a little sign that read "don't lean on the glass." The smell of the old building was a combination of old wood, mildew and mint pipe tobacco. There wasn't any doubt that, to the right collector, this place was virtually filled with treasures.

"Crazy" Bob was a rather round individual who walked with a limp. He was perhaps in his late 60's or early 70's with a ring of white hair that hung down over his ears and an old baseball cap covered the bald spot on top of his head. Beside his desk was an old wooden cane that he sometimes used when he went out of the building.

The wall above his desk gave testimony to the history of its owner, with military decorations and many photographs. He was a prisoner of war in Korea and in the Army he had been a photographer. He shot stills and films of war footage and maintained the cameras for several different divisions. If you got to know him fairly well he might even tell you about the time he worked on the huge camera in the SR-71 spy plane. Of course he only told that story to special customers because at the time it was highly classified and top-secret which he had sworn never to talk about. And then there was the time when he actually shot footage of several UFO's that buzzed the base where he was stationed, but the military took his film and he never saw it again. Though you could never get him to admit it some had even heard it rumored that he was the acting camera operator who shot footage of the UFO crash and recovery near Roswell, NM in 1947. People who knew him well knew he had his own reasons for being strange and those who didn't had nicknamed him "Crazy" Bob. He didn't mind so much though. He knew he wasn't normal, but he also knew he wasn't "Crazy" and if that's what they wanted to call him he didn't really care as long as they kept bringing him business.

Bob had accumulated a good deal of savings over the years with his horse trading, buying valuable things for next to nothing from down-trodden, desperate people on the street and then selling them to someone else for top dollar. He didn't trust banks at all but had to keep some of his money in a business account so he could write a check here and there as well as cash the checks he received. He kept most of his money in the safe in the back room of his pawnshop and, whenever he could deal in cash, that's what he did.

Like the farmers around Megan's grandma's place, Bob had some other problems that made him mad enough to fight about. You see Simon Banister was not only buying up land in the country. Before that he had started several large developments in the city. In fact, for the past three years, he had been trying to buy Bob's pawnshop to level it and build a new shopping mall. Simon Banister was into everything. It appeared that if he didn't own it, he was trying to buy it. He owned the land the Books a Zillion store was on along with the fancy gourmet coffee shop and other stores that were in the same very large building.

Crazy Bob was working on his books when he heard a thump like the sound of something falling in the back of his shop, where he kept many things that people had hocked to him. He got up from his old wooden office chair and walked into the back room. He looked around at the shelves filled with items, then around on the floor. Seeing nothing out of place, he scratched his head and returned to his desk, but before he could take a seat he noticed two young women standing in the front part of his store. At first he didn't say anything, as he wasn't sure if his eyes were seeing what his mind was thinking he saw. The two young women were standing motionless in front of a framed-in newspaper hanging on the wall. They stood so still they looked like mannequins rather than people. They were dressed like something right out of the turn of the century, right down to the handbags they carried. Just when he was certain he was having a hallucination one of them turned her head directly toward him and spoke.

In a very proper British accent she spoke, "Tell me, good sir, do you buy rare coins and Silver Certificates?" she asked.

"Well, yes, I do," he answered as he limped about two steps to lean against the display counter.

The women approached the display case and placed the envelope on the glass. One then removed a single certificate from the envelope and placed it on the glass. "Can you tell me if this is worth anything?"

Bob looked at the piece of paper for a few seconds then took it to his desk where he turned on a light that had a large magnifying glass in it. He examined the piece of paper under the magnifier. Then he picked up a book from his desk and flipped through it to a page that showed the same certificate. Then he looked at the certificate again and picked up his pipe. He filled the pipe with tobacco from a pouch he kept in his top-most, right-hand drawer in his desk that he seldom ever closed. Anytime Bob was about to make a deal on something or give a price he liked to get his thoughts in order with a pipe full of mint tobacco. No one ever complained about the smell and he thought it made him look more honest and dignified as he was giving them less than what the item was worth, while telling them they were getting the best deal in the city.

"Well, the thing is a real Silver Certificate all right. But it's not exactly in mint condition," he said as he lit his pipe. "Tell you what. I can give you fifty bucks for it."

Megan turned around and saw May walking toward her. Then she turned back to Bob. "Fifty dollars, you say?" She paused for a moment as May joined her at the counter. "I had seriously hoped it would be worth more than that. Would you mind if I take a look at your book there, please?" Megan pointed toward the coin book on Bob's desk.

Bob hated it when people would ask to see his coin reference book, especially when they were the ones selling the coins. Now when he was selling coins to them it was another story. Still he handed the book to the young woman and took another puff from his pipe.

"It says here this certificate could be worth as much as seven thousand dollars." Megan pointed toward the value listings in the book.

Bob leaned over to take a closer look, "Oh, what did I say? I guess I read that wrong. I'll give you $500 for it, but that's the most I have ever paid for anything. It's my policy you know."

"I see, and when you sell things like this to someone else do you manage to get what they are worth out of them?" Megan asked.

Bob realized this young woman was not going to be as easy to pull one over on as he had hoped. He knew without a doubt he could get at least six big ones for that certificate from his buyer. "I'm sorry, five hundred is the best I can do. The guy I sell them to doesn't pay very much more than that, so I don't really make that much on them when I sell them."

"Really?" May said as she walked back across the floor to stand in front of the newspaper on the wall. "How much would you take for this picture? Would you take, oh, say fifty dollars for it?"

Bob looked up to see what May was referring to. "I wouldn't take a thousand dollars for that."

"I guess there aren't many of them left around, are there?" May added. "Look, I think this one is damaged somewhat."

"Where?" Bob sounded surprised as he made his way over to see what May was pointing at. "Why, that's a special late edition paper. See there?" he pointed. "This one has a blow up of the two mysterious women that no one could identify on the Titanic before it sailed that day."

"You say no one knew who those two women were?" May asked as she pointed toward the blow up just below the actual deck photo.

"Yeah, that's right," Bob said as he took a closer look at the picture. "What's wrong with it," he asked as he examined the picture then suddenly realized a very uncanny resemblance between the two in the picture and the two young women standing near him. Slowly he turned and looked directly at May as Megan walked up and stood beside her exactly as they were in the picture. "What is this? What's going on here?" Bob mumbled more to himself than to anyone. Pulling his glasses out of his shirt pocket, he took a closer look at the picture.

Megan and May smiled as they repressed a giggle between them.

Bob examined the picture right down to the earrings and necklaces the women were wearing, then the handbags that were hanging over the shoulders of the women. Then he turned and looked at the two young women standing beside him and his mouth fell open and his eyes became wide. "This can't be," he said as he shook his head. "Who put you up to this?"

Megan was holding the certificate in her hand, "Mr. Bob, this certificate could bring you as much as seven thousand dollars and I just so happen to know someone who has 20 or 30 more of them of similar value. Now you know I'm not about to take less than five thousand dollars for this certificate. You will make at least a thousand dollars or more for a few minutes of your time and effort. Either you will do business with us like a gentleman or we will be forced to take our business elsewhere." Megan returned to the glass and replaced her certificate in the envelope.

Bob stood there looking back and forth between the picture in the newspaper and the two young women who were standing there with him. He wasn't sure what was going on, but one thing was for sure, the young woman was right and she knew it. If Bob let them walk away without making a fair deal with them they would find someone somewhere who would.

"Mr. Bob, are you all right? You look rather flushed," May asked as she was still standing near him in front of the newspaper that hung on the wall.

"Uh," Bob mumbled as he leaned over to have a closer look at May's earrings and necklace. "What would you take for those earrings and that necklace?" Bob was doing his best to convince himself that it was just an uncanny coincidence that the two young women in his shop looked identical to the two in the picture.

"I don't think I could part with them right now as they have been in the family for generations," May answered. "Why? Do you think they have some value?"

"Well," Bob rubbed his chin as he strained to extract every tidbit of information that he could from the photo, when suddenly he saw something that caught his attention. It was the wristwatch on May's arm. There it was, the very same one that was in the picture. May had forgotten to remove her wrist watch and after all these years no one had even mentioned it or thought they were out of place. It was the same wristwatch that was in the picture. What were the odds on that? Bob didn't know what to think as he made his way back around behind the counter. "Will you let me take the bill and see what I can get for it and get back to you on it?"

Megan shook her head 'no'. Seeing a photocopy machine in the corner behind the counter she said. "But I will let you take a photocopy of it to show to your buyer."

Bob took the envelope and made a photocopy of the certificate then returned it to Megan. Every few seconds he turned to look at May. "Listen I don't really know who you two are. For all I know, you are trying to pull a fast one on an old man."

"Why would you think that, Mr. Bob?" May asked.

"Because you two look exactly like the two mystery women in that picture over there, that's why." He pointed as he spoke, "Right down to the wrist watch that shouldn't be in the picture."

The two girls looked at each other without showing any expression. Then May raised her arm and both of them looked at the digital wrist watch, then back at Bob. May had forgotten to remove her wrist watch and this was the first time she had realized her mistake, but now was no time to lose control. They had Bob where they wanted him and the last thing they wanted to do was blow it at this point in the game.

"So what are you trying to say, Bob? That they didn't have digital wrist watches in 1912?" Megan spoke without cracking a smile or showing any expression whatsoever.

"Look at it like this, Mr. Bob, if they didn't have digital wrist watches in 1912 then perhaps your paper is a fake. If it isn't fake then it is probably worth far more than you have it priced at now, because it just might be possible that the photographer who took that picture caught something on film that should not have been seen. Something that might defy the boundaries of human understanding."

Bob thought about what she had said for a moment then walked over and picked up the phone and dialed a number. The two girls looked at each other wondering what Bob was up to. "Look, ladies, do you swear to me this certificate is real?"

Both girls nodded their heads that it was. Megan had been paying close attention to the number that Bob had dialed, and it wasn't the number for the police. She ran the number over in her head a few times so as not to forget it.

Bob spoke to someone on the phone for a few moments then hung up the phone. "Wait right here," he said as he made his way into the back room. Moments later he returned with five thousand dollars cash money in his hand. "I'm going to trust you on this. But if this turns out to be some kind of trick, you had better not let me catch you around here again." With that he handed the girls the money and he kept the envelope.

"Thank you, Mr. Bob," Megan said as she took the money and placed it into her purse next to her crown.

"Oh, wait. I have to get something for you to sign for me," Bob said as he ran back into the back room. He had left his safe open and had forgotten to make out the transaction papers.

"Do it!" May said.

In the back room, a flash of blue light could be seen through the door, which caught Bob's attention. When he walked back out front the two young women were gone. "What!" Bob yelled. "I didn't even hear the door bell." Quickly he made his way to the door. When he opened it, the doorbell rang and he ran out onto the sidewalk and looked both directions. The young women were no where to be seen. He walked to both sides of his building and looked around to see if they might be hiding there somewhere but he found nothing, not a trace. "Huh, that's odd. Like they just vanished into thin air or something." He shook his head and walked back in the shop still holding the receipt book in his hand. He stood looking at the picture of the two young women on the wall in the newspaper. "Who are they?" he said thinking aloud as goosebumps rose up on his arms. "Maybe it really was the same two women. But if it was, that means they have to be almost 90 years old," he paused "or else they... Nah, that's just not possible."

Back at the farm, the two girls found themselves standing in their room again with five thousand dollars cash money in their hands. Megan removed the device and placed it back in the box and then in the backpack.

"Ok, now we have five G's and what are you going to do with it? Walk up to grandma and hand it to her?" May asked.

"No, I don't think I want to explain how we came to get it. But I do have an idea that I think will work," Megan said as she started changing clothes.

"I can't believe I never even thought to take the watch off," May said as she was changing.

"Me neither, but it worked out all right just the same," Megan said.

"Speaking of watches, you know we have not been gone all that long. It's not even noon yet," May said.

Megan tucked the money in an envelope and then shoved it in a hip pocket of her jeans. Then down the stairs she went, with May not far behind. They found Martha and the Butler's out walking around in the yard talking about the possibility of starting a dude ranch. Megan called Mr. Butler off to the side and showed him the money she had. "By this time tomorrow, I can have perhaps twenty or thirty thousand dollars, but I need your help."

"Where did you get that money, Megan?" he asked with concern. "And what's that? Are you wearing makeup?"

Megan made a face as she realized that both of them had completely forgotten to wash off the makeup.

"We took one of the certificates and sold it back in the city," May said.

Mr. Butler looked at May then at Megan and understood they had ways of getting things done that normal people couldn't even consider. "What do you want me to do?"

"There's no way I can give this money to grandma right now. She will want to know how I got it and I can't explain that to her. I want you to take some of the certificates and tell grandma you are going to go sell them for her. Don't take all of them just enough to get what we need for now."

"Yeah, to pay off the debt against the farm and things like that," May chimed in as she handed him a list she had made. "This is what some of them are worth. You must at least get somewhere between the lower and middle price on them."

"Then we can do this one of two ways." Megan and May looked at each other for a moment then back at Mr. Butler. "Either you can give us the bills and we can go sell them, give you the money and you can give it back to your Grandma, or you can drive to the city and deliver them to Crazy Bob's Pawn Shop yourself."

"Bob won't give him the money for it," May reminded her.

"He will when you show him this," Megan said as she held up the set of earrings that she had been wearing when the picture was taken. "You show him these and tell him that two young women told you to tell him he had better give you the best price on these or else."

"Yeah," May agreed with a smile.

Megan looked at the envelope in her hand then back at Mr. Butler. "And look, consider it a kind of advance on the work you're going to do on the dude ranch. Help us make it work and we can save the farms," she said as she handed the envelope to Mr. Butler.

"But that's Martha's money," he insisted.

"I think she would want you to have it, or you can consider it a loan because I know you need the money. Just the same I trust you to do the right thing with it," Megan said as they headed back toward the house.

The next day John had convinced Martha to allow him to take some of the certificates and he drove in to the city to the pawnshop just as the girls had instructed. When he got the run-around from Crazy Bob he showed him the earrings, which Bob recognized instantly and changed his tune and amount he would give for each bill accordingly.

As John was headed out the door Bob walked over to the newspaper on the wall. "Say, can I ask you a question?" as he motioned for John to join him.

"Sure," John answered.

"Ever see these two women before?" he pointed at the blow up on the newspaper.

John didn't have to look very close before a smile came across his face. Shaking his head he answered, "You know, they do look really familiar, don't they?"

"Wouldn't happen to know who they are, would you?" Bob asked.

"Sure, they are the mystery women from the Titanic," John answered as he started for the door again.

"Somehow I knew you were going to say that," Bob exclaimed as he watched Mr. Butler walk out the door. "Yes, I could have guessed that's what he would say."

Chapter 23
Things of Cosmic Significance

They got enough money to pay both farms out of debt and start building their dude ranch. Martha, Alma and the girls kept track of every dollar that was spent. The girls kept a fairly accurate list of things that had been done and things that needed to be done. Mr. Butler made everything ready for the horses and started work tearing down the old shed southeast of the house. The hard work of getting things ready didn't damper Megan and May's spirits though, as they were quite pleased with themselves for what they had accomplished. Megan's mother was pleased when she returned to get the girls and gave them a full month extension on their vacation in order for them to help on the farm. There was so much to do that Donna even brought Megan's other brother Gary with her on weekends to work on the farm. Gary hated the entire thing and complained about everything that he could, every chance he got. He blamed Megan for everything, as usual, and little fights would sometimes break out between them any time they were close enough to reach each other. Of course, he crossed the line when he pushed Megan into the horse water tank and that set both girls against him to set the record straight.

Simon Banister bit the end off a lot of cigars when both the Butler's and Martha Martin paid off their loans on time. Then the only expendable henchman,

Jordan Gilmore, up and vanished without leaving a forwarding address and cost Banister another 100 grand. Still he vowed they may have won this round but the battle wasn't over yet. If there was anything he could do to pry them from their homes he would, but just how he intended to accomplish this was never discussed. He even considered raising the price that he was willing to pay in order go buy the farms but never considered paying what they were worth. It was against his policy.

The sheriff issued a warrant for the arrest of Jordan Gilmore for breaking and entering, theft of property, and jumping bail. He vowed that if he ever caught him again there would be no bail and he would be spending a lot of time looking out at the world from behind bars.

Classified Top Secret, somewhere deep in an underground military complex several people were still trying to figure out what the strange random distortions they had monitored were. The spy satellites they were using were designed to track magnetic and gravitational disturbances as well as being able to see things in light and energy spectrums that were not visible to the human eye. To put it bluntly, they were designed to track what they called "alternative aircraft." In common terms, they were tracking what might be called UFO's or flying saucers, most of the time. There were quite a few things about what they did in that place they didn't want anyone else to know about. They didn't want anybody to know they could predict earthquakes with pinpoint accuracy with these satellites. They were able to monitor the build up of electromagnetic energy in the earth and could see invisible "balls of light" or sparks being emitted from the fault lines. Some might wonder why they didn't want anyone to know they were able to see these things. Just think of the lives that might be saved using this technology. Perhaps they just didn't care about saving lives; it wasn't really their department. Then again, if it was known that they had this technology, people would want to see the screen for themselves and then might also see things flying around that certain military minds do not want the public to be aware of.

Deep in the underworld, the foundations had been shaken. But while the dark beings worked to figure out what was going on, they never really figured out where or who. Payah and his friends had been doing a good job of keeping the actual location of the device hidden, at least for now.

All wasn't exactly perfect in paradise as Megan started having nightmares of future events. Great earthquakes and disasters which humanity couldn't even imagine.

One day, shortly before the girls had to return to the city, they sat in the barn loft door looking down at the horses in the lot and thinking about all that had transpired over the summer.

"Did we solve the mystery of the Medallion?" May asked.

"I don't know. I suspect that it did not originate on earth. It came from Mars or somewhere else," Megan answered. "It's a lot older than anyone knows."

"So it's made of Martian gold then?" May suggested as she swung her legs back and forth.

"It could be. And it's not just a decoration either. It means something important. Something that has been passed along not just through time, but also through space," Megan suggested. "Do you remember that big pyramid we stood on while we were on Mars in our vision?"

May nodded her head that she did remember.

Chapter 22

"Well, that big white pyramid represents something very special and that is like the picture on the medallion." Megan was in deep thought as she sat also swinging her legs over the side of the barn. Below them was the entrance into the horse stalls. The door was open so the horses could come and go from the barn as they wanted to. "You know what I think, May? I think that pyramid and capstone is the symbol of something."

"You mean like the King of the universe?" May suggested.

"Yeah, something like that," Megan answered. "And I think there was a huge war on Mars because someone took that symbol and maybe did something with it they should not have done."

May sat there for a moment thinking, "You mean like when someone uses someone else's driver's license or I. D. card?"

"Might be like that," Megan answered still in deep thought. "Might be just like that," she added.

"May, there's something I saw last night in a dream that I didn't tell you about, mostly because I didn't understand what I was seeing. I'm still not real sure what it was but I know it had something to do with that medallion," Megan added

"What did you see?" May asked.

"It was one of the most vivid dreams I think I have ever had. We were standing in the back yard and a wall of fog came up out of the alley and we went to see what it was. While we were walking toward it a bright liquid flowing light came up into the fog and part of it broke off and flew up into the air and made a large beautiful flying saucer shape that flew away toward the East. Then in the fog I saw the bright white liquid light form into a solid shape. It was the shape of the capstone of that white pyramid. It looked like solid white stone and on it there was an engraving cut into the image of the triangle and that image I saw was like that eye looking thing on the medallion." Megan related her dream to May.

May thought for a few moments before she answered, "So you think your dream has to do with the answer to the medallion?"

"Yeah, I think it does. I think that shape I saw in the dream is just one more part of the mystery, another piece of the puzzle. I think it has cosmic significance and I really want to learn more about it."

"Galactic!" May responded still in deep thought on the concept. "If it really is that old and if someone saw the same things you saw then maybe that's like the symbol for the God of Light."

"Maybe so."

May consider this for a moment. "I read something like that in the Bible. I'll have to do some checking on that but I think it has to do with the great pyramid of Giza being the altar to God that was mentioned in Isaiah 19: 19-20."

"Good deal. You check it out and let me know what it says," Megan said with a smile. "While you're at it, check on all the references to UFO's and space ships that you can find. I saw that thing like a space ship and that image all in the same dream. The liquid light broke apart and so the space ship and the image must be related."

"Ok, and you can do some checking on the NASA website for anything you can learn about Mars. NASA said they have reason to believe that Mars once had life on it similar to what we have on earth now and we know that's true because we saw it ourselves. So what happened to it? How would an entire world like that lose its atmosphere?" May asked.

"A really huge explosion, I would guess," Megan answered.

The girls loved the excitement of the secret they held between them and they loved the adventures the strange crown-like device had allowed them to experience. The ability to go places and see things that were impossible for others was a tremendous learning experience. Still it seemed the more they learned about the mystery of the medallion the more questions and new mysteries they came up with. Life was certainly not going to be boring for these two in the future. They had encountered a ghost, apparitions, a mysterious being named Payah, not to mention they had traveled through time and seen things with their own eyes that even in the utmost scientific circles on earth would be considered impossible. Things that many only speculate on and wonder about had become real to Megan and May. With the device they certainly had some evidence and perhaps a way to prove to others what they had learned, but they couldn't tell anyone about it. The device itself contained such powers that in the wrong hands might plunge Earth into the same fate as that which struck Mars. Their only recourse was to keep the secret about the crown like device and hope that Payah could do his job to keep it from falling into evil hands.

"You know, your mom will be here to get us in a day or two," May reminded Megan.

"Yeah, I know," Megan answered.

"So..." May said tilting her head sideways.

Megan looked up to see a sly smile on May's face.

"So, we have just enough time for another adventure," she said as she jumped up and headed for the ladder.

"Where are you going?" Megan yelled as she also got up and followed her friend.

May giggled as she ran for the house.

Back in their room with the door locked, May sorted through some newspapers and Megan gathered up the keys and the crown. Making them ready she put the device on her head and turned back toward May.

"Well, May, where do you want to go today?" Megan asked, trying to sound something like a commercial she had heard on TV.

May turned and took Megan's hand as she held up a picture to show Megan.

"Really?" She asked.

"Yeah, I always wanted to see a spaceship being launched at NASA," May answered.

"That's a Saturn V Apollo rocket, the one that sent the first men to the moon," Megan informed her.

"I know," May smiled.

"Fasten your seat belts and make sure your table trays are in their upright position," Megan called out in an official tone as a bright blue light engulfed the two friends and in a moment they were gone.

The End

About the Author

Since he was a young boy, Bryon Smith has had a fascination with the paranormal. After the death of a neighbor, his father bought the house next door and Bryon soon learned the house was haunted by the spirit of the deceased. In 1970 he had a very close encounter with a UFO and so began a life long quest to find the answers relating to these things.

It was this fascination and his warm memories of his childhood on his grandfather's farm that inspired him to apply some of his knowledge of these subjects into *The Adventures of Megan Martin.*

Over the years, Bryon has held many unusual occupations, including farming, construction work, musician, S.C.U.B.A. diving salvage, boat dock design & construction, electronics technician, radio tower construction, welder, airport lineman, and professional videographer. He and his family are currently working on a new series of television shows called **Spooky Places.**

Today, Bryon lives with his wife and Editor, Dawn; his teenage daughter, Laura, who was the inspiration and "technical consultant" for the Megan Martin character; and his youngest daughter, Kristy.

Presents

Spooky Places

Do you know a real spooky place?

If you know of any really "Spooky Places" where really strange things happen please share your story with us.

Laura and Kristy are in the process of searching out the most interesting "Spooky Places" they can find.

Visit
Spooky Places
at
www.loosecanon.tv
to find out more

Loose Canon.TV
Also Provides Production
Service. Check us out!

Printed in the United States
1021300001B/52-75

9 780971 427297